the
aussie
next
door

the
aussie
next
door

USA TODAY BESTSELLING AUTHOR
STEFANIE LONDON

Entangled Publishing, LLC
2614 South Timberline Road
Suite 105, PMB 159
Fort Collins, CO 80525
rights@entangledpublishing.com
Visit our website at www.entangledpublishing.com.

Amara is an imprint of Entangled Publishing, LLC.

Edited by Liz Pelletier and Lydia Sharp
Cover design by Hang Le
Cover image by Gradyreese/iStock
Interior design by Toni Kerr

Print ISBN 978-1-64063-668-2
ebook ISBN 978-1-64063-669-9

Manufactured in the United States of America

First Edition September 2019

AMARA

ALSO BY STEFANIE LONDON

To Michael, for being one of the most creative people I know. And to Zia, for always believing in your kids (and your nieces!).

CHAPTER ONE

Jace Walters had been ambushed, and by his own mother, too.

He hadn't even seen it coming. The innocent request for lunch—which wasn't out of the ordinary—and the equally innocent suggestion that they drop in on Mrs. Landry "for a minute" hadn't piqued his suspicions. Not even when they'd walked past the stack of suitcases in the entryway, with a brochure for a cruise liner perched on top, did he suspect what was about to happen.

And by then…it was too late.

"My house isn't set up for dog-sitting."

His mother shot him a look across Mrs. Landry's kitchen table. Although who the hell knew what she was trying to communicate. He'd never understood why people couldn't *say* what they meant. Wouldn't that make life easier? Clearer?

Maybe not. His mum had taught him long ago that his bluntness did *not* make *her* life easier.

So instead he sat there, dwarfing everything in Mrs. Landry's house with his broad, six-feet-four frame like he usually did, including the two petite older women. A pot of tea sat in the middle of the table with three mismatched mugs, milk, and a packet of Tim Tams. Eugenie Elizabeth Landry would never, *ever* have people over to her house without serving something to eat and drink.

"They don't take up much space," Eugenie said sweetly.

Jace eyed her beloved dogs. Okay, sure, Truffle—the hyperactive white Chihuahua—didn't take up much space. But Tilly—the German shepherd—looked as though she was really a pony wearing a costume of a dog.

"And really, you won't even know they're there," she continued. "They keep each other amused most of the day. Truffle needs a walk every other morning, but you could always take him to the beach. You go there anyway."

"To surf," Jace said. His gaze flicked to his mother, who avoided eye contact.

"And Tilly, well, she's getting on in life." Eugenie reached for a tissue and dabbed at her eye.

Low freaking blow.

"Exactly!" Jace threw up his hands. "What if something happens?"

What if the dog got hit by a car? What if the dog ate something poisonous? What if the dog decided to chase a bird and somehow made it onto the beach and climbed on a surfboard and got swept away and ended up sailing to Fiji?

"I'd rather her be with people who care. Not stuck in some kennel where they probably feed the poor darlings home-brand dog food." Eugenie shuddered. "You don't even have to buy the dog food. I've got it all prepared."

"It's only a month," Jace's mother said. Her hands were folded around her mug, and a perfect imprint of her pink lipstick decorated the rim. "Well, a bit over a month."

"How long *exactly*?" He knew better than to agree to anything based on such vague terms. Not that he liked anything in his life to be vague— Jace was a black-and-white kinda guy—but he especially didn't like it when his mother was trying to rope him into something.

He'd learned that early on in life: clarify the boundaries of any agreement. Otherwise they'd move, and likely *not* in his favor.

"Two months."

Two. Freaking. *Months?* Jace's preferred level of commitment was something in the realm of a cactus that he needed to water every two weeks— *if* he felt like it. And he was pretty sure a dog would die if it was only watered every two weeks. "Have you asked Adam and Soraya?"

His oldest brother and sister-in-law ran a bed-and-breakfast at the edge of town. Once the school year started in a few weeks, the flow of tourism would reduce to a trickle. And not a moment too soon, in Jace's opinion. He was already dreaming about what it would be like when his little town went back to normal—no struggling to park his car, no jostling with greasy sunscreen-covered tourists on the beach. No sharing his waves with some hog who thinks he owns the place because he rents a beach house for one month of the year.

"They've still got the holiday coming up, so they'll be busy until after that," his mum replied.

"What about Nick?" Now he was moving down

the line of siblings, from oldest to youngest.

"He's at work all day, and Trent's always at different construction sites. Liv is traveling between here and Melbourne." His mother shook her head. "They can't do it."

Jace's stomach sank like a boulder falling to the bottom of the ocean. He was well and truly screwed.

He wanted to point out that even though he worked from home, that didn't mean he had the time to take care of other people's pets. Not to mention it was completely outside his skill set! A cat would be a better dog-sitter than he would. There was a reason he didn't have a dog of his own—and it had nothing to do with how he felt about animals. He loved animals. But his home was his sanctuary. Where he could work and think and create, uninterrupted and unencumbered.

His routine wasn't just important to him. It was *vital.*

And his mother knew that better than anyone. Diagnosed as being on the "high-functioning" end of the autism spectrum when he was in kindergarten, routine was critical to his mental health. But the doctors had also warned his mother that routine could become a prison for someone like him—making him unable to enjoy a full life if even the slightest disturbance to that routine caused an earthquake to his equilibrium. She'd taken those words to heart. His mother had been his champion from day one, and even though she loved and respected his needs, she also nudged him outside his comfort zone from time to time.

Problem was, this *nudge* felt more like The People's Elbow.

Every morning he was at Sorrento Back Beach at seven a.m. for his morning surf. After surfing for an hour, he'd head home, shower, have breakfast—always plain porridge, which had disgusted his siblings to no end when he lived at home—and then work. Even his lunch break occurred at exactly the same time every day.

Having pets meant accommodating things like walks and meal time and vet appointments. So many things to disrupt his life.

"The dogs are used to having people around all the time. You know, for comfort. After Burt died…" Eugenie sniffed. "Well, they're my only family."

Jace sighed. How could he possibly say anything to that? He looked across the table at his mum, and she offered a sheepish shrug. She knew he would do anything for his family. Especially his mum.

But oh, he was going to collect all right. There'd better be some damn good pavlova in it for him.

"Fine." He shook his head. "Two months, but not a day more. If Eugenie isn't back to pick them up, *you'll* be doing it."

"Deal."

Jace glanced at the dogs, already regretting his decision. Truffle was barking at something through the window, his high-pitched yips like a tiny pickax to Jace's brain. Tilly stretched out on the floor, totally oblivious to the noise until Truffle decided to jump down from the windowsill and gnaw on the end of her tail. Then commotion ensued with more barking. And running. And fur flying.

RIP, my sanity.

"Aren't they cute?" Eugenie scooped up Truffle, cuddling him close to her chest. "I'm going to miss them so much."

Ten minutes later, Jace's pristine, peaceful life was already being defiled. His car—which he vacuumed weekly and which looked *way* younger than its ten years, because he'd never been able to pull the trigger on replacing it—was full to the brim with canine paraphernalia. Truffle was sitting in a plush doggy car seat, smug as hell, while Tilly lay over a blanket Eugenie had offered to protect the upholstery. But the carpet was already coated with a fine dusting of dog hair.

Jace got into the driver's seat and pulled the door shut, letting his hands rest on the steering wheel a moment while he drew a long breath. A second later, his mother climbed in while Eugenie made kissy noises at her "furry babies" and ensured everything they needed was accounted for.

The dogs had special brushes, chew toys, water bowls, and timer-activated food dispensers. There was shampoo for Truffle's skin condition and medication for Tilly's arthritis. They had blankets and coats and leashes. Truffle needed to be walked every other day—or he got antsy, which Jace wanted to avoid at all costs. The dog was already more hyper than a toddler hopped up on red food dye. Tilly didn't walk as much as she used to, but she should still go out once or twice a week. Truffle needed a cuddle before bed, otherwise he tended not to sleep well. Tilly was self-sufficient and quiet…unless the possums were acting up.

Jace's head spun with all the information. Two bloody months and he'd be essentially looking after two fur-covered children. Well, technically it was one fur-covered child and one fur-covered old lady, going by dog years.

He started the engine and pulled slowly out of Eugenie's driveway, unsure how fast was safe considering dogs didn't wear seat belts. Frowning, he looked at Tilly and Truffle in the rearview mirror. They'd gone quiet…for now.

His plans for an enjoyable lunch flew out the window along with a fine cloud of Tilly's fur.

"Thank you," his mother said. "Eugenie was desperate. She's done so much for us, and she really deserves this holiday. Her dog-sitter pulled out at the last minute."

The dogs grizzled at each other. Truffle let out a yip so high-pitched, Jace winced.

"I can't imagine why," he deadpanned.

"Don't be like that."

"Why did you feel the need to trick me into it? That was low."

"Yes, it was a bit of a crafty move." She knotted her hands, which Jace had learned was something she did whenever she felt conflicted. "I'm sorry for the subterfuge. But you know how important it is to change things up from time to time. Besides, I thought it might show you that you'd be a great dad someday."

Oh no. They were *not* going to have a discussion about his sex life on top of everything else. Hard pass.

"Speaking of which, how is that cute American tenant of yours?"

"Nice segue," Jace said, shaking his head. "Subtle as a hammer."

And Angie wasn't simply cute. She was sexy as hell. *Sexier* than hell, if that was a thing. Every time she knocked on his door, needing help with something or offering to share the muffins she'd picked up from the local bakery, his head went into a spin.

But Angie made his mum look like an amateur when it came to messing with his routine. If his mum liked to nudge him, his tenant was a steamroller crashing through his life and taking all the exit signs with her. And for that reason, he tried to keep his distance. Unfortunately, even with that decision made, he *still* had trouble not thinking about how sexy her butt looked in those frayed shorts she liked to wear.

No, he couldn't think about that now. Angie was definitely off-limits—both in this discussion and in his own thoughts.

"You didn't answer my question," his mother said. She was watching him very closely, like he was something under a microscope.

"That's because I didn't want to."

She laughed. "Is it so wrong that a mother take an interest in her son's dating life? You never bring anyone home."

"Perhaps it's because nobody in this family understands how to respect personal boundaries."

Jace had grown up in a house of seven. Being smack-bang in the middle of five kids, there had never been a moment of peace. If he wasn't fighting someone for the last piece of pizza, he was squabbling over which TV show to watch or shouting at the others to be quiet while he tried to do his homework. Or draw. Not easy, given he shared a bedroom for far longer than most kids did. His folks weren't exactly rich, and their house was better suited to a typical family with the standard 2.3 children and maybe a small family pet.

But the Walters's house had been utter chaos. They had an "open-door" policy, which meant extended family, friends, and neighbors were always dropping by. They fostered animals and took in strays and never turned anyone away— whether they had two *or* four legs. It was the "Walters way." And honestly, his family *did* try to be helpful and observant of his needs. But one of the things he loved most about them, even if he'd never admit it, was that they treated him like he wasn't different. Like he wasn't…the odd one out. It was annoying at times but also refreshing.

He could be himself, even if that meant locking himself in his closet sometimes just to get a moment's peace.

So while Jace admired how giving and kind his family was, it had made him crave a precious space to call his own—where he could escape the chaos and the noise and the clutter and the chatter.

"Anyway, thank you again for saying yes. I didn't know what else to do," his mother said. "I would have taken the dogs, but we're off camping next week."

Jace didn't bother to point out that one week out of eight would have been manageable, rather than asking him to do two whole months by himself. But that was because this whole thing wasn't about dog-sitting. Not really.

His mother thought he needed to have more in his life than his art. He'd overheard her saying to his dad once that she was worried he'd become addicted to solitude and that he'd lock himself away to the point that he'd miss out on allowing someone into his life. That he wouldn't find love. Apparently that made her sad, because she'd said he deserved love.

And of course she wanted as many grandkids as possible. He had to suppress a shudder at the thought. Jace was perfectly happy with his life the way it was: he had his dream job and a very small but close-knit circle of people he cared about. No girlfriend. No attachments.

Total and utter personal freedom.

But when Melanie Walters decided something needed to change in her child's life, she made it happen. And dog-sitting would force Jace out of his studio *and* out of his routine.

"It's not *that* big of a deal," his mother added with her signature sweeter-than-honey smile. "You're looking after two lovely, well-behaved dogs. What could possibly go wrong?"

Jace raised a brow and checked the rearview mirror, where Truffle the Chihuahua met his gaze. He was sure it was impossible—but he could have sworn the dog winked at him.

CHAPTER TWO

Angie Donovan had seen a *lot* of lawyers. And she'd figured out, over the years, that you could tell a ton about a lawyer based on what their reception area looked like. Several boxes of tissues handy? They probably managed estates or divorces. Somber gray tones usually meant they dealt in wills—because it was softer than black but didn't give the "pearly gates" feel of white.

The ones with water glasses and flowers overcharged. The ones with Herman Miller chairs—usually knockoffs—overcharged even more.

Before coming to Patterson's Bluff, she'd wasted time with one of those kinds of lawyers. The ones with fake furniture, high fees, and absolutely no benefits. The kind who gave shoddy advice to get clients in and out as quickly as possible. Thankfully she'd found Arthur Westerly, because he seemed the sort of attorney who would fight for his clients when they needed him.

She'd been able to tell the second she stepped into his office that this place was different. Instead of the usual muted neutrals, there was a comfy blue sofa that wouldn't look out of place in someone's home. And instead of the usual polite but remote receptionist, the lady at this desk had a beaming smile and called Angie "love."

Australians liked that word, she'd discovered

since moving to Australia from her hometown in Southern California almost two years ago.

"He'll be out to see you in a minute, love." The receptionist, Dorothy, had curly blond hair and earrings made from seashells. "I'm sorry again that Mr. Westerly wasn't here to see you himself. He really hates to miss work."

Angie had been worried when she'd turned up and the kindly Arthur Westerly wasn't in. Apparently he'd been involved in an accident while rescuing a neighbor's cat, resulting in a badly sprained ankle. Which meant Angie had to see Paul Westerly…Arthur's grandson. The guy gave her the heebie-jeebies. Well, some guys gave her the heebie-jeebies, but Paul's heebie-jeebies had heebie-jeebies of their own!

"It's fine," Angie said, hoping she sounded like she meant it. Because she didn't, really. Today was a big, scary day, and Arthur had been holding her hand through this whole disaster so far. She needed him.

Angie shifted on the spot, tugging down the hem of her pencil skirt. Why had she bothered dressing up? It wasn't like the immigration gods were going to smile down on her because she'd put on a blouse and heels. But it had been a last-ditch effort to feel like she had some control over the situation, when she most definitely did not. If this meeting didn't go well, then all her hopes and dreams for the perfect home in this tiny seaside town would be shattered.

You will not *go back to America. No matter what they say, you'll figure this out.*

Only that reassurance had about as much substance as cotton candy. Or what did they call it here? Fairy floss.

Angie watched the view outside. The office looked over the main strip in Patterson's Bluff—a small town on the Mornington Peninsula in Victoria. The street was quieter today, and there hadn't been a wait at her favorite coffee spot. The summer tourism season was slowly drawing to a close. Angie wasn't sure she liked it, because the quiet allowed her time to think…and she didn't want to do that right now.

"Angie?" Paul Westerly stuck his head out of his office. "You can come in now."

He was wearing khakis rolled at the ankle, a collared T-shirt, and a pair of boat shoes. Back home, even the court-appointed lawyers had worn suits. But everything in Patterson's Bluff ran at a different speed. People were relaxed. They made time for trips to the beach and took a moment to chat with people on the street. It was one of the many things she enjoyed about living here.

Angie smoothed her hands down the front of her skirt and took a seat in one of the chairs facing Paul's desk. Well, technically it was Arthur's desk, since this was the biggest office and it was neat as a pin. That's how Angie had known she could trust him.

But Paul, on the other hand…not so much. Paul was around twenty-seven, had a penchant for wearing too much product in his hair and dousing himself in cologne. No doubt it was expensive cologne, but anything of such volume triggered her gag reflex. He was a lawyer, which was something, but mostly he filed paperwork for his grandfather and took on some of the smaller legal matters that concerned the townsfolk of Patterson's Bluff. Oh, and he had a tendency to hit on the female clients.

Angie did her best to avoid him, but she simply couldn't spend another day not knowing what her future held.

"You're looking lovely today. Going somewhere special?" His gaze slid over her in a way that made her want to shrink back into her chair.

"I was supposed to be meeting with my lawyer," she said, cringing at the sting in her voice. It wasn't Arthur's fault he'd had an accident, and she certainly couldn't blame him. But *damn*, she wished it was him instead of Paul right now.

"Seems a shame to be all dressed up without somewhere to go. You know, there's a nice place down in Sorrento where I could take you. I've got the Porsche parked out back."

Angie wanted to scream at him to stop with the cheesy pickup line and get on with announcing her fate. But she held herself in check, in case there was some tiny sliver of a chance that karma might reward her. "Thank you, but I have another meeting after this one. So maybe we should, um...get down to business?"

"I'm afraid it's not great news," Paul said. He leaned back in his chair, as if enjoying the dramatic pause.

Her stomach sank. "Really?"

"I understand my grandfather warned you this

was the likely outcome." He looked at her with a kind of expression that verged on pity.

She curled her hands, digging her nails into the heels of her palms. The pressure calmed her. No matter what she felt, it could not show on her face. She wouldn't do anything to encourage his pity or anybody else's. "What did they say?"

"That the request to extend the expiry date of the work and holiday visa subclass 462 has been denied. For the second-year extension, the applicant must have already completed three months or combined eighty-eight days of specified subclass work during the first 462 visa period." He pushed the letter across the desk. "Given your visa expires in two months and you can't complete that three-months' worth of agricultural work before the end date…there's no option to extend."

For a moment, Angie wasn't sure she'd be able to speak. It felt like her insides had been flash frozen.

"But the other lawyer said I could complete that work in the second year." Angie's voice didn't even sound like her own. She wanted to find the lawyer she'd seen before Arthur and shake him. "He told me people had done it before."

Paul shrugged. "They've really cracked down on visa extensions in the last couple of years and, unfortunately, their word is final."

He said it like it was nothing, like the walls weren't crumbling down around her.

"There's nothing I can do?"

There was that damn pitying look again. "I wish I could fix this for you, but as it stands, you'll need to exit the country in sixty days. You can reapply for a tourist visa if you want to come back for a short-term visit."

The bottom had dropped out of her world. If only she'd gotten the right advice, she could have had an extra twelve months to figure things out. She's been *sure* the heartfelt letter and proof of why she couldn't return home might tug at the heartstrings of someone in the Department of Home Affairs. Why would *anyone* want to return to what was waiting for her in America?

There had to be a solution. Maybe she could convince the Department of Home Affairs to give her a job. Angie Donovan, adviser to the Australian people! Or what if she could convince a family to adopt her? Was that even a thing as an adult? Or maybe it would be easier to find a kangaroo costume and practice hopping around so she could blend in with the wildlife and stay here forever.

Think, Angie. A creative panic spiral won't help you now.

She snapped her fingers. "What about getting a company to sponsor me? I've heard people do that so they can stay longer."

"Some companies *do* sponsor people," Paul said with a nod. "But you're an unskilled worker with incomplete tertiary education. Generally, companies sponsor people in specialized fields."

He was right. Angie was twenty-six years old with three-quarters of a college education, a string of short-term, low-paying jobs on her résumé, and a bunch of employers who'd "let her go" because they didn't want the media scrutiny that followed her everywhere. She couldn't even bear the thought of studying again—not after going to every class and having people stare at her. She couldn't handle crowds anymore, and setting foot onto a university or college campus gave her panic attacks. Hence why her degree had never been completed.

Since coming to Patterson's Bluff, she'd felt like she could live a normal life for the first time ever…and it was glorious. She couldn't lose it now.

Angie felt the tightness building in the back of her throat. The idea of going back to America was enough to give her a panic attack. The thought of those flashing cameras and intrusive questions and microphones being shoved into her face, everyone asking her how it felt to be the poster child for a shitty childhood…no, she couldn't do it. *This* was where she was supposed to be. This was supposed to be her new home.

Her perfect home.

"Is there really no other option?" Her voice was steady from years of practice, but inside she was falling apart. "I don't want to leave. This place is…my dream."

"I wish I had better news." For a moment, Paul looked like he truly meant it. Slimy as he was, there still seemed to be a hint of his grandfather's goodness in him. "You know, you could always find a bloke to marry. I wouldn't be totally opposed to the idea. We could get you a spousal visa, allow you to stay in the country. I'm sure we could find some arrangement that benefitted us both."

Ew. Okay, so maybe that hint of his grandfather's goodness *wasn't* there after all.

"Are you seriously trying to cash in on my misery?" she asked, her fists balling. What kind of son of a bitch—

"Oh no, it's nothing to do with money. I mean, I could give you some options…" He leaned forward, bracing his forearms against the edge of the desk and smiling like a hungry wolf. "We could help each other. People might take me more seriously if I had a wife."

I would literally rather marry a bag of dicks.

"I don't think a fake marriage would work for either of us." Angie clutched the letter to her chest, wanting to cry and scream and pound her fist into a wall.

But if there was one skill she'd learned as a kid, it was to pack her emotions down and swallow them like the bitter little pill they were. Life might have stolen her childhood and her happiness, but it would never take her dignity. And that meant she would never let herself get cornered into being with a man like Paul Westerly.

Angie squared her shoulders and stood. "I appreciate your grandfather writing on my behalf."

Without waiting for his response, she strode out of the office and into the reception area. Dorothy stepped out from behind the desk, tears glimmering in her big blue eyes and her arms stretched wide.

Oh no, not hugs.

Hugs were the worst at times like this. They

always made it harder to keep a handle on her emotions, to keep control of the situation. When Dorothy wrapped her up, the scent of her perfume—roses and lilies—enveloped Angie in a sympathetic pink cloud.

"I'm so sorry it didn't work out," Dorothy whispered. "Make sure you come by before you leave. I know the folks here will miss you, and Arthur would want to say goodbye."

"I will," she promised. "Tell you what, I'll bring some of my heavy-duty rum balls. Give a couple to Arthur and he'll be feeling better in no time." She winked. If only she felt as good on the inside as she knew she could look on the outside.

After settling her account, she headed out onto the street. Her Australian dream was done. Finished. Over.

Finito.

Her bright-blue bike was sitting in the rack, the chain and lock dangling over the handle. Nobody here bothered to lock up their bikes, because everybody knew everybody else. There was a trust that came inherently to such a tight-knit community...the kind of trust Angie had never experienced before.

Her eyes watered as she looked over the chip in the chain stay and the scratch on the handlebar. It had been a little banged up when she'd bought it for twenty bucks from a guy down the road, but she'd worked hard to give it some love. A new set of tires and a new seat made it a great ride, and the little basket with a bright-yellow sunflower that hung on the front had been a steal from the local charity shop.

She rode that damn bike *everywhere*.

Regretting her decision to wear a pencil skirt, Angie slipped out of her heels and pulled the ballet flats from her bag. Her outfit hadn't made a lick of difference to the immigration gods, as suspected. As she climbed onto the bike, she spied something in the basket. A little brown bag with a message scrawled on it.

Hey, Angie, we had leftovers. Thought you might like them. Kel.

Inside the bag were a couple of savory scones—likely the rocket and Asiago that she loved—from the bakery next door. The owner always slipped her extras whenever she came in. They were a thank-you for the help she gave once a week with the store by picking up treats for the Patterson's Bluff nursing home.

By the time Angie made it onto the road, her feet peddling as fast as she could, her breath came in short bursts, and a horrible, tight feeling gripped her chest. She called it "the boulder" because that's what it felt like—a big fat rock squishing her heart and lungs. And she hadn't felt the boulder in a while.

Australia was good for her. Hell, in many ways it had *saved* her. She could breathe here, could be her own person. Have her own life. Live without the constant pressure of being "Little Angela Donovan." Victim. Poster child. Famous for all the wrong reasons.

"I don't want to leave." Her voice was eaten up by the wind as she whizzed along the main street.

After visiting the bigger cities—Brisbane, Sydney and Melbourne—she'd settled here more than six months ago and found the home that had always eluded her. People were friendly, welcoming. She'd made connections and slowly come out of her shell. She'd grown. Gotten stronger. Recovered…at least a little bit.

And now it was all going to be taken away.

Angie made it back to her temporary home in record time and stashed away her bike. She needed a coffee. And then she needed to think, because Angie *wasn't* going to lay down and accept defeat. Over and over and over, she'd been a good girl, followed the rules, and tried not to rock the boat. And what had it gotten her? Diddly-squat.

Leaving her bag in the main room of the little place she'd started to call home, she wandered over to the kitchen and turned on the coffee maker. She would figure this out…somehow.

The sound of something clicking against the floorboards startled Angie, and the hairs on her arms stood on end. She wasn't alone in the house.

"Hello?"

A low, rumbling growl sent a tremor through her as a hulking dog blocked the entrance to the kitchen. Its fur was dark as ink and the beast stood almost to her waist. As it bared its teeth, another low growl rumbled from the back of its throat.

Holy hell, its teeth looked sharp as knives.

Crap, crap, crap!

"Easy." She froze against the kitchen counter.

She was fine against anything the Australian landscape could throw at her—bugs, spiders, snakes—but not a dog. Bad memories started to swirl, like dust kicked up from the ground.

Don't stand there—do something!

Her eyes darted around the kitchen, landing on a frying pan hanging from a hook. She *really* didn't like the idea of hitting an animal, but if it tried to bite her, she would have to defend herself. She reached out, but the dog took a step forward and gave a sharp warning bark.

Angie flinched, her heart hammering against her rib cage. How the hell had it gotten inside the house? She was sure she'd closed the front door behind her.

"Be calm," she murmured under her breath. "Don't let it know you're scared."

"Terrified" was more accurate. All she could focus on was the way the dog's eyes were locked onto her. Like it was hungry and she was a big, tasty bag of bones.

Think, dammit. What would the Dog Whisperer do?

CHAPTER THREE

Jace blinked, wincing as the harsh sunlight blinded his sleep-sensitive eyes. Throwing an arm over his face, he groped for his sunglasses with his free hand. It took him a moment to find them still perched on his head. He'd only intended to come outside for a short while, long enough to brush the cobwebs from his mind.

Last night, he hadn't gotten his requisite eight hours of sleep. Not even close. Truffle had cried until two in the morning—presumably disoriented and missing Eugenie—forcing Jace to break his rule about preserving the sanctity of his bedroom. He kept Tilly in the lounge, where she snored like an old man, and brought the Chihuahua into his room. Despite giving the dog a stern warning, he woke up some hours later with a dog butt in his face.

Unable to break habit, Jace was *still* at the Sorrento Back Beach by seven a.m. for his morning surf. And he still had his standard breakfast when he got home. Routine was routine, after all, and a crappy night's sleep wasn't going to derail his plans. That was, until he'd come outside to think about the latest strip he was working on and had promptly fallen asleep on a lounge chair.

Shaking his head, he sat up. Something was missing—one big black furry source and one little white furry source of his sleep deprivation. There was no movement in the yard. Only the barest hint of leaves rustling as a breeze swept through.

"Tilly?" The dogs were possibly off exploring the huge yard that stretched out behind his house, which thankfully was fenced on all sides. "Truffle!"

There was plenty for a dog to discover around here—lots of wildlife, like rosellas, frogs, cockatoos, and galahs. Maybe the odd possum, though probably not this early in the afternoon. Hopefully they hadn't wandered across a snake.

He couldn't let anything happen to the dogs—as much as he'd woken up this morning cursing his mother for tricking him, a promise was a promise. No matter how much he was coerced into it.

"Bloody hell," he muttered as he got up and strode into the house. "If you come out now, I'll give you extra food."

Nothing.

His place wasn't exactly big, so it didn't take long to search all the nooks and crannies. Where on earth could they have gotten to? Jace wandered back out to the garden and found a T-shirt in a crumpled heap outside the door. Not torn to shreds, thankfully, but there *was* dog drool all over it. Not to mention a decent coating of black fur. Tilly.

Jace tried not to let the burgeoning feeling of panic blossom into a full-blown freak-out. What if one of the people on his street had thought the dogs were homeless and taken them to a shelter? Because that would seem a more likely scenario than anyone who knew Jace assuming he'd agreed to dog-sit.

He walked across the back lawn, his gaze picking over the trees and shrubbery. Maybe they were hiding in the bushes? He glanced over to the small, squat building that sat on the back of the garden. The tiny one-bedroom unit—affectionately known as the "granny flat"—looked relatively undisturbed, except for the fact that the front door was wide open.

"Stay back!" A high-pitched feminine voice cut through the air as a warning growl sounded from inside the unit.

Oh shit.

Jace jogged over and braced his hands against the doorframe. He didn't want to interrupt his tenant, since they certainly weren't on the kind of terms where they'd walk into each other's homes without an invite. Sure, they were friendly. But not *that* friendly.

He'd rented out the flat for a little extra cash, something steady to offset the highs and lows of creative income. But his tenant was prone to distracting him with her long legs and shiny brown hair and pretty, heart-shaped face. Hence why he kept his distance.

"Angie?" he called into the unit. "You okay?"

"Jace!" Her petrified voice rang out. "There's a big dog in here and it looks hungry."

"I'm coming in."

A few footsteps later, his gaze landed on a black tail hanging out of the entrance to the kitchen. He found Tilly hunkered down, facing off with the woman currently renting from him.

Her eyes were wide, her mouth drawn into a thin line as her breath came short and fast, forcing the buttons to strain on her blouse. She'd plastered herself against the kitchen cabinets, and her face was white as a sheet.

"Tilly, sit!" he commanded. Eugenie had taken the dogs to obedience school, so they should know basic commands.

The dog plopped her butt down on the ground and turned her head, looking at him over one shoulder proudly as if to say, *Look how well I'm protecting you.* He nudged her with his knee, and she reluctantly made way for him to enter the kitchen.

Angie sagged back against the counter. "Thank God. You know this attack dog?"

"She's hardly an attack dog." Jace reached down and scratched Tilly behind the ears.

"If you'd given her a few more minutes, you'd be sweeping little chewed-up pieces of human."

Jace stifled a laugh. Angie had clearly gotten a fright from the sudden canine interruption. Even now, with Tilly's tongue lolling out the side of her mouth and looking the furthest thing from dangerous, Angie kept her distance. "Sorry about that. I'll get her out of your hair."

She nodded but said, "It's okay. She startled me is all."

Angie folded her arms across the front of her blouse—which was a pale, summery blue. It was a perfect contrast to her wavy brown hair and sparkly brown eyes. She'd put on a little makeup today, something delicate and pink on her cheeks and that glossy stuff on her lips that made them look totally kissable. Attraction flared deep inside him, as it usually did whenever he was around Angie. Since the day she'd come to check out the flat, he'd found himself unable to stop looking at her.

But, like always, the sensible voice in his head followed up immediately: *Not appropriate to be checking out the tenant.*

Besides, Angie wasn't the kind of girl he should be interested in. She talked a lot and was a social butterfly, and chaos stuck to her like she was made of Velcro. A woman who couldn't seem to go a day without finding some new cause to pour her heart into was trouble with a capital *T*. The last thing he needed was someone trying to "fix" him.

"I'm not great with dogs," Angie added. It looked like she was about to say more, but she chewed the inside of her cheek instead.

"Bad experience?" He slipped a finger under Tilly's collar to make sure she didn't spook Angie further.

"Explain to me how encountering some hairy beast with more teeth than should be legal *isn't* a bad experience? In fact, I'd say that dogs were meant to be earth's dominant species except, you know…no opposable thumbs."

"That's all it took for humans to succeed? Opposable thumbs."

Her lips quirked. "It sounds scientific, right?"

Jace laughed and shook his head. "Well, we might have to figure something out. This is Mrs. Landry's dog, and my mother has told her I have 'plenty of space' to babysit for the next two months."

"*That's* her dog? When she came to visit her aunt in the retirement home, she described the damn thing like it was some little ball of fluff." Angie inched carefully along the kitchen counter. "She called her a lapdog, for crying out loud."

"Given she tried to crawl into my lap while I was working yesterday, I guess you *could* call her a lapdog." Jace frowned. "But I imagine she was probably talking about the little one, Truffle."

Speaking of which, he was still one for two in the dog department. Not a good sign, considering he had fifty-nine days of dog-sitting duties ahead of him.

Angie started to move around the kitchen and reached for the cupboard above her. The cupboards were high for the average person, let alone someone "vertically challenged," as Angie called herself, and she had to rise up onto her tiptoes to reach the mugs. This caused the hem of her skirt to crawl up the backs of her thighs in a way that had Jace feeling suddenly hungry. Angie rode her bike everywhere and she had phenomenal legs.

Jace cleared his throat and averted his eyes. He was about to announce that he should get going to find Truffle when Angie cut into his thoughts.

"So your mom dobbed you in, huh?" She tilted her head toward Tilly. "You're on doggy day-care duty."

"Yeah, she did." He liked the way she said *mom* in her American accent. "Nice use of 'dobbed,' by the way."

"Thank you. My Aussie slang vocabulary is growing. I managed to use 'squiz' in a sentence today." She retrieved two cups, without asking if he wanted a coffee, and set them on the bench.

Despite the banter, Angie didn't seem her usual bubbly self today. Normally, she was the kind of woman who bounced all over the place. She was chatty to the extreme, friendly and warm and sweet like a cup of hot chocolate. But today she seemed a little…off. Maybe it was the fright.

Or maybe it was one of those "people things" he couldn't figure out.

Jace was good at a lot of things—drawing, surfing, keeping promises. He could chop firewood and put Ikea furniture together without looking at the instructions. But he was *not* great when it came to what he liked to call the "fuzzy gray." The "fuzzy gray" was his term for all the things he didn't quite understand. The comments that sailed over his head, those indecipherable facial expressions that weren't obvious enough to be put into categories. Subtext and hidden agendas and ulterior motives. Oh, and him saying things that were true but probably shouldn't be said because it made him sound "blunt."

All that stuff was the fuzzy gray, and he felt certain he was in the middle of it right now.

"Everything okay?" he asked. The question popped out before he'd had the chance to give it due consideration—he still had Tilly in his hand and one potentially missing Chihuahua—but something told him this was one of those times where his own awkwardness should come second to being a good person. And, like his dad always said, the Walters family helped people.

So maybe he could help Angie.

• • •

Tears sprang to Angie's eyes so quickly, they caught her off guard. Oh, hell no. She hadn't kept herself together all through that meeting this afternoon only to lose it now.

She spun around to face the sink—now more concerned about her emotions than the big black dog in her tiny kitchen. Why did she have to act like a melodramatic teenager in front of Jace now? He was pretty much a level of adulthood she could never hope to achieve. He *always* had a cool head about him. He was quiet and composed, thoughtful. And hot...so hot.

Like, *exactly what you think a sexy Australian guy should look like* kind of hot.

Blue eyes, sandy hair. Crooked Hemsworth smile. Tanned skin. Shoulders broad enough to carry the world. She'd seen him in board shorts a number of times and knew that what he had going on under his usual T-shirt and jeans was the stuff of her horny dreams.

Holy freaking physical perfection, Batman.

Except that he most likely thought she was a mess of a human. Which, to be fair, she was. Call it a by-product of the fact that she had only one mode of operation in dealing with nervous energy: grin and bear it. Or, as was more accurate, grin and verbal diarrhea.

In the case of Jace Walters, that meant flitting around with a too-big smile and starting conversations about literally anything that popped into her head. Like that one time she suggested he plant cacti instead of annuals, because they were easier to care for. Except that he should be careful because this one time she fell on a cactus, and pulling the prickles out of her leg was torture. But that it would definitely be worse for a guy because their nether regions were so much more exposed. Which had been super awkward, so then she'd changed the topic and started talking about how strange it was that eggplants had nothing to do with eggs.

She cringed remembering how he'd stared blankly at her. Sometimes it seemed like he had no idea how to react to her or what to say, but who could blame him? She talked sixty miles a minute and changed conversation topics like the wind.

Jace cleared his throat. "Should I go? I don't want to…intrude."

"No, stay. Please." She cursed herself for the desperation in her voice. Warning: stage-five clinger. She turned around and offered him one of her too-big smiles. "I mean…it's been a long day. I could use some company, actually."

Falling apart was *not* an option.

He absently scratched his chest, as if he wasn't sure what to say next. Then he blurted out, "Want to help me look for the other dog?"

She blinked. "You lost him already?"

"I didn't lose him," Jace replied, frowning. "I…

misplaced him."

Angie let out a half laugh. "Sure. I can help with the dog hunt. We're looking for the little one, right?"

"Right."

"And you'll lock up the big one." She eyed Tilly warily.

"Yes, I'll lock her up."

"And you'll let me make you a cup of coffee after."

A crooked smile pulled at Jace's lips, making a dimple form in one cheek. "Sure."

"Give me a second to change." She darted off to her bedroom and quickly wriggled out of her pencil skirt and blouse. She wanted to burn the damn things—useless talismans that they were.

She reemerged in jean shorts, a white T-shirt, and thongs…which she *still* couldn't say without giggling. Although now, not even the Aussies' funny word for flip-flops could lift her spirits. The meeting today had left her feeling like a husk. Like someone had hollowed her out and taken a match to her future.

You could always find a bloke to marry. I wouldn't be totally opposed to the idea.

Paul's words swirled in her head, but she shut the thoughts down. There was no way she could marry a guy for a visa. She'd always known she would marry for love—because her life would have been very different if she'd had love…from anyone.

No way would she shortchange herself where *that* was concerned.

Not even for the life of your dreams? Not even for the chance to live anonymously and happily?

No. She deserved more.

"I'm outside," Jace called, and Angie jogged through the front door, then slammed it shut behind her. "Big dog is locked up."

"Well, *that* is a giant relief." She also didn't love small dogs. Angie didn't hate them, of course, but she'd had such a bad experience earlier in life that she'd never bonded with any other dog since. "Okay, Dr. Watson. What's your read on the situation?"

"How come you get to be Sherlock?"

"Because Sherlock would never have lost the dogs in the first place."

He stared up at the sky as if he were training to be a meteorologist before finally answering. "Good point."

Jace's property was huge. If there was one thing Australia wasn't short on, it was land. And Patterson's Bluff had some of the best in the country—rocky ocean views, streets thick with native foliage. The kind of sunsets that could make even the most emotionally remote person shed a tear.

But all of that meant plenty of space for a small animal to explore. The property sloped down at the back, with thick bushes and shrubbery creating seemingly endless hiding spots. There was a huge old tree with a legit tree house. It looked better than some of the houses Angie lived in as a kid.

"Tell me about the dog," she said, rubbing

her chin in what she guessed was a Sherlock-like gesture.

"Chihuahua. Two years old. Male. White fur, big pointy ears. Buggy eyes."

It pleased her immensely that Jace was playing along. She needed this distraction right now. "There's no way he could have left the property?"

"No." Jace shook his head. "The front door and all windows were shut. Gate around the side was also shut and locked."

"Back door?"

"Not locked. I came outside to think and...I fell asleep."

Angie raised a brow. Jace was Mr. Diligent. Mr. Always Working. "Rough night?"

"Yeah." He raked a hand through his hair. "I had a guest."

"Oh." For some reason, the thought of Jace having someone stay over sent a hot poker lancing through her. Which was ridiculous, since she never begrudged people's happiness. But her mind spun on the idea of him naked and sweaty and up all night, torturing her with vivid images of his surfing-honed body. "Well... Uh... Good for you."

He looked at her strangely. "I had a *canine* guest. Truffle was crying, and I caved around two a.m. and let him sleep in my bedroom."

She didn't know what was worse, the jealousy that was both unwarranted and unexpected...or the fact that Jace suspected she had her mind in the gutter. "Right, well. Yes. I totally knew what you meant."

Angie marched forward, heading toward a cluster of bottlebrush trees nestled along the fence that ran closest to her unit. The bright-red flowers swayed lightly, their spiny tendrils shuddering in the breeze. Crouching, Angie pushed the branches to one side. No dog.

"He might have been chasing a bird," she mused. "Dogs do that, right?"

They inched along the fence, checking behind clusters of trees. A small shed was tucked away in the back corner of the property, where Jace kept the lawn mower and other gardening tools. But the padlock was firmly in place, so he couldn't be hiding in there.

"Truffle!" Jace called. His deep baritone carried across the yard. "Here, boy!"

Nothing. The breeze picked up speed, sending Angie's hair scattering around her shoulders. Overhead, dark clouds threatened. Summer was like that here—a week of blistering heat followed by a thunderstorm to cool everything down. Then the temperature would start to climb again.

"Shit," Jace muttered. "I need to get him inside before that storm hits. Eugenie said he can catch a cold easily if he gets stuck out in the rain for too long."

"We'll find him," she said in what she hoped was a reassuring voice. "Truffle! We've got treats for you! Doggy treats and steak and…pizza."

Did dogs eat pizza? Probably not. Maybe it was one of those things they weren't supposed to eat but still enjoyed. Like chocolate.

They went farther down into the more densely

wooded area of the property, where trees grew up and out, creating a shadowy patch. They walked quicker, pulling back bushes and branches and calling Truffle's name. The temperature dropped rapidly, and Angie shivered. Jace let out a sharp whistle.

"What if he got hurt and he can't move?" he said.

Angie's heart clenched at the worry in Jace's voice. "He's probably having the time of his life. You know, he's like a little explorer navigating new territory, and he's probably so ready to come back to the big dog and tell her all about it."

"Eugenie will *kill* me if anything happens to them. They're like her children." A deep groove settled between his brows. "This is why I stick to cacti."

If he hadn't looked so genuinely concerned, Angie might have laughed. That was Jace in a nutshell—he liked living a quiet, low-maintenance life. Cacti were *perfect* for him, which was why she'd suggested them in the first place. The fact that he'd listened to her and bought a few for his garden had filled her with a soft, squishy kind of warmth in her chest. She got the impression that Jace usually did what he wanted, regardless of what people said.

A fine mist descended over them as they emerged from the trees. The storms here could hit suddenly, scattering people who didn't know well enough to always have an umbrella stashed somewhere close by. They probably had less than five minutes before the rain turned nasty.

A loud clap of thunder filled the air, and Jace charged up toward the house, calling Truffle's name. They were almost at his door when the sky opened up, rain teeming down in sheets. And still no dog.

"You go inside," he said, ushering her toward the door. "See if he snuck back in."

Angie hesitated a second, terrified at the thought of being stuck in a house with the big black dog...especially since she knew dogs liked storms about as much as she did. But she'd also never seen Jace so worried in the six months she'd lived here as his tenant.

"Sure." She steeled herself and headed up the stairs to his house, shielding her face from the rain.

She wanted to help Jace, because even though he was a little distant, he'd been nothing but kind to her since she'd arrived. Then, after they'd figured out where that furry little critter had gotten to, she could go back to worrying about the biggest problem of all: her future.

CHAPTER FOUR

Angie stepped into the house and looked around, her body tense as a tightly coiled spring. The prospect of watching Tilly the Big Black Beast filled her with dread. And worse, it made bad memories churn in her head. One of her foster fathers had been a mean son of a bitch who let his kids go hungry and did even worse to his four Rottweilers. It had been no wonder that they were aggressive, the way he treated them.

"Tilly?" she called out.

She took a moment to look around Jace's house, because she'd never been inside for long before. Her verbal diarrhea usually sent Jace packing whenever they caught each other in the yard. He was 100 percent business. No personal chitchat. No trading of "getting to know you" tidbits.

He wasn't rude about it, but um, yeah, she'd gotten the point. Of course, that hadn't stopped her from popping over to see him…a lot. There was something that drew Angie to Jace — something inexplicable that always set her tummy aflutter.

Now they had a routine. She'd knock on his door a few times a week, looking for coffee or sugar or a wrench (he'd almost had a heart attack *that* time, thinking she was doing some DIY plumbing, until she'd explained it was for her bike). Being that close to him would make her prattle on about something silly until he'd smile and say he had to get back to his work. But she couldn't seem to stop herself from finding an excuse to visit him.

Clearly the man had phenomenal pheromones.

She shook her head and refocused on her surroundings. The place was neat, not a speck of dust anywhere. It put her to shame, because even though she wasn't dirty, Angie thrived in organized chaos. She knew her house keys would be safely nestled in a little pile of receipts and change on her countertop. She knew her missing shoe was usually under the couch. Or the bed. Or there was that one time when she found a stiletto tangled in one of the potted plants, and that was *totally* inexplicable. Later, she'd had nightmares about her plants coming alive to steal her personal belongings.

Jace probably *never* had dreams about plants stealing his personal belongings.

There was a framed photograph on the little table between the couch and armchair, five kids all with matching sandy mops of hair, suntans, and big toothy smiles. Well, four had big toothy smiles. Angie smiled at young Jace's expression— apparently he was serious as a judge, even back then. His eyes seemed to be looking at something beyond the camera.

"Tilly?" Angie delved farther into Jace's house as a crack of thunder ripped through the air, making her jump. She inched toward his bedroom. For some reason, going into someone's bedroom without strict invitation felt like a violation of privacy.

Like lawyers' offices, a person's bedroom said a lot about them. And she would know, because she'd lived in *a lot* of houses. This bedroom was as tidy as everything else in Jace's life. He had only the minimum number of pillows on his king size bed—because he preferred function over form. The bedside table housed a lamp and a book with a leather bookmark hanging out the side. Since the book didn't have any dust on it, it was likely he actually read on the regular. While practicality reigned as king in the land of Jace, he still made time for his hobbies, it appeared.

"Tilly?" Angie looked around, oh so tempted to snoop. But she knew better—after wanting nothing more than a home where she felt safe and secure, she'd never breach that security for someone else. "Come on, girl. I don't like storms, either."

But Tilly was nowhere to be found.

The sound of something banging in the depths of the house had Angie turning on her heel. "Jace?"

A howling wind whistled through the house, so loud it felt like the very foundations were trembling. Oh man, this was *perfect* weather for reading spooky books. She'd had a total fascination for the Goosebumps and Fear Street series when she was a kid. This weather was living out an R. L. Stine fantasy.

"More like Cujo," she muttered to herself as she continued hunting for the dog.

Rain fell in thick sheets, sending huge white hunks of ice pelting down. Hail. Only it was hail like she'd never seen it before. The stones were as big as golf balls and they bounced against the grass, thumping down on the verandah out back and tearing through the netting around the apple trees next door.

Dear God! What if the little dog was crushed by giant ice balls?

She yanked open the door and winced as the cold air slapped her face. The temperature had plummeted. Jace stormed toward the house, his face bowed against the rain. Angie let out a sigh of relief when she saw a very wet, miserable-looking white bundle in his arms. She wasn't a dog person by any stretch, but there was something about a muscular hunk of a man taking care of a tiny animal like that...

Hello, hormones.

Jace strode into the house, and water pooled on the tiled floor. "He's terrified, poor thing."

Understatement of the year. The small dog was shaking so hard, Angie worried he might give himself a concussion. His little doggy brain was probably rattling around like a pinball.

"I couldn't find Tilly. I think she's hiding." Angie bit down on her lip. "I'll keep looking."

"Here." Jace handed over the Chihuahua, who looked up at her with terrified eyes. "Find a towel and get him dry. We'll need to warm the little fella up."

Angie went straight into the bathroom and found the fluffiest towel she could. Then she bundled Truffle up burrito-style so that only his little face poked out. Her top was soaked through, and she'd started to shiver, too.

"It's okay; it's okay," she cooed as she carried him to the couch. "You're fine now. Although I was told Australia had beautiful weather. Funny how they don't put crazy thunderstorms in the travel brochures."

Unsurprisingly, Truffle did not comment.

A minute later, Jace walked back into the main room. He had a dog in his arms again—only *this* dog was easily sixty pounds... What was that in kilos? A lot, anyway. But she didn't appear to be any less scared than her tiny counterpart.

When he set the dog on the couch, Tilly buried her head into the cushion, wedging her face under Angie's thigh. For a minute, Jace stood there, the beginnings of a smile on his lips. Angie, on the other hand, was still as a statue while she tried not to think about how many teeth were in her immediate vicinity. Yet, under Jace's watchful eye, she felt totally safe. Like his mere presence calmed her and made her memories go quiet.

Outside, the storm roared, heavy black clouds rolling past with the continual *thunk, thunk, thunk* of hailstones. But even masquerading as a drowned rat, Jace was smokin' hot.

"You should get changed," Angie said. "Put on something dry or else you'll catch a cold."

He shook his head. "You sound like my mother."

"I've met your lovely mother, so I'll take that as a compliment."

"You should." He peeled his soaked T-shirt

over his head, and droplets of water flew in all directions around him. They dribbled down his chest, sliding over the ripples of muscle at his stomach and clinging to him all over. "The rain was coming down so hard, I couldn't see properly."

As if to illustrate his point, he dragged the back of his hand across his forehead, but it didn't do any good. That's when she noticed a nasty red mark on Jace's cheek. "Looks like you got one in the face."

He fetched a towel from a small closet on the other side of the room. "Hurts like hell, too."

Momentarily, her fears about the dog situation were overtaken by a dryness in her mouth and a thumping in her chest. Watching Jace rub the towel over his naked torso was doing strange things to her insides, making them feel all flippy and twisty. The air evaporated from her lungs, leaving her feeling tight and…needy.

As he walked toward his bedroom—which unfortunately she could now picture clear as day—she watched how the muscles moved in his back as he continued to dry himself off. Wow. Surfing sure made for a good body.

Please don't let me go into verbal vomit time now…

"Thanks for helping," he called from the bedroom. The sound of something slapping forced her imagination into hyper speed. He was already sans T-shirt, then off would come the socks. Then his jeans…

"Did you know three dogs survived the sinking

of the *Titanic*?" She almost slapped her forehead. God, could she ever talk like a normal person? Or keep her trap shut altogether? "Never mind, it was a fun fact that sprang to mind. And you're welcome...although I didn't really do much."

Angie pressed deep into the corner of the couch, trying to put some space between her and Tilly's snout. No dice. The dog practically crawled into her lap, her heavy body pinning Angie to the couch and her wet tongue swiping wherever it could reach. Burrito Dog, on the other hand, was still a canine vibrator.

"If I hadn't heard your screaming, I might have been sleeping out there when the hailstorm hit."

"So I saved your life?" She grinned to herself, feeling a little tingle of the warm and fuzzy variety that he was grasping at straws to make her feel better.

He walked back out into the living room in dry jeans and a fitted black T-shirt. "I see you three have become best buds."

"Fear is a bonding experience." She looked down at Truffle. "So what now?"

"You're not going anywhere until the storm dies down." He didn't sound too happy about it, and Angie tried not to take it personally. Although it stung a little, if she was being honest.

He's probably frustrated that you're both stuck here when it was supposed to be sunny and warm.

The lights flickered overhead, and Jace groaned, a frustrated plea on his lips. But the gods were cruel, and the power flickered once more before dying completely. The hum of the refrigerator cut out, and the lights went dark.

"That's the *last* thing we need," he said, raking a hand through his damp hair. "Bloody hell."

"Is this normal?" she asked over her shoulder.

"Storms are normal, but this hail isn't. And no power means no internet and no fridge."

"I guess we can't call for a pizza, huh?" she joked.

Another loud crack of thunder rang out, followed by a huge *boom*. Not the kind of boom that came from the sky, either. Angie jumped off the couch and, still cradling Burrito Dog, went to the window.

"I'm guessing that tree isn't supposed to be horizontal?" she asked as she and Jace stood in front of the large windows.

Branches covered the road near the end of the driveway, and some of the smaller debris blew down the street. Leaves billowed up, swirling as if in a mini tornado. Like Sharknado...but for leaves.

Please don't think about the possibility of a tornado with dangerous creatures. You are in the wrong *country to survive that kind of thing!*

"We're stuck on the property until the storm slows down enough for the council to clear the roads." He shook his head. "But that'll take a while. At least a few hours."

"Is there likely to be power at my place?" she asked.

Jace shook his head. "If it's out here, it'll be out there as well. And I don't like the idea of you doing a mad dash across the yard with all those big hailstones coming down."

"So you're stuck with me?"

He looked over her shoulder. "More like the other way around."

Somehow she doubted that very much.

• • •

Jace lit the gas stove with a match and set a pot of water to boil. Yesterday morning, his life had been in order: clean house, no obligations, plenty of time to work. He was in the middle of plotting out a new script for his comic series, *Hermit vs. World*, and had started sketching a rough storyboard. In fact, he was *ahead* of schedule, which was exactly how he liked to work.

But now...

Jace looked out to the living room, where Angie had moved onto a single armchair in an attempt to get away from Tilly. The big dog wasn't having it, however, and had followed her, promptly settling in a heavy lump at her feet. Truffle appeared to be the only one who was totally comfortable, as he was still wrapped in a blanket and settled against Angie's chest like a newborn baby.

Cute as it was, Jace's whole day had been hijacked. He was now approximately four hours and thirty-five minutes behind schedule, due to him fitting in a walk that morning with the dogs and then falling asleep and *then* going on a rescue mission. Now Angie was here, and he couldn't very well leave her alone while he worked. Jace glared at the black clouds clogging the sky. Not that he would be able to see a damn thing in his studio anyway.

"I think he's asleep," Angie said quietly as she laid down the bundled-up dog and came toward the kitchen. "Do you think we should take him to a vet?"

A loud crack of thunder shook the house, reminding them they weren't going anywhere.

"I think he got a fright, that's all."

"Didn't we all." She let out a weak laugh. "So, uh…it's probably not a bad thing we got stuck together. I had something to talk to you about."

"What is it this time?" he asked. "Save the koalas? No, we did that one already. Sea turtles? Oh, let me guess. It's the quokkas, right?"

Angie was a bleeding heart, always trying her hardest to save one group or another. Always jumping in to help the latest charity effort. In the six months she'd lived here, she'd taken part in bake sales, fund-raising walks, tree planting, charity brunches, and raffles. She'd also been volunteering at the local retirement home, doing her best to give the people who lived there some companionship. Her care was poured into everything like she was overflowing with it.

And, being a bubbly person, she was never satisfied to act alone. She roped everyone into her charitable activities. Jace couldn't even remember the amount of fund-raising Freddo Frogs he'd bought and then given away after listening to another impassioned speech from his tenant. But he couldn't seem to say no to her. Ever.

"Well, actually, I *was* going to talk to you about an event I'm planning for the retirement home after my disaster of a meeting at the town hall," she replied with a funny expression. "But that might have to wait."

"You mean they pooh-poohed the Grannies on Poles pole-dancing class?" He chuckled. "I'm not surprised. You probably scandalized Mrs. Marconi."

"Feeling sexually confident isn't only for young people, Jace." She huffed. "And yes, you're right, they pooh-poohed Grannies on Poles. But that's not what I need to talk to you about right now."

There was a waver in her voice that stopped Jace in his tracks. He might not have known Angie that long, but he knew one thing about her—she was *always* upbeat. A little kooky, sure. Passionate and idealistic? Hell yeah. And always positive. That little waver, however, was an anomaly. And this from a guy usually not the most observant when it came to social cues or nonverbal communication.

But the difference in her was so stark, it was like a physical jolt.

He wanted to ask what was troubling her, but he also felt himself sinking into the fuzzy gray. What was the right thing to say? How did he ask without being too blunt? His gaze drifted outside, as though the trees might offer advice. Sadly not. Then he took a deep breath, looked her in the eye, and asked, "What's going on?"

Angie bit down on her lip and turned, as if checking on the dogs. But it looked like she was trying to compose herself. "I have to leave."

"Right now?" He frowned. The storm was raging like an angry toddler, and although the hailstones had lessened, he could already see downed branches and debris all over the yard. No doubt the streets would look just as bad. "It's not safe. I mean—"

"No. I have to leave Australia."

For a moment, his mind was blank. It oscillated like the Spinning Beach Ball of Doom that appeared when a program crashed on his MacBook. "Why?"

"My visa extension was denied." Her voice was flat, brittle. But he knew it must have hit her hard, because she'd been talking about everything she was going to do once the extension came in.

She'd planned to fit in trips to some of the places in Victoria she hadn't been yet—to the Yarra Valley for wine tasting, to Ballarat and Sovereign Hill for a touch of Australian history. Not to mention all the grand plans she had for making improvements at the retirement home.

The thought of her leaving was...surprisingly sad.

Water hissed as it bubbled over the pot's edge and onto the hot stovetop and snapped Jace back to reality. He poured it up to the fill line on his French press. Then he gave the coffee and water a stir, his spoon clinking against the glass.

"How long until you have to go?" he asked, already dreading her answer.

Because it's going to mess up my routine. We'll have to post the flat online, interview new tenants, do background checks… It's nothing to do with her not being here.

"Two months." Her voice was barely above a whisper.

"And there's nothing you can do? You can't appeal the decision?"

She let out a harsh laugh. "If I had another option, I wouldn't be here telling you I have to leave."

"Right." He bobbed his head. "What can I do to help?"

The question popped out before he even had time to think about it, because that was the Walters way. He would do what he could—packing boxes, organizing a moving company, helping with a garage sale. Even if it meant sifting through the stuff in her place, most of which seemed to have no real purpose…like the seashells she had lined up along the windowsill in the front room. Not to mention the bowl she kept on the coffee table, which was full of random things like ticket stubs and loyalty stamp cards that had been finished. Who kept that crap anyway?

"I appreciate the offer, but I don't even know what needs to be done yet." She sighed. "Paul Westerly suggested that he and I get hitched so I can stay in the country and because people would take him 'more seriously' if he had a wife."

His spoon clanged against the French press loudly. A stone settled in the pit of Jace's stomach, setting him on edge. "He's a dickhead."

"Right?" Angie watched him closely. The

feeling of her eyes boring into him was like someone had taken a match to his blood. "Too bad it's not someone other than Paul *Gross*terly offering."

Jace tried to process her comment as he pushed the plunger down on the French press. Making coffee helped quiet his mind. He liked the process of it—the ritual. But right now, he couldn't think of anything else except the idea that Angie might marry someone for the sake of being able to stay in Australia.

That was the one thing he could not help her with—because marriage wasn't for him. Not now, not ever.

"I mean, you're single. Ever thought about getting yourself a wife?" She winked. Was this one of those times where the words sounded serious but were meant to be a joke?

"Marriage is bullshit." He spoke a little harsher than he'd meant to. "Two people decide they need a piece of paper to make it real. And for what, so one of them can inevitably walk away anyway?"

She blinked. "Cynical much?"

"It's not cynical—it's realistic." He shook his head. There wasn't much that Jace got fired up over—but this was one of them. "It's hard enough to make it work when you're in love, let alone when you're *only* doing it for the piece of paper."

"Wow. Okay, one, I was joking. And two, it's a little insulting that I'm not even *hypothetical* wife material." She walked into the kitchen and yanked the fridge open like she owned the place.

"It took you less than a second to discount the idea."

Jace was sure this was one of those verbal traps he had a tendency to walk into. When he was younger, his mother joked that she was going to give him a tattoo on his foot that said *insert into mouth* for how often he spoke without thinking. It wasn't that he didn't think, more that he only had one speed: straightforward. It had taken him years to develop a filter, and even now he hated using it. Why couldn't he answer questions truthfully?

The thought of marrying anyone was…just no.

And it wasn't for the reasons anyone, including his family, might assume. It had nothing to do with accommodating another person into his routine. It was simply…him. What if one day the woman he chose to let into his life decided that she couldn't deal with his idiosyncrasies anymore? What if his quirks became too much?

Even his own family, who loved him dearly, teased him when a joke on television flew over his head. He could tell they were disappointed when he wasn't up to going to the pub if he'd had a rough day. And sometimes he felt like he let them down when he didn't know the right thing to say if they were having trouble—like when his big brother admitted that he and his wife were struggling to get pregnant.

The fuzzy gray was no place for a marriage to thrive.

"I don't do hypothetical," he said. "Besides, we both know it wouldn't work in the real world."

Angie pulled out the milk and wandered over

to where he'd poured the coffee into two identical white mugs. "You're right. I'm deflecting because I don't want to leave, and it's easier to make jokes than to think about reality."

"For what it's worth, I don't want you to go," he said, meaning every word of it.

"That's sweet," she said, then turned to him and narrowed her eyes. "You were going to make a crack about steady rent, weren't you?"

He wasn't, actually. But it was probably better to let her think that. So he grinned and she swatted him, rolling her eyes and taking her mug back out to the living room. He *didn't* want Angie to leave, that much he knew. She made the place brighter. Happier.

Maybe that was why her news made his stomach feel weird.

Regardless, there wasn't anything he could do about it. Because there was no way in hell he'd ever expose himself to the inevitable rejection that would come with being married.

CHAPTER FIVE

The following day, Angie had to put on her best and brightest—and fakest—smile. Luckily for her, it was something with which she was very familiar. Wearing a fake smile was kind of like pulling on an itchy sweater when it was cold out. Sure, it wasn't the most comfortable thing ever...but it served a purpose.

And that purpose was making the residents of the Patterson's Bluff Retirement Home feel good. She volunteered three days a week as a "companion" to the elderly residents. This sometimes involved playing cards or board games, watching movies, talking, and making cups of tea. Mostly, her job was to keep people company. A lot of the residents said having young people around made them feel young again themselves. Like her youth was contagious.

It suited Angie. She'd never had grandparents as a kid, so this made up for the relationships she'd never gotten the chance to cultivate in her own life.

The main roads had been cleared late last night, after the storm finally subsided. All the downed trees and other dangerous things had been removed, but there was plenty to keep the emergency workers busy—blocked drains, branches, and other debris littering the residential streets, injured wildlife, and damaged traffic signage. Angie had taken a slight detour on her bike, avoiding the paths covered in gumnuts and likely to send her A over T if she hit one with her front tire.

But the weather was pleasant. Cooler than it had been in days, with a slight breeze that carried the salty tang of the ocean right to her nostrils. She peddled at a leisurely pace, taking in all her favorite sights of the town. The quaint little pub that sat on the corner of the main strip, the ice-cream store with its old-fashioned blue-and-white-striped awning. Then there was the "yellow house," a unique two-story beauty that was painted the prettiest shade of buttery yellow, with lacy white fretwork to match. It reminded her of a cake, like it was too sweet and too perfect to be real.

She turned off the main road and peddled up the final hill of her journey, waving to Mr. Singh, the retired chemistry professor. Next door were the Clarks and their five rascal boys. And next to *them* was the sweet Jane and Tom and their baby, Michelle. The big house on the next corner belonged to the "mayor" and his wife. Glen Powell was actually the *former* mayor of the Shire of Mornington Peninsula but still acted like he ran the place.

As Angie pulled into the retirement home, her heart sank. She knew so many people in this town, knew all the quirks and politics, knew the relationships that ran deeper than the sand at the bottom of the ocean. In only six months, she'd been welcomed with open arms and made to feel like one of them. And now she'd have to announce she was moving on. It would be like ripping out the stitches on her heart, making her feel the pain of all the old wounds she'd hoped might have healed properly this time.

Maybe it was smarter to rip off the Band-Aid in one fell swoop? She could keep on peddling. Head straight back to pack her bags and call a taxi to the airport? She could get a flight to LAX from Melbourne and avoid two months of dragging out the inevitable. Two months of pain and denial.

"Hey, Angie."

A feminine voice made her turn around. It was Nadesha Chetty, one of the managers for the retirement home and the person who'd helped sign Angie up for volunteer work when she'd first arrived in Patterson's Bluff. She was also one of the only people who knew about Angie's past, on account of her doing Angie's reference checks. And, unlike a lot of people she'd met in her time, Nadesha had actually kept Angie's secret safe.

"Crazy weather, huh?" Nadesha was dressed in her uniform—black pants and a pale-blue shirt with a name badge pinned to her chest. Her black curly hair sat in a fluffy cloud around her shoulders, and her lips were decorated with her signature poppy red. Like always, she wore a gold chain around her neck with a small ruby pendant that matched her lipstick perfectly. "I was worried I wouldn't be able to get out of my street this morning."

So much for riding away and packing her bags. No way she could flake out on her shift now. "I thought Australia was beautiful one day, perfect the next."

They walked into the building together, and Angie gave a wave before heading into the home's communal living space. There were several common areas dotted around the property, including a quiet library and a room that had big comfy couches and a huge TV. But the main area was where Angie found herself during her volunteer hours. Maybe being around the sweet people who lived here would help lift her mood. Even though they were all grateful for her presence, most had no idea how *they* positively impacted *her*.

As soon as she walked into the room, Angie was waved over to where three women sat around a small square table littered with cards.

"We need a moderator," said Meredith, a seventy-six-year-old woman who never left her room without her two trademarks: a pair of chunky earrings and a cloud of Chanel No.5 wafting around her. "Betty is cheating again."

"I am not!" Betty pressed a palm to her chest and gave a dramatic gasp. "The fact you even *think* I would cheat is an outrage."

Angie looked to the remaining player. Jean never missed a trick, and she cleaned unsuspecting poker players out more often than not with her gentle voice and unassuming smile. "The silent assassin," Angie jokingly called her.

"Jean? What's going on?"

The older woman shrugged. She was bundled up in a fluffy blue cardigan and wore a pair of glasses with a chain connected around the back of her head. "I didn't see anything."

"You *always* take her side," Meredith said, shaking her head. "I swear I'm going to stop playing with you two one day."

"She says that"—Betty winked at Angie—"but she's still here every week."

Meredith huffed but motioned for Angie to take a seat. "Deal you in?"

Angie nodded. "Sure."

"So tell us about the meeting," Betty said as she shuffled the cards. "How did it go?"

The town planning meeting felt like a lifetime ago, but it had only been last Friday. Angie cringed at the memory. She'd gone with grand plans about how she could help improve Patterson's Bluff, thinking that as someone the town had embraced, she would have a voice in that forum. Unfortunately, Glen Powell had been quite "appalled" at some of her ideas for the changes they should make in the retirement home, thinking that allocating their annual development budget to learning opportunities for the elderly was a "misuse" of funds.

"It was…not great." She sagged back against the seat as Betty flicked the cards across the table like a proper casino dealer. "Mr. Powell shut me down."

"That old fogey," Jean said with a grunt. "Needs to pull the stick out of his backside, he does."

Angie couldn't help but laugh. "Agreed. I get the impression he thinks I'm some upstart coming in here with my grand plans, trying to make his life difficult."

"Well, *I* was a big fan of Grannies on Poles," Meredith said, fluffing her hair. "Why should you young ones have all the fun? Water aerobics is fine, but I want to try something new. I hear Zumba is good."

"I don't understand why Glen Bloody Powell gets to determine what goes on here," Betty chimed in. "He's *not* mayor anymore, even if he thinks he owns the damn place."

Angie looked at her cards and tried not to remember Jace's smile at the pooh-poohed idea. Or the fact that the hail had let up only thirty minutes later, and she hadn't been able to think of a good-enough reason to delay going back to her place. Unfortunately.

She focused on her cards. They played Texas Hold'em, and it was *not* her forte. And her cards were less than ideal. But Angie had decided long ago that she wasn't a quitter—not even when she had been dealt a shitty hand.

Weren't you about to run back home and pack your bags so you could slink off to LA without saying goodbye? That is the very definition of quitting when life deals you a shitty hand.

Ugh. Stupid logical brain.

"It wasn't just the pole-exercise thing that got knocked down, either. Glen also hated the idea for the yoga and meditation class—hippie mumbo-jumbo, he said. Oh, and apparently the community vegetable garden is a lawsuit waiting to happen because people might poison one another with pesticides." Angie rolled her eyes. "I didn't even get through all my ideas."

"I'd like to poison *him* with pesticides," Betty grumbled as she tossed some of her chips into the center. "Raise, by the way. I've got some lovely cards here."

"You always talk such a big game. And I call, because you're bluffing." Meredith tossed her chips into the center. Angie matched, and Jean decided to fold. "What kind of ideas *was* he interested in?"

"A billboard on the Nepean advertising the pub. Says we're losing too much traffic to people bypassing us and going straight to Sorrento and Portsea."

"Never mind that he has a share in the pub," Jean muttered. "Self-serving so-and-so."

"Anything else come up at the meeting?" Betty asked. "Aside from Glen Powell looking out for number one?"

The rest of it was a blur. At the time, it had all seemed so important, like Angie was trying to ingrain herself in the town. Like she was going to be the kind of resident who worked hard to make their community better. But now it was a jumble in her head, overtaken by her present worries.

Before she had the chance to respond, the poker game was interrupted when a male resident came over. Angie hadn't seen him before, so maybe he was new. The man was tall and handsome, though he walked with a cane, which made him look older than his strong features and sharp gray eyes would imply.

"*Buonasera signorine*," he said. "Who's winning?"

Meredith looked at Jean with a scowl. "Our resident card shark is winning."

Jean's cheeks went bright red and she huffed, waving a hand angrily at her friend. Angie had never seen the woman have such a reaction before—usually she was quiet and reserved. Unruffled. But she would barely meet the gentleman's eyes.

"I'm Angie. I volunteer here." She stuck her hand out, and the man clasped it in his, giving her a firm shake.

"Marcus Andretti." He smiled. "I moved in recently."

"It's lovely to meet you."

"Have a good game." He inclined his head in a single nod and continued on his way toward a group of men who were sitting by the window, overlooking the courtyard.

Angie's lips curved up into a wicked smile as she turned to Jean. "You have a crush on him!"

"Shh." Jean slapped her arm. "Silly child. I have nothing of the sort."

"She does." Betty put her hand over her mouth and laughed. "And the feeling is mutual."

"Stop it." Jean's cheeks were red as tomatoes. "I've told you before, my heart belongs to my Winston. Forever. Wedding vows were not made to be broken, not even by death."

The table quieted then. Over her six months of volunteering, Angie had gotten to know the rich and vibrant histories of the people who lived here.

"When I met him, I knew we would get married

on our very first date," Jean said. Her eyes were misty, but she sat with her shoulders squared and her back straight. "People these days seem to think it takes years to figure out if you love someone. Phooey! I knew on that first night that Winston was my forever. We were married within a month."

"One month?" Angie hadn't known *that*.

"And I would still be with him now if it wasn't for…" She swallowed. "When it's right, you know."

When it's right, you know…

"I'm sorry, Jean. We were only teasing," Betty said softly, reaching over to pat her arm. "I know you loved him very much."

Meredith nodded and turned her attention back to the cards. "All right, time for the river, ladies."

The last card was turned over—nine of hearts. Angie officially had nothing…less than nothing. But she didn't want to fold now, not even at the end. She waited for Betty to place the blind, and then she called. So did Meredith, who crowed in victory.

"Full house!" She slapped her cards down, faceup.

Betty groaned. "Dammit, I thought I had you with two pairs."

Angie flipped her cards over and Jean chuckled, patting her on the back. "Dear, you were never going to win with that hand. You should have folded from the start."

Sighing, Angie looked at her cards. Her two

of spades and seven of clubs. Nothing cards. Jean was right—she'd never stood a chance. But it was worth trying, right? Wasn't it always worth trying?

"Next time," Jean said with a smile. "You'll learn."

CHAPTER SIX

Jace hunched over his desk, staring at his latest work-in-progress. The four-panel strip featured his hero, Hermit—a figure with a rounded head and stern expression—clutching his head in disbelief as his thoughts spiraled out of control. At this stage it was all in pencil, and Jace's desk was littered with versions that didn't quite convey what he wanted.

In fact, he had a whole page with slightly different versions of Hermit clutching his head. This was an important moment in the *Hermit vs. World* story, the introduction of a new "big bad" and another challenge for his misanthropic hero to tackle. Jace's comic had started years ago as nothing more than a doodle in the back of his high school chemistry notebook. It was the only way he'd been able to make it through the class, since his teacher, Mr. Potts, had the kind of voice that could put a professional insomniac to sleep. And so, *Hermit vs. World* had been born. The character had started out as a high school misfit, like Jace, and had grown up alongside him.

When Jace had started publishing the comics online, he'd found a cult following who eagerly awaited the weekly installments. Between places like Reddit, Boredpanda, and Instagram, he'd gained quite the audience. Eventually two Australian newspapers had picked up the strip and now, the *Washington Post* Writers Group was considering syndicating *Hermit vs. World*. This storyline had to be *perfect* if he was going to cement this deal—a deal that could lead to bigger and better things, like possibly a National Cartoonist Society award. Or, what if his comic became the next *Peanuts* or *Calvin and Hobbes*?

More importantly, maybe he could help young boys and girls know that it was okay not to be extroverted and loud. That it was okay to prefer books over people, like he did. That being quiet and spending time on art instead of going to parties wasn't weird—it was simply another way to be.

Jace sat back and stared at his storyboard, drumming his fingers against the edge of his desk. Something wasn't quite right. He knew where the story needed to go—Hermit had found out the mayor of the town, a stuffy older guy with a ridiculous mustache, had decided to build a bridge from their little island to the mainland. This posed serious problems for Hermit's desire to keep his hometown as quiet and peaceful as possible. And, more importantly, protect the cabin he'd built for himself so he could live in solitude.

"Yip. Yip, yip, yip!"

Speaking of disturbed solitude…

Jace pushed back on his desk chair and headed into the living room. Truffle was perched dangerously—his front paws balanced against the windowsill overlooking the front yard and his back paws braced against one of the sofa chairs. How he'd gotten into that position, Jace had no idea. Because his tiny Chihuahua body was stretched out in a way that would make it tough for him to move without plunging down into the gap between the chair and the window.

Suddenly realizing he was stuck, Truffle swung his buggy eyes in Jace's direction as if to say, *Uh-oh. I've made a terrible, terrible mistake.*

"Yeah, yeah. I'll save you, little buddy."

He wasn't sure which dog got themselves into more trouble—Truffle and his propensity for climbing on furniture and getting stuck or Tilly, who couldn't seem to control her wagging tail and kept knocking things off the coffee table. Needless to say, all drinks were now to be kept above Tilly height.

Jace scooped up the Chihuahua. With peace restored, he caught a glimpse of what Truffle had been barking at. Angie stood out front of the mailbox, one hand resting on her bike and the other toying with her hair. Jace's younger brother, Trent, was talking to her.

He had that wide-smile, hands-shoved-into-his-pockets kind of flirting that had been known to lift any skirt in a hundred kilometer radius. Trent had always been the "lady killer" of the Walters family—a natural-born charmer who could talk his way into, or out of, anything.

For some reason, watching him turn that charm on Angie made Jace feel...well, he wasn't sure exactly what. But it was...uncomfortable. Given the knowledge that Angie would soon be leaving swirling around in his brain and wreaking havoc on his ability to concentrate on work, maybe it was time for a break.

"What do you think? Should we go and say hi?" He looked down at Truffle. "I think we should."

Jace strode out to the front yard in time to hear Angie's tinkling laughter. The sound was like pure happiness, like catching that first perfect wave in the morning when the sun was still the color of butter and the ocean was his alone to conquer. Her cheeks were pink, her hair tied back in a bouncy ponytail that swished this way and that as she shook her head. She was utterly captivating, and she *looked* utterly captivated…by Trent.

"Hey, bro." Trent raised a hand in greeting. "I was hoping you'd be home."

Trent must have come straight from the construction site, as he was still in his work gear — a T-shirt, shorts, and dusty steel-capped boots. His car, a Holden Ute, sat in the street, also streaked with dirt. When they were young, Trent and Jace had often been mistaken for twins instead of brothers despite the two-year age gap between them. That lasted only until Jace got his growth spurt at sixteen, when he'd towered over everyone. All of his brothers, included.

"I didn't hear you knock," Jace replied.

"That's because I got distracted." Trent turned to Angie and winked. "I was hearing all about some grand plans to revive the activities at the retirement home."

Jace raised a brow.

"Angie's on a charge to make Patterson's Bluff the place to be." Trent grinned.

"But what about after—" Jace stopped short when he caught Angie shooting him a look and shaking her head behind Trent's back. That was definitely a "stop talking" face. So she was keeping her departure a secret? Interesting. "After...the town hall."

"I'll soldier on," Angie replied, looking relieved that he hadn't blown her cover. "Glen Powell isn't going to knock me down."

"Ugh, that power-hungry moron." Trent made a face. "I wish he'd stayed in Mornington. And, for the record, I think your ideas sound great."

Angie beamed. "Thanks."

"If you're free tonight, you should come to the beach. We've got a twilight party planned." He leaned in and nudged her with his elbow. "You can be on my team for cricket."

The twilight parties were a summertime staple in Patterson's Bluff—evening beach get-togethers that consisted of volleyball and beach cricket, huge picnic blankets, and food. People often smuggled in beer, even though it was technically against the open container laws. But the local cops turned a blind eye, so long as things didn't get too rowdy and everyone cleaned up afterward.

It was that kind of town.

"Sure, that sounds great." She turned and looked at Jace. "Do you want to head down together? We could bring the dogs."

"Jace?" Trent raised a brow. "Have you met this guy? I'm pretty sure the last time he went to a party, people were still playing music on cassette tapes."

It was like Trent knew exactly what to say in order to fire up Jace's competitive streak without meaning to. More than likely, his brother was giving him an out, in case he didn't want to go. But maybe this time he did. Sure, he didn't *often* go to parties. And yeah, maybe he wasn't the most social person on planet Earth. But that didn't mean he wouldn't go if he happened to feel like it. And right now, looking into Angie's pretty brown eyes, he damn well felt like going to a party.

"Let's bring the dogs," he said, looking down at Truffle, who seemed as happy as a pig in mud with his little pink tongue lolling out of his mouth. "You sure you're okay with them?"

"I'll take the little one," she said with a cheeky smile.

"You must have some kind of voodoo, Angie." Trent shook his head. "I've been afraid for years Jace would eventually figure out how to live without needing *any* outside contact with the world."

Ah, little brothers. The people who had the most power in the world to push your buttons. Jace loved him, but sometimes he wanted to kill him. Right now was one of those times.

"Well, anyway, I need to get out of these work clothes." Angie gave them both a wave and started to wheel her bike down the side of the house. "I'll come by later, Jace."

"See you then." He gave a nod and watched Angie disappear, the sound of her footsteps on the gravel path quietly crunching away.

"Take a hint, bro." Trent rolled his eyes and

punched Jace on the arm. "I was inviting Angie to the party for a reason, and it wasn't to have you hanging around."

"You're into her?" Even saying it aloud made Jace want to throw something. Not that he was surprised—Angie was cute. And funny. And yeah, sure, she seemed to use more words in a day than he would in a decade, but *damn* did she look good in those little denim shorts. He was tempted to spill the beans about her need to leave the country to put his brother off, but that would be a dick move.

"Yeah, I'm into her. She's hot *and* she's sweet as hell. Mum likes her, too."

Jace blinked. "Since when do you give a shit what Mum thinks?"

"I don't know." Trent shrugged and looked very sheepish all of a sudden. "Might not be such a bad thing to date someone the family will like."

Trent's last girlfriend had *not* fallen into that category. Although Jace's brother was the kind of guy who seemed immune to worrying too much about his relationships—which had less staying power than the latest viral cat video. Along with his famous charm, Trent had the attention span of a goldfish, hence why their eldest brother, Adam, called him the One-Month Wonder.

And Angie has two months…

Jace shook the unsettling thought out of his head. Those two would be a catastrophe together—flighty Trent and overly optimistic Angie? Total disaster waiting to happen. It was his duty to protect them both.

"The dogs need some outdoor time, and it's probably good that Angie doesn't walk all the way there on her own," Jace said. *All the way there* being barely seven hundred meters in possibly the safest small town in Australia. But one couldn't be too cautious.

His brother raised a brow. "Seriously?"

"What?"

"You're so full of shit. You like her."

"Of course I do. She's nice."

Trent shook his head. "No, man. You *like* her."

"I don't," Jace insisted. "Not like that."

He was…protective of her. That's all. She was on her own in a foreign town. Totally reasonable.

Plus, according to his ex, he was no good in a relationship. She'd wanted a dreamer and a romantic, and Jace was neither of those things.

"Then you don't mind if I ask her out?" Trent folded his arms over his chest. Why did he wear his T-shirts so damn tight? It looked like he was a grown man trying to shop in the kids' section.

"It's your call. I think she's really sweet, and I'd hate to see you chew her up and spit her out like you've done with every other woman you've dated."

For a moment, Trent didn't say anything. Yeah, okay. Maybe this was another one of those instances where he was being too blunt.

"Tell me how you really feel." Trent shook his head, but then his expression changed like the wind had blown his worries out to the ocean. "Anyway, I didn't come here to shoot the shit. I need a hand. My laptop's playing up."

Sighing, Jace let his brother lead him over to his Ute, where the computer was sitting on the front seat. He would have to get his head in the game. He couldn't let Angie fall under his brother's spell, not when she was going through so much stuff in her own life. And it wasn't like he was being a horrible person by cockblocking his brother. He was simply helping Angie avoid the pain of inevitably getting dumped by Trent when some shiny new thing caught his attention. Really, he was being a Good Samaritan.

Yeah, buddy. Keep telling yourself that.

• • •

Angie stood in front of the mirror in her bathroom. For some reason, she was feeling a little anxious about the twilight party. There wasn't any rhyme or reason to it—she'd been to several of these parties earlier in the summer. They'd even had a huge one on New Year's with a fireworks show.

But both of those times she'd gone for fun, not because someone had invited her. Was Trent asking her on a date? Angie had panicked, and that's why she'd immediately turned around and invited Jace. But why should she be worried if it *was* a date?

It's not like Jace was interested in her romantically, that much was clear.

After changing outfits more times than she would *ever* admit, Angie had settled on a black floaty dress with a tie around the waist. It was the perfect cover-up to the bikini she had on underneath in case the water was still warm. She'd left her hair down after washing it, and the natural wave had come out. The strong Australian sun had given her a decent tan, and all the freckles had come out along her shoulders and arms and cheeks.

She looked happy.

For the first time in years, the reflection staring back at her was satisfied and calm and healthy. Physically *and* mentally. But soon that wouldn't be the case. Last night, she'd barely slept, tossing and turning into the wee hours of the night, counting sheep like it would make a difference. It didn't. Because it was like being back home all over again, reliving the nightmares of her childhood. Doing everything she could think of to fight off a panic attack.

"You're past all that," she said to her reflection as she tucked her hair behind her ears. "You've battled those demons already. No matter what happens, you *will* survive."

But what if she regressed the second she got back to America? Australia had been so good to her—partially because of the sheer distance and partially because of the connection she felt to this beautiful part of the country. To this town. Every cell in her body was screaming at her to stay. To find a way to make it work.

To make it her home.

But how?

I knew on that first night that Winston was my forever. We were married within a month.

Jean's words rang in her ears. When she'd asked Jace if he'd ever thought about getting a wife, he'd looked at her like she was crazy. But was it? Really? Jean had known right away that Winston was the man for her, and they'd been married for more than fifty years when he passed away. What if this scenario was the push she'd needed to find the right person? What if this was fate shoving her in the right direction? Forcing her to find all the things she'd truly wanted in life—love, family, home.

The solution to her problems could very well be here in Patterson's Bluff. Right under her nose.

She shook her head. It was a silly idea—who would she marry anyway? She didn't even have a boyfriend. And who fell in love and got married that quickly *these* days? Nobody. Okay, maybe drunk people in Vegas...but they weren't exactly a shining example of how to start a quality relationship. And the last thing she wanted to do was defraud the Australian government.

But no matter how much she tried to rationalize away the thought, her brain kept whispering, *What-if?*

What if she fell in love? Legitimately. What if she found the right guy and they simply expedited the relationship process? The possibility of getting two dreams for the price of one swirled in her mind. A family to love *and* the chance to stay. Forever.

But the first image that sprang to mind jolted her. Not because she was wearing a white wedding gown and everyone from the town was surrounding her. But because the groom was Jace. Now where did that thought come from?

She shook her head. They'd be terrible together. Like oil and water. Fire and ice. Like… brussels sprouts and peanut butter. She couldn't stop saying or doing the wrong thing around him.

As for Trent… She'd never even thought about him in that way. Technically, he was handsome—he was tall, though not as tall as Jace. Golden hair, naughty smile, chiseled jaw. But he did nothing for her. There was no zing. No sizzle.

But there *were* other men in this idyllic town to consider.

Some guys were clearly a pass—like Paul *Gross*terly and that guy Rick whom she'd dubbed Creepy McCreeperson for the way he leered at the waitresses at the local pub. Then there was another category—the potentials. *This* was where she needed to concentrate her focus. Because she had less than two months to go before D-Day. Devastation Day, as it was now going to be called. Less than two months to potentially fall in love and convince that guy to put a ring on it.

"Just Beyoncé the *shit* out of this," she said to her reflection.

Her false confidence was exactly that—fake, and a coping mechanism. But stranger things had happened in the world. One of her foster moms—a pink-cheeked Avon saleslady named Beth—had once said to her, *Good things happen to people who are open to possibility.*

So that's what she would be. Open to the possibility of finding love and a solution to her problems all wrapped in one package. Open to letting the unpredictability of the world guide her to the right outcome.

Feeling optimistic and renewed, Angie headed out to the front of her house and slipped her feet into a pair of sandals. Then she grabbed a denim jacket, in case it got chilly later, and her bag.

Jace was already waiting for her, holding a canvas tote that probably had some snacks and drinks. The two dogs were on their respective leashes. He was staring off into the distance, looking like some handsome doggy wrangler. Worn blue jeans hugged his strong legs, and he wore a pair of white Converse high-tops and a T-shirt that had a Stark Industries logo on it. She almost hadn't believed he was a surfer the first time they'd met—because he didn't seem the type at all.

But that was Jace in a nutshell…he was pleasantly unexpected.

"Ready to go?" she asked as she came up beside him.

Tilly turned and appraised Angie with a cool, uninterested stare. Apparently the dog had a short memory about the whole nonconsensual cuddling on the couch thing. Truffle, however, was pleased to see her and immediately jumped up to say hello. He was wearing a little jacket that also served as a harness. It was quilted and floral. Like, Grandma's curtains floral.

"Yep. Want to go halves?" He held out both the leashes, and she immediate took Truffle's. "Chicken."

"Sticks and stones, buddy. I thought you might be happy to be rid of this floral monstrosity anyway." Truffle trotted along happily, totally oblivious to the fact that he looked like a craft-store reject. "Doesn't exactly seem like it's your style."

"Is it *anyone's* style?" He wrinkled his nose in a way that was far too adorable to be sexy, and yet…

"Eugenie's, clearly. I don't understand why people always dress up little dogs in those ridiculous outfits. I lived in this place once where we had three Shih Tzus with glittery bows in their hair. One time, one of the dogs decided to eat the bows. I'm pretty sure it was a form of protest."

"What happened?"

"The dog shat glitter for twenty-four hours, but he was fine otherwise."

Jace snorted. "What did your mum think about you glitter bombing the dogs?"

Crap. She'd almost forgotten for a minute that Jace didn't know she was a foster kid. When Angie had come to Patterson's Bluff, six months into her Australian travels, she'd wanted to keep her backstory private. Vague. She came from a broken home, they moved around a lot, etc. People assumed she moved with her family, and when they asked more questions, well, the weather was an interesting topic.

"Oh, do you know what's worse than a glitter-shitting dog? The time a kid I knew had an allergic reaction to a bird and his whole face swelled up to twice its normal size." Distraction, that was her tactic. "Are you allergic to anything? Seems like everyone has some kind of allergy these days. Peanuts, animals, lactose. I even met a guy once who was allergic to orange foods. Couldn't have carrots, sweet potato, or pumpkin. Might have been something to do with the enzymes? Or maybe it was a vitamin thing."

Angie stopped suddenly; her motormouth was in *fine* form today. She peered up at Jace, who was staring straight ahead. Was that the beginnings of an amused smile on his lips? It was so hard to read him sometimes.

"Sorry, what was the question again?" he asked. Okay, yeah. He was *definitely* amused.

"Are you allergic to anything?"

"You mean other than my family?" he deadpanned. "Nah, I'm pretty much invincible. Basically a superhero."

He turned his head and held her gaze for a beat, and she almost tripped over her own feet. Jace seemed to live in his own world. Maybe it was an artist thing. But when he did grace her with a sudden hard look, well, there was no other way to put it… Butterflies. He set a kaleidoscope of butterflies loose in her belly.

As quickly as it happened, he steadied her, then looked away.

They continued to walk in companionable silence along the road they lived on—which was leafy, with houses set back onto the blocks so they felt private and peaceful. It was the perfect place to live, with its rugged coastline views and incredible sunsets over the water. It had greenery everywhere and wildlife and heart. It had a unique smell of eucalyptus and briny air, and it felt so very much like home.

"It's so beautiful here." Angie trailed her hand along a big wattle tree as they passed, her fingers catching on the small yellow blossoms. "I wish I could stay forever."

"Are you keeping the visa thing quiet?"

She bit down on her lip and sighed. "For the moment. Thanks for not spilling the beans to Trent earlier."

"It's okay. But if you want me to keep a secret, first I have to *know* it's a secret."

"Yeah, you're right. I was going to tell him..." They turned a corner onto the main road that led to the beach where the twilight party was taking place. "And I was going to tell the people at the retirement home, too. But I chickened out. I need a little more time."

The sun was still out, since it stayed light until well past nine p.m. in the height of summer. And it was gloriously warm, with a hint of cool ocean breeze. In fact, it was so perfect, it was almost like the universe was calling to her: *Stay here. Stay forever.*

But she could only do that if she fell in love.

CHAPTER SEVEN

By the time they made it down to the beach, the party was in full swing. Music floated on the breeze from a pair of portable speakers, drawing people to the action. Picnic blankets and brightly colored beach towels were spread around, containing food and drinks and clusters of friends deep in conversation. A game of beach cricket was in progress along the firmly packed sand at the water's edge.

Angie paused to kick off her shoes before digging her toes into the sand. It was still warm, like it had trapped the day's worth of sunshine beneath it, and the sensation immediately relaxed her muscles. The beach was magic here, she was sure of it.

The waves rolled in, lazy and slow, and the cracking sound of a bat hitting a tennis ball was followed by a chorus of both cheers and groans. Trent sprinted up the beach toward the "stumps" — which was actually a cooler, or an "Esky," as they called it here. His strong legs pumped as he ran, his feet digging into the sand and kicking up particles with each stride. His hair flopped as he turned, and when he bolted back, his bat stretched out in time to beat the ball to raucous cheers from his teammates and he crowed with victory. Then he raked his hand through his hair and took a bow.

"What's that?" Jace held a hand to his ear. "The sound of women's undies dropping all over the country."

Angie snorted. Tilly plodded along with them, while Truffle strained forward, his leash pulled to maximum tautness. The little guy was sniffing everything in the vicinity, distracted by each new person that cooed in his direction.

"You're very different, you and Trent." It wasn't the first time Angie had observed it. "You don't like being in the spotlight, do you?"

"Nope. I hate it."

They found a spare patch of sandy ground to spread out their blanket. In addition to some snacks, Jace—ever the Boy Scout—had also come prepared with mosquito repellent, dog treats, bottled water, and two hoodies. Angie's lips lifted in a smile. He'd worried about her getting cold.

"Which suits Trent fine," he added. "He likes to hog the attention."

Was it her imagination or was there an undercurrent of tension there?

"Did you and Trent have a fight or something?" she asked as she laid down her things and found a comfy spot to sit. Truffle immediately jumped into her lap.

"No." He unclipped Tilly's leash, and Angie immediately tensed up. But the older dog was content to head down to the water alone and get her paws wet. "Fighting with Trent is pointless because he never sees how he might be wrong."

Yeah, there was *definitely* some tension. As much as Jace's relatives frustrated him, he was totally a family guy. But since he was *also* a private person, she decided not to push it.

"Hey, you two!" Chloe Lee waved and headed over. Her long hair hung in a braid over one shoulder, and she wore a pretty floral dress that swirled mid-thigh. "Mr. Jace Walters, you have officially been summoned. Beach cricket and beers await."

Jace wrinkled his nose. "I've been summoned?"

"By Trent. The team is down one, and your skills are required. Go!" She gave him a gentle shove. "Your country needs you!"

Rolling his eyes, Jace shot Angie a resigned look and then headed off toward the commotion farther down the beach. Angie tried not to stare at him as he walked away—she'd never really thought board shorts were an appealing piece of clothing, but you could literally put a potato sack on that ass and it would look good.

"Mind if I join?" Chloe plopped down without even waiting for Angie to respond. Those kinds of questions were rhetorical in this place, because making a spot for your neighbor was part of the DNA in Patterson's Bluff.

"Is that some serious vibes between you two or am I misreading things?" She swung her head over to where Jace was jogging toward the game.

"You're totally misreading things." Angie tried to brush off the flutter in her stomach. "Unless you're picking up on some very unreciprocated vibes."

"You think?"

"I *know*." He couldn't have made it clearer the

day of the storm—he wasn't into relationships, and he wasn't into *her*.

Chloe's nose wrinkled. "I don't know about that, Angie. He looked pretty interested to me. I could see him watching you while you spoke before, and he was the definition of riveted."

"You're seeing something that isn't there, trust me." He hadn't even made butterfly-inducing eye contact, so how could he have been "riveted"?

Jace laughed as the cricket team cheered at his arrival. The sound carried across the beach as he whipped his T-shirt over his head. The sight was a shot straight to Angie's gut, sizzling and simmering and making her feel all warm and gooey inside. How could a guy who claimed to want a lonesome, solitary life look totally perfect doing the opposite?

"You asked him?"

"In a roundabout kinda way... Well, I hinted at it," Angie said. "Kind of."

"You know guys are bloody useless when it comes to hints, right?" Chloe rolled her eyes dramatically. "They do *not* get subtlety."

Angie chuckled. "Well, Jace isn't like any other guy I've ever met, that's for sure."

He cared. He was honest...brutally so, at points. And sure, he probably wasn't everyone's cuppa—as the Aussies liked to say—but he was decent. Good, down to the marrow of his bones. A man nothing like the ones she'd known growing up. His only downside was that he wasn't interested in her. Not like that anyway.

Plus, he most definitely was not interested in

marriage and forever—and Angie didn't have time to waste on a fling. She was fighting for her dream now.

"Anyway, it's fine. I've got other things keeping me busy," Angie said with a forced smile. She picked up one of the strawberries Jace had packed in a Tupperware container and took a bite.

"Yeah, I heard they knocked back your proposal for the nursing home." Chloe wrinkled her nose. "That sucks. I was going to suggest we team up. Figured the residents might want a yoga class to stretch out after all that pole dancing."

Chloe was one of the youngest business owners in Patterson's Bluff. Her yoga and meditation studio, Unwind, had become something of a hot spot on the main strip. Known for her firm but kind approach to health and well-being, Chloe had people coming in from all over the peninsula to take her classes.

"That would have been great." Angie sighed. "I know I feel like a million bucks after one of your yoga flow classes, so I'm sure the residents would have really benefitted from it."

Chloe leaned back on her forearms and tipped her head up to the sky. Even lounging, she was the picture of effortless chic. She had on a fine silver anklet with an anchor charm dangling off it, matching the silver polish on her toes that would have looked cheesy as hell on anyone else. But Chloe could pull off the things that other mere mortals couldn't.

"You know," she said, "I've been trying to think about how I could do something more for the community here, but I've been struggling to find something to fit in with my schedule, since I'm so busy with the business. But maybe I could donate a class once a month to the retirement home? I'll come in and do it for free, and that way you don't need Glen bloody Powell to sign off on it because there's no money involved."

"You would do that?" Angie pressed a hand to her chest. "That's so generous."

"Of course. Business is booming, but I haven't forgotten what helped me get started. People here came to my studio when I was still running it out of my mum's garage. It's only right to give something back."

"You're amazing," Angie said. "Seriously, thank you."

"Anytime. Just tell me what you need me to do."

Their conversation was interrupted by a loud chorus of cheers, and Angie found herself laughing as she watched Tilly race off down the beach with the tennis ball. Jace, Trent, and three other guys were all shouting after her.

She might be old, but she could still run like the wind when she wanted to.

"Boys," Chloe said with a grin. "Always making a commotion."

"You went to school with the Walters, right?"

"Sure did. Pretty much everyone here went to Patterson's Bluff High." Chloe looked at Angie closely. "They're a nice family. Good people. Why do you ask?"

Angie quickly shook her head. "No reason."

She knew the denial was too swift the moment Chloe's lips quirked up into an amused smile. "Bullshit."

"Just curious, I guess. Jace is... He doesn't talk too much about his family, but they've always struck me as being close. Although I get the impression he and Trent butt heads a bit."

"I don't know if I would say that. But they're probably the most different of the bunch." Chloe cocked her head. "Trent is as extroverted as Jace is introverted."

"Know anyone in the middle of those two things?" she asked with a pointed look.

"Are you asking me to set you up with someone?" She clapped her hands together. "You have no idea how happy this makes me. If I didn't have a yoga studio, I would *totally* be a matchmaker. I'm very good at figuring out what people like."

"So we're clear, I'm not looking for a one-night-stand kinda thing. Nothing against it, but I feel like I'm ready to...I don't know, set down roots." Saying the words filled her heart with warm, fuzzy hope. Roots. She'd never had them before. Never had a place that she could see herself growing old in, until now. "God, I haven't had a boyfriend in years."

The trial had shattered her privacy, attracting flocks of users and weirdos to her. She'd actually gone on a date with one guy who told her he'd been attracted to her because he liked to "fix" things, as if she was some shoddy fence work that needed redoing.

"I'm very out of practice."

"Well, you're a gorgeous person inside and out, and I won't set you up with someone who's going to treat you badly. So you have *nothing* to worry about." Chloe tapped a finger to her chin, her gaze sweeping over the beach.

An excited fizzy feeling bubbled up in Angie's stomach. Logically, she knew she was grasping at straws. Trying to fall in love in less than two months was ridiculous. Despite Jean's story, Angie knew that kind of fast and true love was the exception. Not the rule.

But she couldn't stop asking herself, what if she was one of the special few?

And the fact was, Angie knew how to fit in. It was her superpower, actually. Being carted around to home after home as a kid had helped her become a chameleon of sorts. In one house, she was quiet and thoughtful, and in another she was energetic and chatty. She knew how to make people like her. It wasn't a skill for her…it was a survival mechanism.

And all of that meant she could expedite the process of building a bond with someone.

"Well, the Walters boys *are* an option. Not Adam, because he's married. But Trent is hot and super fun. Jace was born serious, as you know. I can't remember the last time he went on a date, though. And Nick is super ambitious and successful." Chloe shook her head, a cute frustrated expression on her face. "The hotness genes run strong in that family."

"And beyond the Walters family?"

"Theo Hasikos. Not sure if you've met him before, but he's got some kind of tech start-up business. Nice guy. Cute, too. Oh, or maybe Elijah McCormack?"

"I know of Elijah." Angie bobbed her head. He ran one of the hottest restaurants in Patterson's Bluff. Range was a farm-to-table place that used only local ingredients, and he was a big advocate for supporting Australian farmers. He also totally had a lumbersexual vibe going on.

"Super hot, especially if you're into beards and broody eyes. He's a really decent guy...comes into the studio occasionally, too. In fact, if I'm not mistaken, he's usually comes to our Monday morning class." Chloe sat up, her eyes wide and mischievous. "You should join us."

"What? And chat him up while I'm all sweaty and gross? No thanks." She rolled her eyes.

"While you're *glowing*. Do it! Have a chat, ask if he wants to grab a coffee, and go from there. See if there's any chemistry."

Angie laughed, shaking her head. Could this crazy plan possibly work? Or was she unduly getting her hopes up?

You spent your whole life having your hopes dashed, and you're still putting yourself out there. It's a testament to your resilience.

Angie certainly hoped so. Because this conversation with Chloe—who was excitable and kind and giving—further proved that *this* was the kind of community she wanted to be part of. Where people put up their hands to help and volunteered their time.

Just as Angie was feeling totally relaxed and happy about her decision, she was suddenly thrust from her rose-colored-glasses mood when her dress became wet. "Truffle! Goddamn it, the dog freaking peed on me."

• • •

After a few games of beach cricket, Jace had sand everywhere—in his shorts, in his hair, and under his fingernails—from a dive that was athletically impressive, if he did say so himself. Some of his tensions from earlier in the day had faded—which tended to happen when engaged in an activity that allowed him to focus. Sports had always had that effect on him, though he generally preferred more solitary pursuits like surfing or running along the beach.

"So how's the dog-sitting going?" Nick cracked the tab on a can of beer and handed it over before grabbing one for Trent and then himself. "The little mutts crapped all over your house yet?"

"Little? Have you seen the size of the German shepherd?" Trent laughed. "I was going to ask if you wanted to rent her out for kiddie rides at the summer market. Much easier than getting a pony in."

"One, she's old and grumpy. Two, I'm pretty sure Eugenie didn't ask me to dog-sit so I could figure out how to turn a profit from it." Jace sipped his beer and turned to watch Angie jogging toward the water, holding the skirt portion of her dress out in front of her.

What on earth is she doing?

Nick tilted his head. "Why *did* she ask you? No offence, bro, but you're probably the last person I'd expect to take care of another living thing."

"Gee, thanks."

"Remember that time he tried to flush the goldfish before it was actually dead and it came back to life in the toilet bowl?" Trent slapped a hand down on his leg. "Oh man, Olivia was *furious*. She called you Attempted Fish Murderer for weeks."

"I was twelve! How was I supposed to know it wasn't properly dead?" Jace rolled his eyes.

"To be fair," Nick said, "I remember Adam finding a dead possum on the side of the road and trying to bring it back home so Dad could barbecue it because he overheard them talking about bills."

"Oh God, I'd forgotten about that." Trent made a gagging face. "Mum made him scrub his hands for an hour before she'd let him touch anything."

The memory made Jace smile. That was Adam in a nutshell, big brother always trying to do the right thing…even if it led him to making some bad choices. Despite the ribbing, he appreciated his family. Responsible Adam, ambitious Nick, charming Trent, and dreamer Olivia. Which made him what? Steady Jace. Yeah, that sounded about right. They'd made for a chaotic house growing up, and they certainty contributed to Jace's desire for a peaceful, fuss-free life…but they *were* thick as thieves. And he wouldn't have it any other way.

"So…I bumped into Julia the other day," Nick

said all of a sudden.

And like that, Jace's easy, relaxed feeling evaporated. His brother might as well have grabbed him by the throat. He hadn't heard that name in years. Hadn't wanted to *ever* hear it again.

Trent blinked. "*Julia* Julia?"

Nick nodded.

"What the hell is she doing back in town?" Trent raised a brow. "I'm surprised she has the guts to show her face around here after what she did."

It was amazing how one little statement could shatter everything about a man's world. All the security he had walking down the street without worrying about bumping into his ex...gone. The comfortable feeling that people had forgotten about the most embarrassing moment of his entire life...also gone.

"She moved into one of the townhouses in that small development at the edge of town. You know those cookie-cutter, construction-by-numbers jobs." Nick turned up his nose. "Blander than a cereal box, they are."

Trust Nick to be more upset by Julia's choice of housing than her return to the town where she'd broken his brother's heart.

"Anyway, I thought you should know." Nick took a pull on his beer. "Better that you hear it from one of us than stumble across her at the shops."

"What did she say?" Trent asked. Of all Jace's siblings, Trent had been most affronted by Julia's abrupt and public departure, having thought of her as a sister, since they'd all grown up together.

If only he knew that he'd inadvertently contributed to their breakup.

Jace didn't want to remember that time. He'd never told his siblings why his ex had left him, and he'd hoped to take that secret to the grave.

"Not much. She seemed quieter than I remember. But maybe she was uncomfortable." Nick shrugged. "Who knows? I heard her dad wasn't doing so well, so maybe that has something to do with it."

So far, neither of his brothers had acknowledged that Jace hadn't said a word. Probably because they were used to it—he always went quiet when he was processing news. But right now, his mind was spinning like a tire losing traction in mud. It was as if the universe was conspiring to take everything he enjoyed about his life—routine, stability, patterns—and crush it all to smithereens.

First the bloody dogs and then Angie's news and now this.

"You all right, mate?" Nick's gaze narrowed. "I can hear your cogs turning from here."

"I'm fine." Jace's standard response.

"*Fine* fine? Or fine, you're going to build a blockade in front of your house and never leave it again?"

Probably closer to the latter.

"Jace?" Trent waved a hand in front of his face.

He blinked, shaking his head to dislodge the memories he'd spent the last five years trying to scrub from his brain. "I said I'm *fine*."

"All right. No need to get your jocks in a twist." Trent brought the beer can up to his lips and tipped his head back. "We're looking out for you."

The twilight party continued on the beach, music dancing on the night air and the waves rolling in dark and foamy under a dusky star-speckled sky. All that remained of the day was a thin, rapidly disappearing band of fiery orange on the horizon.

It would only be so long before he went home and tried to sleep while ugly memories of his ex-fiancée haunted him. Jace knocked back his beer in the hopes the alcohol might loosen the tight, uncomfortable feeling taking over his muscles.

For some reason, the thing that worried him most was Angie finding out about what had happened. The whole thing had been a nightmare—from finding out that she secretly harbored feelings for his brother to the fact that she left him waiting while everyone he cared about looked on with horror.

He didn't want her to pity him. He didn't want *anyone* to pity him.

• • •

By the end of the twilight party, Angie was feeling optimistic about her plans. *Surely* after all she'd been through, the universe had saved up a big bundle of karma for this exact moment. Was she grasping at straws? Absolutely. Shooting for the moon? Yup! Hanging all her hopes on a plan so thin it would snap in a faint breeze?

One hundred percent yes.

But sometimes the barest hint of hope was all a person had. And if she didn't at least *try* to find a solution, then did she really deserve to stay?

What if you are *unlovable?*

She mentally waved away the dark thought and watched as the party began to wind down. All the sports had come to an end when it got too dark to play, and now people were curled up on blankets, talking and relaxing. One couple was making out in the ocean. How could you *not* fall in love in a place like this?

The sky was a rich inky shade, and a delicate blanket of stars glittered overhead. Truffle was curled up in Angie's lap, not seeming to understand that she wanted some distance after the peeing incident. She stroked his fur, enjoying the feel of his velvety ears beneath her fingertips. Okay, so not all dogs were scary.

"Ready to head back?" Jace had come over with Tilly, and he had a finger hooked into her collar. She wasn't sure why, but she felt like he'd held on to the dog like that to make Angie feel safe.

"Yep. It's pumpkin time." She handed him the leash, and he crouched down to clip it onto Tilly's collar.

At this distance, the shifting light of the dark, broken only by the stars and flickering lanterns that some of the other guests had brought, Jace looked even more handsome. Even more starkly masculine. The shadows made his jaw sharper and his nose prouder. The flickering light caught the faintest undertone of red in his sandy hair. Or maybe it was an illusion.

Sometimes she couldn't tell the difference.

They padded quietly up the beach, the sand squishing between her bare toes and her dress flapping against her legs in the breeze. She'd put the hoodie on that he'd thoughtfully packed for her, and it smelled like him—clean, comforting. A hint of something that made her insides flip.

"So what did you and Chloe talk about?" he asked. "Looked like you were very deep in conversation."

She swallowed. Technically she didn't owe him an explanation of her newfound plans, because it was her damn life and she could do with it what she wanted. But he'd kept her secret when she'd asked, and he'd been good to her ever since she arrived. Were they friends? Yeah, she supposed they were. She liked his company and enjoyed spending time with him. She respected him. So why should she feel the need to clam up like she always did?

Maybe he'll think you're an idiot.

"Well," she said, stretching the word out as though it had five syllables instead of one.

The sound of their feet—and paws—hitting the wooden steps that led up to the main road filled the stinging silence. Jace's ability to keep his mouth shut and listen was at a level that Angie had never encountered before.

"I don't want to go home, which you know. Uh…" She desperately wanted him to understand her position. It felt important. Like, *really* important. "There's a reason I don't want to go home, and it's something that's very personal. Something I've kept a secret."

She didn't dare look at him. They were bathed in pools of light from the streetlamps, and it felt like an interrogation spotlight. Any time she told this story—which was so infrequently in the last few years, she could count the instances on one hand—it made her cry. She didn't want him to see that side of her. That weak, vulnerable side. The little girl inside her who had been exploited and neglected so many times, she'd lost count.

So she had to keep staring ahead, keep staring at Truffle's adorable little doggy butt wriggling with each step and at the lines in the sidewalk and everything else that reminded her she was moving forward. That she could get through this.

"I made a decision when I came here that I was going to keep my past a secret. I wanted to feel like a woman going on a normal overseas adventure and not like I was running away when that's *exactly* what I was doing." She rolled her lower lip between her teeth. "I never had a mom. Not like people assumed anyway. I guess I had *lots* of moms, technically. And dads."

"You were in foster care?"

She nodded. "My real mom died from an overdose when I was a baby, and my dad didn't want me. So I was put into the system. I thought it was because there was no more family left."

Although that hadn't turned out to be the case, she'd found out years later.

Jace let out a puff of air that managed to convey everything she was feeling—the hurt, frustration, resentment. It was like he could encapsulate the complexity of her life in one tiny breath. He didn't even need words.

"I bounced around a lot. Bad stuff happened…" Should she tell him the rest? It felt too much for the beautiful night they were having. It felt too much for the life she'd made here, because it was the stuff of nightmares. Not of dreams. "One of the people who was supposed to care for me…uh, didn't care for me properly."

It was like swallowing gravel. She couldn't say it.

"Then I ended up with a lawyer who wanted to use my situation as an example of why reform was needed in foster care. He took Child Protective Services to court, and it was a big deal. The case blew up."

Like, *reporters and microphones and flashing bulbs and invasive questions* level of blowing up.

"People said all kinds of things about me," she added, her throat tight with unshed tears. "It made national news. Everywhere I went, people recognized my name and they knew…they knew what happened to me. Do you have any idea what that's like? To have everything bad that happened to you splashed across newspapers and morning talk shows? To have every secret I ever wanted to keep ripped from my hands and made public? To have the whole world know that my own family didn't want me?" She shook her head. "I guess the only benefit was that I got a big, fat payout that allowed me to leave the country…not that I wouldn't give it all back in a heartbeat if it would erase the court case from people's minds."

A heavy hand slipped against her palm, strong fingers intertwining with hers. Yeah, he didn't need words all right. The gesture was like a warm blanket and a cup of cocoa and a hug and a fireplace and hot apple cider.

"I don't want to go back there," she said again. "And I figured maybe if all these bad things happened to me, some good things might happen if I put myself out there—the universe would balance me out. So I thought, what if I try to meet someone, and maybe we'd fall in love, and I'd be able to stay."

Jace squeezed her hand and took a deep breath. "I don't think that's how it works, Angie."

"You're right: I need someone to marry me. But a marriage needs love, and *that* is something I want. Something good." She blinked, still keeping her eyes laser-focused ahead of her. "Marriage is just a piece of paper, isn't it? You said it yourself. The love is what matters."

"I think that's true."

"So if I find love now, then the piece of paper might come a little quicker, and I might *finally* be able to have a home. A proper home." She sucked in a breath and took a chance looking at him. There was no judgment on his face. No harshness marring the handsome blue eyes and strong jaw and curved lips. "If I let these two months go to waste without even trying…then why did I even come here?"

"So you're not…looking for a fake marriage?" Of course Jace was worried about doing things the right way.

"No. If I was looking for that, then I could have taken Paul Westerly up on his creepy offer." She shuddered. "I want real love. I know, it seems foolishly optimistic. But life has handed me so many lemons. So many bad things. I wondered… if maybe this was my time to have what I want."

Jace frowned, and his heavy brows knitted. "Aren't you worried you might end up getting hurt?"

"Of course."

Angie didn't know much about Jace's dating history. He was locked up pretty tight about his personal affairs, but Angie would have put money on him having had his heart broken in the past. He gave off that vibe—and she could spot someone protecting their heart from a mile away, because she knew what it meant to live life on the defensive.

"But I'll *definitely* get hurt if I don't try," she said. "So I refuse to go to my grave without chasing after what I want."

If anyone could pull this off, she could. She had the drive, she knew how to fit in with people and make friends quickly, and she could sift the bad from the good.

They'd made it to the front of Jace's house, and he hovered by the small gate that protected the path to her little flat out back. "Aren't you worried about hurting the other person if it doesn't work out?"

She blinked at the slightly accusatory tone in his voice. "What do you mean?"

"Did you ever consider how the other person might fare in all this? What pressure you'd be putting on him to decide so quickly that he was in love?" He shook his head. "Some people need lots of time to make decisions, you know? And then what, you'd leave him if he couldn't make a decision in your timeframe?"

"If that happens, I won't have a choice but to leave," she said softly. "And don't worry, I won't be knocking down your door, trying to change your views on marriage. I promise."

Part of her had hoped he might make a joke that maybe she *should* knock down his door...or something to that effect. Maybe hint there was some reciprocation of attraction between them— even if only a sliver.

Jace was staring off into the distance, not letting her in. Not letting her see what was going on in that strange, beautiful brain of his. It hurt. Because she'd spilled her story to him, voluntarily told him more than anyone else here. Anyone else in her whole life, which was admittedly a small bunch.

Somehow, she felt like her words had hurt him, and she didn't know why. He'd already made it clear that he wasn't interested, so it wasn't like she was asking him to make a decision here and now.

"You think you can find someone here, in this town?" he asked. When his gaze swung back to hers, the connection was like being shocked with electricity. It wasn't just butterflies now but great winged beasts churning her up inside.

The way he made her feel when he looked at her like that, like he saw past every careful defense she laid down, past every fake smile she'd practiced in the mirror as a kid and all the times she said "I'm fine" when she was anything but... Hell, he made her feel so seen. So real.

She swallowed, reaching deep for her voice. "I hope I can find someone."

Why can't it be you?

Nodding and muttering something that sounded a whole lot like *I'll never understand women*, he reached for Truffle's leash and walked the dogs into his house. For a full minute, Angie stood there, rooted to the ground and wanting to go to him.

If you do that, then you will definitely *get hurt.*

CHAPTER EIGHT

Angie woke up the following morning full of energy, and the rose-colored glasses were firmly back in place. After an hour of soul-searching when she'd gotten back into her place last night, she'd come to the conclusion that Jace's comments were nothing more than a product of his concern. Lots of people would disagree with her plans. Even Chloe didn't have the full story and might have responded differently if she knew.

So she was going to act like there was nothing weird between her and Jace, and if he didn't like what she was doing, well…that was on him.

If she wanted a pre-Tinder-era kind of love, then maybe that's where she needed to look for inspiration. After a quick trip to the retirement home, she rode her bike back to the flat, the bucket full to the brim with VHS tapes. She'd seen them in one of the cupboards a few weeks back, like some forgotten relic of the nineties. Nobody was using them, since the movie room had both streaming services and a Blu-ray player. The staff members were more than happy to off-load the tapes on Angie so they could reclaim the shelf.

The only problem was…Angie didn't have a VHS player.

Hoisting the pile of tapes in one arm—using her chin to stop them from spilling out of her hands—Angie knocked on Jace's door. The sound immediately caused a ruckus inside, barking and yipping and footsteps and a kettle whistling. A second later, the door swung open, and she almost dropped the whole damn pile.

Jace stood at the door, his hair damp and poking out at all angles. The barest dusting of golden prickles coated his jaw, and a pair of jeans rode low on his hips. So low she could see those incredible V muscles pointing down toward heaven, disappearing into the waistband of his pants like an invitation to sin.

"Hey. Hello. Good morning!" *Smooth, Donovan. Real smooth.*

"Three greetings. Must be a good day." Jace held the door for her, then disappeared into the bedroom. He reappeared a moment later, stretching a white T-shirt over his head as he walked. "Did you go to a garage sale this morning?"

She almost wanted to sigh in relief at his easy question. He must have decided to let go of the strange tension from last night, too.

"No, these came from the retirement home." Angie began stacking the tapes into a neat pile. They were all in their original cases with the brightly colored spines indicating a wealth of romantic information: *Clueless*, *You've Got Mail*, *She's All That*, *Never Been Kissed*, and more.

"And why are they now in your possession?" Jace picked one up, inspecting it like it was a fossil from an archaeological dig. "Also, did they not have a single decent movie?"

"Excuse me, Mr. Grumpypants. Romantic comedies are my personal favorite." She turned

over the cover for *There's Something About Mary*.
"This is a classic."

Jace didn't look convinced. "I'll take your word
for it. I guess this is the point where you ask me if
I have something that will play those things?"

She grinned. "You're so smart."

"Let me see what I can find. You know this
place used to belong to my grandparents, right?
There must be fifty years' worth of useless shit
under the house. I'm sure there will be a VHS
player."

"Not useless. *Retro*." Angie began sorting the
pile by order of interest. "Oh man, *so* much Drew
Barrymore in this pile. And Meg Ryan...and
Alicia Silverstone. Why don't we see these women
in movies anymore?"

"Misogyny in Hollywood?"

"Too right. The nineties was a gold mine."

Jace headed outside, and Angie followed.
There was a small door that led to the crawl
space under the house—which Angie would
not be going under. But Jace, in true Aussie
"bloke" fashion, didn't seem perturbed by the
cobwebs and dust and the very likely outcome of
encountering an eight-legged foe.

A few minutes after he went in, he came out
triumphant with a cardboard box. Black Sharpie
indicated that this box contained videos and a
player. Score!

"I think we've got a winner," Jace said as he
brushed the dust particles from his hair. He had a
grimy smudge on his cheek, and Angie's hand shot
out before she had a chance to think.

Her thumb connected with soft skin over the sharp angle of his cheekbone. The touch wasn't anything to write home about, and yet it made her body tingle as if someone had poured champagne into her veins. For some reason, Jace made her feel like a giddy teenager who'd never been kissed.

"You had a smudge," she said, pulling her hand back and rubbing it against her leg.

"Tends to happen when you go foraging." His smile was crooked and the barest hint of sexy. "Shall we open her up?"

"Yes, let's do it."

They took the box back into the house like two excited treasure hunters. The tape keeping the lid closed was weak and yellowed, and it offered little resistance to the scissors Jace ran over it. When the flaps popped open, they peered eagerly inside.

"Oh, Liv is going to die when she knows I've found these." Jace grinned, pulling out a homemade VHS tape complete with self-designed cover. "Mum made a compilation of all her dance performances."

"My God. That is some serious eye shadow." Angie ran a fingertip over the cover, which contained a picture of Jace's little sister at probably about nine years of age. She was all elbows and skinny legs, with an epic sequined outfit and electric-blue eye shadow that went all the way to her eyebrows. Topping it all off was the adorable gap between her front teeth. "She's too cute."

"There is literally nothing more terrifying

than an army of little girls in sequins." Jace
continued digging through the box, pulling out
other homemade videos labeled with dates and
occasions, as well as a few without boxes or labels.
An old packet of photos was stuffed inside, and
Angie instantly made a grab for it before Jace
could stop her.

The small bundle of photos included some
negative strips. "Aw. You guys are so adorable."

The photos appeared to have been taken
at someone's birthday, and the Walters kids
were all dressed in fashion atrocities of the late
nineties. Oversize basketball jerseys, baggy shorts,
and chunky sneakers. Like a bunch of NSYNC
wannabes.

Jace looked about ten and distinctly like he did
not want to have his photo taken. A younger Trent
and Olivia held melting ice creams and the eldest
two, Adam and Nick, stood tall and proud in the
back.

"You were serious, even as a kid. And Trent
looks like he was the family clown back then,
too." She put the photo to the back of the pile
and kept looking through them. Many were out of
focus or had someone with their eyes closed, but
100 percent of them were charming.

Sadness hit Angie in the gut, out of nowhere.
Looking through these shiny, happy memories
was such a foreign thing to her. She imagined
people with real families and proper childhoods
did this on the regular—flipping through albums
and reminiscing about the good old days.

Angie had a small collection of photos from

her past that she couldn't bring herself to throw out, despite the fact that they never made her smile. But it almost felt like throwing them out would erase what little childhood she'd had. Never mind the fact that all she saw when she looked at those photos was how poorly her fake smile hid the loneliness in her eyes.

"Mr. Serious. That's me." Jace dug out the VHS player from the bottom of the box and frowned. "I have no idea if this will work. It's probably clogged with dust."

"Only one way to find out." Angie held her hands up, but Jace carried the player to his TV unit.

Funny, she'd expected him to hand it over and send her on her way. When she'd first moved in, Jace had been very firm that he kept a tight schedule with his work, and she'd tried to respect that.

"Which one do you want to test?" Jace was on all fours, digging behind his entertainment unit for somewhere to plug in the VHS player. From here, Angie had to stop herself from drooling over the way his jeans stretched tightly across his butt.

Dammit. She had to stop putting herself in a position where she was looking at his backside.

"How about *Never Been Kissed*?" She plucked the tape from the top of the pile. "But I don't want to keep you from your day. If it's working, I can take it back to my place."

"It's fine. I'd scheduled some time off this morning to do my washing and cleaning."

Angie stifled a smile. Who scheduled time to

do their washing? And he could very easily have given her what she asked for and sent her packing. Was it possible he *wanted* to spend time with her?

He opened the video cover and pulled out the tape, slotting it into the VHS player. When it played, the end of the movie was rolling, where Drew Barrymore kissed the leading man to the tune of "Don't Worry Baby" by the Beach Boys.

"Spoiler alert: The girl gets the guy." Angie grinned and settled onto the couch.

"Whatever happened to *be kind, rewind*, huh? Kids these days don't know the torture." He set the video to rewind itself and stretched up from his crouched position. His jeans were worn and soft and had the kind of lines in them that highlighted his muscular thighs. "Hell, you probably didn't have to do that."

"I'm only five years behind you," she reminded him. "And actually, the homes I grew up in were not exactly very technologically advanced."

"So tell me," he said. "What's this one about?"

"Oh, it's a classic. Josie is a twenty-five-year-old reporter who goes undercover as a seventeen-year-old high school student—"

"And nobody notices?" He raised a brow.

"Well, it was the late nineties. Everyone playing a high school kid in movies back then was at *least* mid-twenties," she replied. "And anyway, *21 Jump Street* had already done it a decade before. So it's got precedent."

"Right."

"Anyway," she said, ignoring his disbelieving tone. "Josie was called 'Josie Grossie' in high

school because she was the class nerd, and now she gets a second chance to try to be cool."

"Even though she's moved on and presumably has a successful reporting career and shouldn't be giving a crap what some high schoolers think?"

"Doesn't everyone wish they could prove people from high school wrong? But *then* she falls in love with her teacher and gets to have the high school experience she wished she could have had the first time around. Only, by the end, she understands what's truly important."

"That teachers shouldn't be hitting on their students?" This time Jace's tone was betrayed by a small quirk of his lips. He was pushing her buttons on purpose. "Even the fake ones."

"Are you going to watch the damn movie or not?" Angie asked, folding her arms over her chest.

Jace grinned his adorable, crooked grin, which always made her pulse flutter. At that moment, the VHS player made a sound, and the whirring stopped, so he pressed Play and then joined her on the couch. Truffle came from out of nowhere and leaped up between them, rolling onto his back and exposing his splotchy pink belly to the world. Jace reached down to scratch the dog, like this was a routine they'd created. There was total trust. Total comfort. The dog had a blissed-out expression on his face, and for the first time in her life, Angie found herself being a little jealous of an animal.

"Why do you like these movies?" he asked as the video started. It looked like it had been watched over and over, giving the screen a slightly fuzzy quality.

"Rom-coms?"

"Yeah."

Angie shrugged. "I don't know. I guess there's something comforting about knowing that everyone deserves a happily ever after. It's a universal thing, right? We all want the comfort of thinking our lives will turn out well even if we don't always feel like good things will happen to us."

That was far more insightful than she'd intended, but it was true. The first time she'd sat down to watch a rom-com with her foster mom was after she'd moved houses for the fourth time in as many years. It was right around the time a boy at school had told her that she was a loser because her family hadn't wanted to keep her.

Yet watching that silly, funny movie about the girl who everyone thought was odd had made Angie wonder if perhaps *she* could have that moment of coming down the stairs, dressed up and transformed and suddenly noticed. Suddenly important. That maybe one day she would be loved and accepted.

"Don't tell me this is part of your grand fall-in-love-instantly plan?" Jace frowned. "Does this quantify as research? You're not planning to go undercover at the local high school, right?"

She reached across Truffle's stretched-out body to give Jace a gentle shove. "To quote another classic rom-com, *as if*! And if you shut up for five seconds and watch the darn thing, you might learn something, too."

"Doubtful." His lips were doing that sexy quirking thing again.

As the movie continued, Angie found herself unable to stop stealing glances at her landlord's profile. The strong nose and hard jaw, the thick eyelashes that most women would kill for. The way his hair curled stubbornly around his ears, the place where a cowlick always made it look like he'd just rolled out of bed.

Maybe Angie watched these movies because she needed hope—hope that someone with a good heart, someone who made her feel that exciting flutter, would fall for her. Hope that even though her family hadn't wanted her, maybe that didn't mean she wasn't lovable.

It allowed her to dwell in the fantasy that she'd fall in love…maybe with someone like Jace who had a good heart and a gaze that could burn her up?

There's no point fixating on someone who isn't interested. You'll waste this opportunity and end up going back home alone and miserable.

True that. No matter how much he got her hot under the collar and made her giggle in that perfect giddy-schoolgirl way, her plans did not allow for a guy who wasn't interested. So she had to officially cast him out of her mind and get back to the movie.

It was time to enter study mode, and Angie was determined to be top of the rom-com class.

• • •

Jace officially did not get women. To be fair, he didn't really get people, but he *especially* did not get women. The whole Josie Grossie thing was... confusing. Which made Angie's plan to fall in love and get married in two months something *beyond* confusing.

Hell, Jace took more than two months to make a decision about which pair of sneakers to buy after they discontinued his preferred style. Marriage? That was something that should be entered into with the utmost care. Maybe if he'd taken more care the first time around, it would have ended up differently.

But after he'd left Angie last night, a bad feeling had eaten him up all night. He could tell she wanted something from him—support, maybe. A hug? Who the hell knew? That whole conversation was smack-bang in the middle of the fuzzy gray, and he was *way* out of his element. So far out of his element, he would have been more comfortable going undercover in a high school.

"Isn't it beautiful?" Angie pressed a hand to her chest as the couple on-screen kissed.

Jace still couldn't get past the fact that the teacher had fallen for one of his students, even if she was legal. How the heck was *that* romantic?

Now that he looked closer, Angie had tears in her eyes. They were like shimmering little crystals, glinting and catching the light. They made her lashes stick together in little clumps, and for some reason, that was one of the most beautiful things he'd ever seen.

When Jace was a kid, his mother had had a

chart stuck to the refrigerator that had different facial expressions on it. He'd never been too good at deciphering those on his own, so his mum had helped him. There was a smiling face, which meant someone was happy. A frowning face, which meant someone was angry. And a face with tears, which meant someone was sad.

As he'd gotten older, the expressions had become even more challenging to decipher, because people didn't always let their face represent exactly what they were feeling. How the heck was he supposed to know that not all frowns were angry?

Watching Angie closely, the tears continued to glimmer, although she blinked a lot so they wouldn't fall. And she bit down on her lip. Maybe the movie was having the opposite effect than she'd intended. Whenever Liv was sad, she liked to be hugged. She said it made her feel better.

So Jace slowly reached his arm along the back of the couch, waiting to see if Angie pulled away. She didn't. For some reason, this made his heart feel like it was rushing. Now his arm was fully stretched out behind her, and his hand dipped down to touch her shoulder.

Still, she didn't move away.

She had on a top with no sleeves, and the skin on her shoulders was perfectly smooth. Perfectly warm. It felt good against his fingertips. Freckles dusted her skin, like someone had flicked a paintbrush against her, and she had a tiny white scar that looked like a crescent moon. How had he never noticed that before? It was almost like looking at the sky—star specks and moon, a galaxy on her skin.

Angie inched along the couch toward him, and he let his hand drape over her shoulder. Eventually, she leaned into him, her head coming to rest on his shoulder and her hair trailing over him, like bands of silk.

It felt so good to have her curled up against him, her gentle curves pressing into his body. And she always smelled good, too. He'd seen her perfume bottle on her bathroom countertop once, a pretty glass thing with a yellow ribbon. It made her smell like lemons and sugar. And *that* made him hungry.

God, he was so hungry.

The movie was totally lost on him now. The television could have been blaring hard-core death metal, and he wouldn't have even noticed it. All his brain could process was Angie. The feel of her, the smell of her. The sound of her sniffle and the way it wrinkled her nose in the most adorable way.

Holding her felt so right, as if his body was somehow tense and perfectly relaxed at the same time—like he didn't dare move a muscle in case it caused her to pull away.

Stop. Angie is not the girl for you—she talks too much, chaos follows her everywhere, and…she's leaving.

But he couldn't stop. It was like he was committing every part of her to memory, using his eyes. His fingertips. He traced the line of her arm, and she turned to him, tilting her face up to his. The tears were less now, still a faint glimmer but replaced by something…hotter. Her lips were parted and glossy, her cheeks flushed sunset-pink.

He wanted to kiss her. Need struck him with the force of a hammer, pounding relentlessly in time with his pulse. Filtering through his system in a way he hadn't experienced in a long, long time. Too long.

It felt like time had ground to a halt, as if someone had hit Pause on his life. Could he kiss her? Would that be so wrong when he knew she was looking for so much more than he could give? Their needs were opposed but…he wanted to. So badly.

Angie's eyes fluttered shut, her beautiful spiky lashes still damp. He leaned closer, inching his face toward hers until—

"Oof!" There was a wet dog nose in his crotch and two giant paws on his thighs. Dammit, Tilly! Truffle raced across the room, barking loudly as if demanding that nobody forget he was here. As if that was even possible.

Angie immediately pulled away, putting as much distance between her and the bigger dog as possible. Her expression was hard to read, but she laughed in a way that sounded odd. Like it wasn't a real laugh.

Tilly looked up at him, her big brown eyes unwavering in their contact. It was almost like she was saying, *I know what you were about to do. Don't worry—I protected you.*

Without a canine running interference, he would have kissed Angie. And that would have been a *huge* mistake. Thankfully now the moment had been lost, and Angie was fussing with a throw pillow, avoiding looking at him.

The awkward tension was back. It was probably for the best, though. Angie was trouble with a capital *T*, and even though he very much wanted to kiss her, it wasn't a good idea. They wanted different things...*needed* different things.

"Thanks, girl," he whispered to Tilly, giving her a hearty scratch behind her ears.

He would have to be more careful from now on, because it was clear he was attracted to Angie even more than he first thought. And when she got too close to him, his brain ceased to function properly.

Or at all.

"I, uh...should go." Angie got up from her seat and hustled out of his apartment so quickly that she left the VHS player and all her tapes behind. The back door shut with a bang. Jace sagged back against the couch, his head spinning and his body feeling all wound up.

Yeah, he *really* didn't understand women.

CHAPTER NINE

So it turned out that Truffle had a problem. A *humping* problem.

Jace's morning had been turned upside down when his post-surf shower had been interrupted by aggressive pounding on his front door. His elderly neighbor, Mrs. Marsh, had stood on his doorstep, still wearing her nightgown and slippers, her hair wrapped in a silk scarf and Truffle on a leash.

Turned out he'd escaped by jumping onto the couch, climbing up the back, and making a death-defying leap to the sideboard under the window, where he'd climbed out. That's what Jace got for leaving the windows open at night. But the prison break–style escape wasn't the worst of it. Mrs. Marsh said she'd found Truffle humping her beloved beagle, Archer. Or, in her words, bringing "the devil" into her home.

Jace wasn't exactly sure how a Chihuahua that was no bigger than a loaf of bread was able to bring the devil into anyone's home, but he promised he'd do his best to prevent any further canine sexual acts. But as much as he wanted to keep his promise to Mrs. Marsh, he didn't want to sully his internet browser history by Googling "dog humping." Who knew what kinds of weird ads *that* would bring up on his computer? So he'd stuffed a few treats into these weird ball things that were in Eugenie's bag of tricks that would hopefully keep the little guy occupied for a while so Jace could work.

He'd been trying to figure out an issue with his currently storyline, *Hermit vs. the Bridge*, but he couldn't find the right feeling. Yesterday, he'd sketched scene after scene, trying to get into Hermit's headspace. But nothing was working.

Maybe it was because he kept playing the "almost kiss" with Angie on loop, letting the image repeat over and over and over until he was sure if he reached out, he would touch her. He'd even started sketching out a scene with Hermit meeting a woman, but that just made him think about all the ways he could possibly screw things up with Angie, so he'd balled the paper in his fist and tossed it across the room.

In the end, he'd started sketching Hermit stumbling upon a dog with an injured paw. *That* felt a whole lot safer than trying to put a romance subplot into his comic. After a morning of free sketching, he'd ended up with a funny scenario about Hermit finding a dog who also didn't like people—a canine version of himself.

He found himself chuckling as he worked. The dog—whom he'd decided would be called T, as in short for *trouble*—was lost. Nobody in the town wanted a dog who didn't like people, so Hermit agreed to look after him for the time being. After all, he knew what it was like not to fit the mold. By the time the afternoon rolled around, he'd completed the draft and was inking on top of his pencil.

All comic storylines took detours now and then, and Jace figured the introduction of a new character might boost interest for his readership. People on the internet loved dogs. So it was a strategic move in his mind. An acceptable diversion. But tomorrow, he'd have to get back to the real storyline.

Speaking of dogs…

He glanced through his studio's open door, which looked out into the living room, where Truffle was humping the leg of the coffee table. The little guy was really going at it, too. He'd hooked his front paws around the leg of the table and his head jerked around with the movement.

"You've got some pent-up energy, huh, bud?" He scratched his head. What was one supposed to do to discourage that kind of thing? Eugenie Landry had *not* prepared him for this. "Hey, enough!"

Jace clapped his hands and Truffle trotted over, tail wagging like he was feeling pretty good about getting some.

"Don't look so damn pleased with yourself."

But Truffle continued to look *very* pleased.

"All right, let's go for a walk. See if we can't burn off some of that energy."

At the sound of the *W* word, Truffle's ears pricked up, and his tail wagged. At least if he was all tuckered out, then he wouldn't have energy to foist himself on unsuspecting dogs or inanimate objects…hopefully.

Jace narrowed his eyes at Truffle, who had taken up post by the front door and was patiently waiting. No wonder he was distracted from work—maintaining his routine was like pushing shit uphill at the moment.

"You're cute and all, but *man*, you're a lot of work." Jace crouched down by the front door to help Truffle into the harness he wore to prevent him from choking himself when he tugged on his leash. The dog slapped his tiny paws on Jace's knee and looked up at him adoringly. "Okay, so you're *real* cute. Still way too much work for me. Can you *please* stop humping things?"

Somehow he doubted Truffle's compliance. They headed out into the midday sunshine, leaving Tilly behind because she was happily curled up in her doggy bed and snoring like an old man. He'd take her out later.

Jace's house wasn't far from the main strip, and the walk took him along streets he could draw purely from memory. The buzz of lawn mowers mixed with birds chirping and the ever-present squawk of seagulls was Patterson's Bluff's eternal soundtrack. Truffle stopped to sniff at each corner, dutifully marking his territory with a quick raise of his leg.

Jace made it all the way down to the main strip before he had the sudden worry that he might run into Julia. For a moment, he'd been so wrapped up in looking after the dog, he'd forgotten the bombshell that Nick had dropped the other night. What if she was here now? Doing her groceries and walking around like this was *her* town when it wasn't?

The thought of it made him tense. The last time

he'd seen her was the afternoon of their rehearsal dinner. She'd had her makeup done, her reddish hair piled up on top of her head. There'd been a strange energy about her—one of those things he was hopeless at describing. But he'd put it down to nerves about their big day. Totally normal, right?

That was until he'd gone to the dinner with his family, as planned. She'd only invited her dad, since her mother wasn't in the picture anymore. His parents, siblings, and a handful of their close mutual friends sat at the beautiful seaside restaurant, waiting...and waiting.

And waiting.

He'd called her at ten minutes. Then thirty. Then an hour. Julia wasn't the most punctual person, so they hadn't been *too* worried, initially. But by an hour and ten, his imagination had churned, convincing him that something bad had happened.

The food had come out, but Jace couldn't eat. When he'd gone home, he'd known it was over. Her side of the bedroom had been totally cleaned out...and there'd been a note.

Dear Jace, I'm sorry to do this to you. But I can't marry you. I think I'm in love with Trent. I have to leave.

He swallowed against the uncomfortable lump in his throat that came whenever he thought about that day—though he tried not to. But the shame and embarrassment were still so easily brought to the surface. He'd never gotten an explanation beyond her note, never heard from her again. Not that he'd tried to contact her. The whole thing had sent him further into his work. Further into his own world.

Jace walked up the main street, pulling his shoulders back like he was a man who owned his space. Regardless of Julia's reasons for coming back to Patterson's Bluff, he wasn't going to let it affect him. He'd moved on.

"Hey, Jace." Chloe gave a wave as she headed over to him. She had on her usual attire—hair in a messy bun, yoga pants, and a T-shirt that said you had me at namaste. In her hands was one of those reusable Keep Cup-style coffee mugs. "Walking a cute little dog like that is a great way to pick up women."

He snorted. "If you knew the reason I was taking this guy on a walk, you wouldn't say that."

Chloe laughed. "It was great to see you out at the twilight party the other night. I feel like it's been ages. What have you been up to?"

"Work. I've got interest from a comic syndication group in the US for *Hermit vs. World*." He paused when she looked like she was expecting him to continue. What more was there to say about that? "Um, that's comic-nerd speak for a really great business opportunity."

"That's awesome. I always knew you'd do something with your art. And I'm usually the one making people have that glazed-over look." She sipped the drink in her right hand, leaving a glossy pink imprint on the lid. "There's only so much *savasana* one can take before people wonder if they're dead. Sorry, yoga humor."

Jace didn't quite get the joke, since his experience with yoga would have rivaled his experience with horny dogs before today. "The studio looks like it's going really well."

"It is!" She grinned. Across the road, Unwind was bustling. A group of women with colorful mats stood outside, chatting. Through the front window, a class was taking place. People stood with their arms raised above their heads before sweeping down to bend in half. "I'm really pleased. I wasn't sure the locals would buy into the whole yoga and meditation thing, but they've embraced me and apparently I haven't embarrassed my mother *too* much."

"Is she still mad that you gave up on the family business?"

"Uh, yeah. Understatement of the century. But being the black sheep has its perks. They don't expect anything of me anymore." Chloe rolled her eyes, but then something caught her attention, and she paused. His gaze followed hers across the street.

Oh.

At that moment, Angie came out of the yoga studio, wearing a pair of skin-tight lilac leggings that showed off her cycling-toned legs to perfection. On top she wore a black tank, and her hair was swept loosely into a ponytail that hung over one shoulder. A sky-blue yoga mat was tucked under one arm. She looked…radiant.

"They're totally vibing." Chloe seemed über-excited. "I knew they would hit it off!"

"Angie told me about her plan." Elijah reached up to pick something out of Angie's hair, and Jace frowned. "This whole thing is dumb."

Chloe stared at him long and hard. He knew he sounded jealous, but she didn't know Angie was leaving soon. It was a dumb idea because she was leaving. No other reason. Absolutely nothing to do with the almost kiss.

He watched Angie and her Romeo, who now had her giggling about something. Probably how many pizzas he could toss at once.

Did they even sell pizzas in his restaurant? Jace wasn't sure.

"Oh shoot, my class is about to start. It was nice chatting with you, Jace." She gave a wave. "You should come by sometime, stretch out your muscles. It's a good idea when you've been sitting at a desk all day!"

Over his dead body. Jace had as much flexibility as a lump of coal, and he wasn't about to put himself in a situation to show that off in public. His gaze lingered on Angie and Elijah.

Judging by the way she was talking to Elijah, smiling sweetly and toying with the end of her ponytail, she was definitely "vibing," as Chloe put it. An ugly, foreign feeling surged up inside Jace that made him feel the exact same way as when he'd watched his brother flirting with her.

Turn around and walk away. It's none of your damn business.

But before Jace fully thought through the consequences of his actions, he was crossing the road with Truffle leading the way. As soon as the little white dog caught sight of Angie, his tail started going a million miles a minute.

Stop. You're not going to get involved. Don't be a hypocrite. Other people in this town meddle and you *hate* it.

It was true. He came from a family of meddlers, and it drove him nuts. But maybe there was some meddling-specific chromosome that had been passed on from his parents without his knowledge, remaining dormant all this time and waiting for the right moment to strike.

"Jace." Angie looked at him with wide eyes, almost like she was a kid with her hand stuck in the cookie jar.

"I was taking Truffle for a walk." He raked a hand through his hair like he was totally relaxed and going about his day. The truth was, he had no bloody idea *what* he was doing. "How was yoga?"

"Awesome." For some reason, Angie's voice seemed an octave or two higher than normal. "Super great, actually. Excellent."

Hmm. Three ways of saying the same thing. She did that whenever she was nervous.

"Are you into yoga?" Jace asked Elijah.

"Yeah, man. With all the firewood I have to chop for the pizza oven, my back gets real tight."

Jace resisted the urge to roll his eyes. How did he manage to say shit like that *without* coming off like a total douchecanoe?

"But I could always use some tutoring." Elijah shot Angie a flirty look, and her cheeks turned the prettiest shade of pink. "Any opportunity to expand my skills."

"I'm sure Chloe could help with that," Jace said stiffly.

Out of the corner of his eye, he saw Truffle sniffing around Elijah's leg. He'd done the same thing to the coffee table earlier that morning—inspecting his target. Jace really should put a stop to it…

"I wasn't talking about Chloe," Elijah said, his eyes still trained on Angie.

Angie laughed and gingerly stuck her hand in the air. "I volunteer as tribute."

Jace forgot the dog and stared at her hard. Was this one of those gray-area things he'd never understand, or did Angie really like this guy? He had no freaking clue.

Just then, Truffle jumped up on his hind legs, hooking his front paws around Elijah's calf. His hips started to hinge back and forth, and Elijah glanced down, a *what the hell do I do now* expression on his face as he and Angie looked down at Sir Hump-a-Lot.

"What the hell?" Elijah stumbled back, and Truffle dropped down to the ground, looking mightily miffed that his sexy times were interrupted.

"Truffle!" Angie snort-laughed. "So inappropriate."

"It's a dominance thing," Jace said to Elijah. "He tends to do that whenever he thinks he can overpower someone."

Angie shot Jace a raised brow, but she squatted to give the dog a scratch behind the ears before he could figure out exactly what she was thinking. Was the comment too much? He'd blurted it out without thinking, and Elijah seemed off his game now.

"I'd better get going before any other animals

decide to make love to my leg," Elijah said. "But I'll see you tomorrow, Angie. Looking forward to it."

Why would Elijah be seeing Angie tomorrow? And why did the thought of them meeting up make him feel a little ill?

"You heading home now?" she asked, pasting on a big smile and acting like this whole situation wasn't strange and awkward as hell.

"Actually, I was going to take Truffle to the dog park. He…uh, needs to work off some energy."

"Want company?" she asked.

"Sure."

Don't mention the date. Don't mention the date. Don't mention the date.

"So you've got a date with Elijah." Shit.

Maybe there was somewhere he could *buy* a verbal filter. Surely Amazon Prime would have something. At the very least, some electrical tape might work to keep his mouth shut.

"Yeah." She fiddled with her ponytail. "We're grabbing a bite to eat. He seems like a nice bloke."

Jace didn't even react to her use of "bloke" like he normally would have. "He has an unnatural amount of muscles, you know."

That's the best you can do?

Angie blinked. "Unnatural?"

"It means he spends too much time at the gym," Jace explained, trying to dig himself out of the verbal hole. "What does that say about a man's priorities in life?"

"That health is important." Angie's brows furrowed.

"Some gym is good. Too much gym is bad." *Dude, that made literally no sense.* "What I mean is that you want a guy to do things with you, right? Other than, like..." He tried to think of something weight-related. "Squatting."

Angie shook her head. "Somehow I don't think we're going to do squats on our date."

"*And* he's a small-business owner."

"What's wrong with that?"

"It takes up a lot of time." Yeah, this sounded more legitimate. "He works long hours and has a lot of responsibilities for the people he employs. And, uh...legal stuff. Running a business is serious work, Angie. Very time-consuming."

"So you're telling me that I should find a guy with no job *and* no hobbies?" She laughed. "I'm not sure that sounds like someone whose company I'd enjoy."

"No, well, not *no* job. But maybe..." *Dig up.* "Someone who works at home so he's...around more."

She narrowed her eyes at him. "Someone like you?"

"Oh no, definitely not me." If there was a time to shut up, it would be now. But Jace was on a roll, and he couldn't seem to stop himself. "Like...Rob Halpert."

They turned a corner at the end of the main strip of shops, heading toward the dog park while Truffle trotted happily in front of them.

"Rob Halpert is at home all the time because he's retired. And *seventy-two*." She laughed. "You want me to date someone old enough to be my grandpa because he'll be 'around more.' Seriously?"

"What about someone who's creative?" Oh no, that sounded like he was describing himself again. "Like a model-train builder."

"Is this model train builder *also* seventy years old?"

"It was just a suggestion. All I'm saying is, Elijah might not be the best choice. You know marriage is a big commitment." He cleared his throat. "You want to enter into it with someone who'll be able to spend time with you and not be…doing weights and working all the time."

They came to the edge of the park, and Angie shielded her eyes as she looked up at him. He wasn't so good at reading all her expressions, but this one had a definite tone of WTF about it.

"If it's all the same to you, Jace, seventy-year-old creative model-train builders are not my type. I know, shocking." She shook her head. "And perhaps it's best if I go on my date with Elijah and determine for myself whether we're a good match."

Jace looked down at Truffle, who peered back up at him as if to say, *You're on your own with this one, buddy.*

"Who knows," Angie continued. "Maybe I'll be able to see if all that time spent in the gym has made him good husband material or not."

Ugh. Jace wasn't sure what he wanted to do more: throw up or sabotage her date.

CHAPTER TEN

"Earth to Angie!"

A hand with flashing diamonds yanked Angie from her thoughts. She'd been a space cadet all morning, frequently letting her mind wander to what might happen on her date this afternoon. For some unknown reason, she was having mixed feelings about the whole thing. It was exciting, but something felt…off.

"Sorry." She shook her head. "Whose turn is it?"

"Yours!" all three of her poker buddies chorused in exasperated unison.

"All right, all right." Angie glanced at her cards, which were a whole lot of nothing. "Fold."

"What's wrong with you today?" Meredith asked with a frown. "You come in here with your head floating in the clouds, and you can't pay attention for more than three seconds."

"I know. I'm sorry. It's… I'm distracted."

"*That* much is obvious," Jean huffed, adjusting her glasses. "You're slowing down the rate of play."

"You got somewhere to be?" Betty asked her friend with a raise of her silver brow.

Jean looked down at her cards and shook her head, but a telltale pink flush colored her cheeks. Now that Angie thought about it, something looked different about her. Was that…lipstick?

"You look pretty today, Jean." Angie cocked her head.

It wasn't only the lipstick, either. Jean's usual outfit of slacks with a sensible short-sleeve shirt had been updated. Today she wore a blouse that was baby blue—to match her eyes—and covered in a fine print of yellow and white flowers.

She made an indignant snorting sound as if the compliment was ridiculous. "I don't look any different than normal."

Angie leaned over and sucked in a breath, catching a whiff of something delightfully floral. YSL Paris, if she wasn't mistaken. One of her foster moms had worn it religiously.

"You smell nice, too." Angie narrowed her eyes. "*And* you're wearing mascara!"

Jean looked like a deer caught in headlights— her widened eyes magnified by her thick-rimmed glasses. Her snow-white hair was curled and cropped, and she even had on a pair of simple pearl studs, rather than her usual thin hoops.

"She's dressing up *and* she wants to rush through our game." Betty tapped a finger to her chin. "Most unusual. What's on the schedule after this?"

"The barbecue lunch." Meredith snapped her fingers. "Marcus is going to be there. I overheard him chatting with Davis about his prowess on the grill."

"Stop it." Jean shook her head. "All of you. Nothing is different. I simply felt like putting on a nice top today. Is that such a crime?"

"It's okay if you have a crush on someone, Jean." Angie pressed her palm to the older woman's arm.

For some reason, Elijah wasn't the face that popped into her head. Oh no, she got a crystal-clear image of a crooked-smiling, blue-eyed comic artist instead. Most inconvenient.

"I think it's sweet," she added.

"You're all talking bloody nonsense." Jean folded her arms across her chest and glowered at them. "You should hear yourselves."

"Oh, come on. I can't be the only one who's got a date planned for today," Angie said with a wink.

Three sets of eyes turned to her.

"You do? Tell us everything." Meredith put the cards down, and the poker game was forgotten for some good old-fashioned gossiping.

Maybe it was a sad indictment on Angie's life, but all she'd ever wanted was an older relative to talk to about this stuff. A big sister, a mother, an aunt...someone who cared enough to listen to her hopes and fears, to her dreams. To offer advice based on their years of experience. To have these women as part of her life now, like three amazing grandmothers...well, it made her even more determined to stay in Patterson's Bluff.

"Yes, I have a date. He runs a restaurant, and he's very successful...and good-looking." She felt the need to tack that on as if it somehow validated her choice. But the circling thoughts that had distracted her all through her volunteer shift surrounded the total lack of chemistry she felt running into Elijah yesterday.

It didn't make sense. He was devastatingly handsome—that was a fact. And he seemed thoughtful and intelligent, if a little serious. His business was one of the most well-regarded in Patterson's Bluff. So she'd plowed on and suggested they meet up, following Chloe's advice. Elijah had said yes without hesitation. And yet...

Wasn't there supposed to be a zing? Some kind of tingling sensation that told her they'd work well together? Butterflies?

Give it a chance. You talked to him for all of five minutes, and half of that was while Truffle humped his leg. Not exactly the most romantic setup.

True. Maybe she was too worked up about this whole thing—too stressed about her looming deportation date—and that was killing the vibe.

"What are you doing on your date?" Betty asked.

"Grabbing a bite to eat. He's invited me to come to his restaurant and sample some of the new dishes they've been working on."

Meredith frowned. "So he's taking you to work?"

"Well, no...not exactly." *But yeah...kinda.* "It's going to be fun. I love trying new food."

Her comment was met with three unconvinced faces. Betty shook her head. "That's not a date. Back in my day—"

"Here we go." Meredith rolled her eyes good-naturedly.

"A date was dinner and dancing," Betty continued. "My John had all the moves. Still does, when his arthritis isn't flaring up. He made me feel like a princess on the dance floor."

"People don't really go dancing anymore,"

Angie replied. "Although I wish we did; it sounds like fun."

"That's what a date should be. Fun, something different than what you do in your normal day-to-day life." Betty reached over and patted her hand. "If he's taking you to work on date number one, imagine what it will be like on date a hundred and one. He'll probably suggest you help him sort his recycling."

Maybe Betty had a point. Elijah had seemed so excited about showing her the new menu, though, and from all accounts he was extremely passionate about what he did. His restaurant was responsible for keeping two local farms in business when they'd been on the brink of bankruptcy. *And* he'd been at the forefront of championing the reduction of single-use plastics in the town.

Angie admired Elijah...but was that enough?

"If he's the right guy for you, you'll know it," Jean added. "That feeling is unmistakable."

"I dated a man once who took me in a helicopter on our first date." Meredith's gaze had drifted away, as though she were watching the past play like a film on-screen. "It was so romantic. We flew over the countryside and had a picnic in this open field. He'd brought wine and fresh bread and cheese."

"Sounds magical," Angie mused.

"It was." For a moment, Meredith only twisted her ring around her finger. But then the dreamy gaze disappeared, replaced by her usual sharp and focused expression. "But, alas, it was not to be."

"How come?"

"He wanted marriage, and I didn't." Meredith winked as the retirement home's event planner came into the room and announced that the barbecue was about to start.

The common area was already mostly vacated, and the remaining residents got to their feet so they could all file outside. Angie offered to help take one of the gentlemen, who needed assistance with his wheelchair. As they slowly made their way out to the courtyard, Angie caught sight of Jean fluffing up her hair in the reflection of a window.

There was a sparkle to her eyes, a mischievous excitement that gave her the aura of a woman decades younger. Despite her adamant denial, it was clear there was *something* going on. Marcus stood at one of the barbecues, turning sausages with one hand, his other holding his cane close. But his eyes kept flicking to the line of people snaking through the open double doors. When they landed on Jean, a smile softened the sharp angles of his handsome face. He gave her a subtle nod, and she pretended not to notice. Typical Jean, stubborn as ever.

But her eyes skimmed over him the second he turned away, and she fiddled with a slim chain-link bracelet around her wrist. Twisting and turning so the links caught the light.

Angie couldn't help but grin. There was something so exciting about a crush—even if she wasn't the one experiencing it. Maybe Patterson's Bluff *was* the right place to fall in love? It certainly seemed as though there was something in the air.

But as her volunteer shift drew to a close, Angie found herself not particularly looking forward to her date. In truth, she'd rather go back home and watch another rom-com with Jace while the dogs were curled up at their feet.

Now you know *you're going crazy. Since when do your fantasies include dogs?*

• • •

By the time Angie made it home from her "date," she was starting to wish she'd never told anyone about it. No doubt there would be questions. It wasn't like the night had been horrible—in fact, she'd most certainly had worse. But Elijah had been distracted, being interrupted every few minutes by staff from the kitchen. At one point, he'd left her sitting there so he could deal with a problem, and she'd contemplated sneaking out. It was obvious to them both that they had about as much chemistry as overcooked spaghetti.

Angie was unlocking the little gate at the side of Jace's house, still in her outfit from the date, when she spotted him heading up the path. Ugh, she couldn't act like she hadn't seen him. That would be rude.

Tilly and Truffle trotted happily in front of him, and Angie waved. "How is the terrible twosome doing today?"

"Truffle hasn't humped anything, so that's a win." His crooked smile set flutters in her stomach.

"You're a pro." She brushed her hands down

the front of her dress, feeling even sillier that she'd gotten all dolled up. It had all been for nothing.

"New dress?" he asked as if reading her mind.

"Yeah." Suddenly self-conscious, she wrapped her arms around herself. "So what's your recommendation for a post-crappy-date activity? I would usually cry into a bucket of ice cream Bridget Jones–style while watching a romantic movie."

Better to get it out in the open, she figured. Cover her disappointment with a self-deprecating joke.

Jace nodded. "It didn't go well?"

"Uh, no. Not really."

His expression was hard to read. "I haven't had dinner yet. Do you feel like going for a drive?"

In spite of her mood, the thought of getting away from the flat and distracting herself sounded like bliss. "Actually, yeah, I do."

Five minutes later, they were on the road in Jace's car—a practical Ford SUV with a rack on the roof that held his surfboard. It was a funny contrast—like most things about Jace—because the car itself had a distinct "soccer mom" vibe, right down to the meticulously clean interior. But the brightly colored surfboard would look better suited to some peace and love Volkswagen van.

"So," he said, drumming his fingers against the steering wheel as they paused at an intersection. "The date was a bust?"

"It was…fine." She bobbed her head, trying to

figure out what exactly had gone wrong. Elijah was a great guy—charming but serious, passionate about his work. Hell, the guy was A+ loving-relationship material on paper.

But in person…fizzle city.

"Not exactly a rousing endorsement." Jace's gaze slid over to her, his lip pulled up into a smirk.

For some reason, that pissed her off. He'd been baffled about the whole "expediting true love" thing from the second she admitted her plans. Clearly telling him was a mistake.

"I *should* have enjoyed myself," she muttered. What was wrong with her? A cute guy had taken her to his lovely restaurant, where she'd picked at her food and counted down the seconds until it was over. Sure, he'd been a bit distracted, but was that *so* bad in the scheme of things? He was ambitious. It was an admirable trait.

You were bored.

There was no denying it. A handsome face was not enough to give Angie the "snap, crackle, and pop" she'd seen in the movies.

"What went wrong?" Jace asked.

"Honestly? I don't know. There wasn't anything particularly bad about it." She sighed. "But there wasn't anything particularly good about it, either."

Flipping the visor down in front of her, she inspected herself in the mirror. A lick of mascara, a bare dusting of bronzer, and tinted lip balm enhanced her features, but she felt a little plain despite the overtly feminine dress. A little…not her best.

Maybe the problem is with you. You don't feel attractive.

"What would have made it better?"

The coast blurred past. The sky blended into the water at the horizon and the little parking lots that dotted the side of the road were full of people coming and going. Families, mostly. She pulled her gaze away.

"I guess it was missing that spark. I didn't feel like I was anticipating anything."

He turned his beast of a car into a sweeping corner that revealed the main strip of Sorrento. Jace hadn't told her a word about what they were doing, only that she should get into the car and trust him. Which she did.

"Like, when you meet someone you're attracted to and your stomach gets that twisty-turny feeling." She looked at him, her stomach feeling more than a little twisty turny at that very moment. "And when the date ends, you're already hoping for another chance to see them."

"You're not hoping to see Elijah again?"

"Not in that capacity. But maybe I should have been prepared with more questions to ask. I can't put all the blame on him." She watched the scenery change as they pulled onto the main strip. Sorrento was a beautiful town farther along the coast, bigger and more popular than Patterson's Bluff. The street inclined up the landscape, and a grand old building crowded the bottom corner. Cars lined the street, where shops and restaurants sat in a colorful row. "Are we here?"

"We certainly are." He pulled the car into an

empty parking spot next to a Ferrari.

An actual Ferrari.

"Gee, I bet you feel good until you come here," she said, and to her surprise, a laugh burst forth from his lips.

"It's changed a lot since I was a kid." He killed the engine and pushed open the door.

Angie stepped down from the SUV, being extra careful not to let her door anywhere near the lipstick-red sports car. The only person she'd ever known to drive a Ferrari was the lawyer who'd upended her life—and he wasn't the kind of guy Angie wanted to go near ever again.

"So what are we doing here?" She looked up and down the street, which was bustling with people, many of whom looked as though they'd come from the beach. Given she'd been so uncomfortable on her date that she'd barely eaten, she was now officially starving.

"We're going right here... Well, kind of." He nodded toward a small fish-and-chips place in front of them. It didn't have any seating, but a line snaked out the door and spilled onto the street. He ran a hand through his dark hair and the perfect waves sprang stubbornly back into place. "I'm introducing you to a Walters family tradition."

"Which is?"

"Fresh fish and chips overlooking the ocean. We used to do it every weekend during the summer as kids. We'll order our food here, and then I'll drive us to the Sorrento Back Beach." He nodded. "It'll be fun."

She couldn't help but laugh at the way he said it, like what he deemed fun was a fact rather than an opinion. He was certainly a black-or-white kind of guy like that. Which, honestly, in a world where everything felt so uncertain, she found to be totally and utterly comforting.

"I thought this might cheer you up," he added. "You can be part of my family today. This is what we do when someone is feeling down."

Angie caught herself staring up at him, her heart full with his sweet and unexpected gesture. But that sweetness was edged with something else. A deeper attraction that made her heart beat a little faster and her hands tingle with anticipation. She wondered what it would be like to taste him, to swipe her tongue along the soft, pillowy edge of his lower lip as she kissed him. Like if he'd actually responded to her silent invitation the day they'd watched the movie together.

Bad thoughts. Retreat!

She swallowed and focused her gaze on the menu for the fish-and-chips restaurant. It wouldn't do any good thinking about kissing Jace, no matter how delicious she was sure it would be. Because he'd made it clear he didn't do relationships.

And she would never settle for less.

CHAPTER ELEVEN

Half an hour later, they were dinner enabled and the SUV made a steady climb up to a car park that overlooked the Sorrento Back Beach. Jace reversed the car into a parking spot and dropped the rear seats down so they could sit in the back with their legs dangling out over the edge.

Truffle had perked up at the possibility of food and trotted around happily, tail wagging, confident in his assumption that he would get himself some treats. If Angie had half his confidence, she'd go far in life. Tilly made a whining noise when Jace nudged her to make room for Angie.

"She's going to eat my face off; I can feel it," Angie said, perching herself at the very edge of the car to get as much space as possible between her and the huge dog.

It was fine while they were outside, standing up with plenty of space around them. But in the back of the car, her old fears bubbled to the surface. Tilly's pointy teeth were definitely within chomping distance.

"You can't still be scared of her. She's a total softy." Jace pulled the bag containing their dinner onto his lap and started sorting through it.

Angie met the dog's warm amber gaze. But pretty eyes weren't a reason to trust anyone — canine or otherwise.

"Says the man who didn't even want to dog-sit

in the first place."

Jace shrugged. "I'm starting to see why people like dogs. Though I'll be very happy to reclaim my routine when Eugenie comes back."

Angie raised a brow but didn't have a chance to respond as he started dividing up their food.

"One piece of flake and two potato cakes," Jace announced as he handed her an open piece of parchment paper containing her dinner. He took the package containing the chips and shook a generous amount into her pseudo dinner dish. "Sauce?"

"Yes, please." She held her hand out, and he loaded her up with packets of ketchup. "I shouldn't be so hungry. There was so much nice food at Elijah's restaurant, but I was too nervous to eat any of it."

Jace was holding a stack of napkins, counting them meticulously so they could have exactly half each. Clearly having grown up with four siblings had made him very good at sharing. Or maybe it was because he was processing something. She got the impression that he seemed to retreat into himself when he was thinking.

Normally a silence like this would set Angie's nerves on edge—this was often where her verbal diarrhea would kick into full force. Jace handed her half the napkins. He had artist's hands—smooth skin, long fingers, and one callus where his sketching pencils would rest. Her heart beat quicker, the warning sirens turning to a call of longing. Turning to whispers of temptation.

"Why were you nervous?" he asked.

"I don't know." She popped a chip into her mouth. "I guess I knew there wasn't anything special there."

"How could you possibly know that so soon?"

"Just a feeling...or a lack of feeling, as it were." She sighed when she bit into a piece of crispy yet buttery flake with the perfect amount of saltiness. Pure heaven. Angie licked her lips and took another bite, suddenly ravenous. "I'd hoped I might find some spark as we got to know each other, but one date was enough to tell me it wasn't going anywhere."

Tilly lifted her nose in the air and sniffed. Jace held out a few chips, but she placed her head back on her paws without taking them.

"What's wrong with her?"

"Maybe car rides don't agree with her," he said, his dark brows creasing, and he gave her a loving pat.

Watching the two of them interact was sweet. He seemed to genuinely care about the dogs. There was so much more to Jace than she'd first thought—he was this serious, artsy guy who was a bit lost in his own world. A kind loner. But there was such a genuine base to him. When it seemed like everyone who'd come in and out of Angie's life had carried an ulterior motive, there was Jace with his pure goodness and blunt honesty.

"So no date number two for Elijah?" He tore off a piece of fish and dipped it into a dollop of ketchup.

"Why are you so interested in my dating life?" she asked. "You made it clear you thought I was sending myself on a wild goose chase."

"Can't a friend disagree and *also* be interested?"

"I guess." She tried to concentrate on the salty deliciousness of her meal instead of her own tumultuous feelings. Friend. It was the line between them. "But you think I'm doing the wrong thing."

"I never said that."

"You implied I was being idealistic and setting myself up for failure."

"I don't imply things. I *say* things if I want to say them." He frowned. "But yes, I do think this is a plan that has more chance of failure given the... constraints."

She sighed. "But I *really* don't want to go home. I'm not...the best version of myself there."

It was 100 percent the truth. At home, she was Angela-Marie Donovan. A paranoid woman who always screened her calls and never answered the front door and avoided relationships of any kind and rarely left the house without dark sunglasses and a baseball cap.

Like being a celebrity but without any of the perks.

"Here, I feel more like myself," she added.

The parking lot was up high, and they had an incredible view of the beach. Rocks jutted out of the water, and green vegetation sprawled across the hill, broken only by the wooden path and stairs that allowed people to climb down to the beach below. She watched the ocean roll into the shoreline, the crests crashing into white foam which ran up the sand.

The air was salty and fresh. Crisp, despite the heat.

"There are rock pools down there," Jace said, as if he sensed that she didn't want to talk about serious stuff anymore. For someone who seemed to think people were a foreign species, he was certainly doing a solid job of being a good friend now. "It's low tide now, so you can see the outline of them. They kind of look like honeycomb."

She followed his pointed finger until her eyes caught the interesting pattern along the far edge of the beach.

"We would go swimming in them as kids, but they're full of seaweed." He grinned. "I used to freak Olivia out by grabbing some and trying to tuck it into her bathing suit."

"And here I was thinking you would have been the Goody Two-shoes in the family." A smile curved on her lips, easing some of the tension from her body. "Since you've grown up to be so serious and all."

"Being serious isn't all bad." He munched on a chip, looking content.

It was all too easy to pretend they were a couple in love, coming to the beach with their fur babies. Angie felt a deep tugging in her gut—a longing that called out for her to lean over and kiss the salt crystals from his lips. To run her fingers through his thick, wavy hair. To let him press her down to the bed of the SUV while he devoured her. Consumed her.

Made her feel whole again.

Nope. Unsafe thoughts! Back away. I repeat, back away.

She couldn't waste her precious time lusting after the wrong guy.

. . .

Jace tried to stop his thoughts from cycling out of control—that happened sometimes when he really wanted to say the right thing. Part of him wanted to know more about Angie's date and why it hadn't worked, and part of him never wanted to hear about it again.

What he did know was that he wasn't so good at talking.

It was an aspect of his autism that had always been a struggle, and he never quite knew if his words would make things worse instead of better. But part of it was also that growing up with three brothers meant talking wasn't the way things got sorted out. In fact, more than one time, a discussion had been settled with a furious round of *Mario Kart* instead.

It would be so much easier if he didn't care about Angie's situation—or the way she wanted to fix it.

A small flock of seagulls had gathered around on the ground by their feet. They scuttled back and forth, hoping for food scraps. Angie tossed her remaining few chips to them before scrunching up her parchment paper and tucking it away in the bag it came in.

"You'll have us swarmed if you feed them," he warned.

Tilly lifted her head and started barking, scattering the birds to the wind, but not before they'd gobbled up the chips. Truffle joined in at the last minute, wanting to claim the glory without actually putting in much of the effort. With a slight amount of renewed energy, Tilly started sniffing around Angie.

"No food left," she said, holding up her hands, though her shoulders bunched around her neck.

When Tilly plopped her head in Angie's lap, she glared at Jace. "If she starts growling at me again, I'm going to scream."

"Yeah, she's *so* ferocious." He chuckled as Tilly sighed, nudging her head against Angie's arm. "She wants you to scratch her head."

"I don't think so."

"Oh, come on. She really is harmless. All bark, no bite."

"Jace, she really scares me, okay? I get not everyone is afraid of dogs, but I *am*."

He immediately felt like a jerk. There'd been plenty of occasions where people had dismissed his fears growing up—like that one time he couldn't stand being in the movie theater because it was too damn loud and some teenagers laughed at him—and now he'd done that to her.

Bloody hell. Why couldn't he *see* things like other people did? Why couldn't he read a situation and understand the subtle nuances that other people did? He'd gotten so used to people's words and feelings not matching up that sometimes he didn't listen to the words. He didn't know what he could trust, what aspect of a person was most accurate—was it their eyes, their mouth, their hands? Was it their words or that fluctuating tone of voice that he never got quite right?

"I'm sorry, Angie." He shook his head. "Do you want to go home?"

Please say no.

She sighed. "No, I'm having a good time, but… what if she bites me?"

Maybe this was something he could help Angie with. Because he'd learned in the past few days that dogs were actually *much* easier to read than people.

"You'll be able to tell if she's upset." He reached out to grab her hand but paused. "Can I show you?"

Angie's whisky eyes were big and round. But she nodded, her bottom lip drawn between her teeth. He gently took her hand in his, sucking in a breath at the way the contact made him feel like everything was lighter. Better.

Slowly, he guided her hand to Tilly's head and pressed her palm down, moving it back and forth. The dog seemed to be enjoying the attention, and she let out a big sigh. "See," he said softly. "She's totally relaxed right now."

Usually Jace struggled with eye contact— apparently that was a common thing for people like him. He'd never been too good at looking right into a camera when someone was taking a picture, or maintaining eye contact during a conversation. Right now, however, he couldn't look anywhere but at Angie. It would be so easy to lean in and kiss her, just like he'd wanted to during the movie. Would she tasted as good as she looked? Fire burned through him, the deep pulse of want spreading around his body and settling between his legs.

Making him yearn to pull her close.

"I got bit by a dog when I was little," Angie said. "So they scare me, but I don't hate them."

"How did it happen?"

"One of my foster dads wasn't a very nice man. He had a couple of big dogs and didn't treat them well. I was young, and I was stealing a sausage from the grill. The dog tried to snatch it out of my hand, and I was frightened, so I pulled back, but it got its teeth into me. I had one hell of a Tetanus shot and never went near a dog for years after."

He admired how easily Angie shared things with him. It made him want to open up to her, made him want to explain why he was the way he was. He could tell her why he didn't see that her fear was so sharp, why he wasn't always good at coming up with the perfect response to her questions. He wanted to explain why he was so reluctant to even think about being in a relationship again.

But the beauty of his interactions with Angie was that she *didn't* know about his autism. That she treated him like any other guy. Any other guy who *could* do all the things he couldn't. And if he shared that part of his life with her…what if she pitied him?

He couldn't take it, having someone so strong

and resilient and positive as her pitying him. Making him feel different, even if she didn't mean it. What if things changed, like they did with his ex when she started to focus on his flaws instead of his strengths?

"I understand why you were scared," he said, and the statement made a beautiful smile bloom on her lips.

What if she stopped looking at him like that?

It would be better if he didn't tell her. Let things be the way they were so he could feel normal around her. He liked it that way.

They sat in silence for a while, the heaviness of the dog's slumbered breathing mingling with the slow back and forth *whoosh* of the waves. If only they could stay here forever.

But that wasn't in the cards for him, unfortunately. There would be no forever with Angie, and possibly no forever with anyone. Maybe *Hermit vs. World* would end up being an auto-biographical comic after all. Because if Julia couldn't put up with his quirks, a girl he'd known most of his life, then who would?

"I don't know what I'm going to do," she said softly, almost as if she was speaking to herself. "I've never felt as good as I do here."

Angie had been through so much, and she deserved to be happy.

She won't be happy with you.

What had his mum told him once? Caring for someone meant sometimes putting their needs before your own. Maybe that's what he had to do here—focus less on hating the idea of Angie being with someone else and focus more on what *she* wanted. To fall in love and stay in a country she'd determined was her dream home.

"Maybe you need to do a little more research before you jump into the next date," he said eventually. That was how he usually dealt with big decisions—gather as much information as possible first. "Try and figure out *before* if there's likely to be any chemistry."

"Research?" She wrinkled her nose. "How would I do that?"

"See if you can observe them. Maybe interact with them in a way that's causal before suggesting a date?" He shrugged.

"Is that what you would do?"

"I wouldn't do anything because I'm perfectly happy being on my own," he replied, scratching Tilly behind the ear. It had been true at one point, but now he wasn't so sure. Since Angie had barreled into his life, he didn't usually have whole days where he avoided talking to another human being anymore. A year ago, there was no way he would have blown off his preplanned meal to have fish and chips. But she'd made him want something different. "But we're talking about you, right?"

"Right." She nodded. "Research. I don't suppose you feel like accompanying me on a field trip?"

His gut reaction was a resounding *no* in flashing neon. But maybe this was exactly what he needed to get over this strange hold that Angie had on him—maybe seeing her happy with someone else would be the catalyst he needed to move on. To forget about the idea of a relationship, because he wasn't sure he ever needed to go through the pain of rejection again.

So, in a way, helping her would also be like helping himself.

"Sure." The word popped out, and he immediately wanted to snatch it back.

But now that it had been said, there was no taking it back. A promise was a promise. Talk about wading into the fuzzy gray. He was so *not* qualified to do this.

And there was only one way it could end: He was going to have to set up the woman he'd almost kissed…with some other lucky bastard.

CHAPTER TWELVE

Jace tilted his eyes up to the ceiling of the Bright Bluff Café, where funky Edison bulbs dangled next to clusters of potted plants. Exposed beams gave the space a barnlike feel, and everything was painted a crisp, clear white. It was all so neat and orderly…just like his life used to be.

Instead of working, which was what he should be doing at eleven a.m. on a Wednesday, he was here…stalking some poor, unsuspecting guy. He'd spent a good fifteen minutes before leaving the house rearranging his daily schedule to ensure that he could still get in the requisite number of work hours.

Angie came back to their table with two coffees in hand—a flat white for her and a long black for him. "Any sign of our target?"

"Can we please not call him a target? It sounds like we're about to put a hit on him," Jace said dryly.

Why had he agreed to help on Angie's ridiculous mission? Oh, because he had a moment of personal crisis and decided the best way to "get over" his crush on his annoyingly sexy tenant was to help her find a man.

Maybe it's also the fact that having Angie here is what you want, even if it means she's dating someone else?

"Sorry." She laughed. "Any sight of our…

research subject?"

Now it made the guy sound like a lab rat. "He was there a minute ago and his laptop is still sitting at the bar. Maybe he went to the men's room?"

The lab rat in question was Theo Hasikos, thirty-two, tech start-up whiz. Named one of Patterson's Bluff's biggest success stories. He'd come from little—with a family who'd struggled to make ends meet after immigrating from Cyprus—only to sell his first software creation at age sixteen. He paid off the family's mortgage at twenty-one, and now he was working on some top secret project that had tongues wagging all over town. Unlike a lot of people who found success in business, he hadn't left his town behind for greener pastures.

Jace knew him in passing, enough to know that he worked from the Bright Bluff Café every Wednesday morning without fail. Jace had seen him here a few times when he'd stopped in for a coffee if he was having a particularly hard time with *Hermit vs. World*.

"Thanks for doing this," Angie said. "I didn't want to sit here all morning by myself like a creep."

"Always better to creep in pairs, right?" he quipped.

She snorted and took a sip of her coffee. "Smart-ass."

"What exactly are you looking for with these guys?" he asked, his eyes lingering on the front door, which tinkled with a tiny bell each time a customer came or went. "Other than a fast track to marriage."

"The same thing anyone wants in a relationship. Someone they can trust, someone who makes them feel good about themselves. Someone who makes them feel alive."

"I never understood that. Isn't the fact we're all breathing enough to make us feel alive?"

Whenever he used to say things like this to Julia, she would roll her eyes and call him an emotionless robot. But he was genuinely curious. This mythical "alive" feeling that people chased was put in the same confounding bucket as the fact that people talked about wanting to "find" themselves.

It didn't make a lick of sense.

Angie cocked her head. "It's not really as literal as that. It's more... How should I put it? You know that feeling you get when you meet someone who truly understands you? When you don't have to explain yourself all the time? They just...see you, all the good bits and the bad bits, and they accept it all."

Jace wasn't sure he'd ever experienced that. People were always a bit confused by him—by his need for solitude and privacy. By his need for schedules. His general cluelessness and advanced ability to generate awkward moments. Oh, and the fact that he wasn't inspired by any ridiculous motivational sayings that skirted the edge of logic.

"You come from such a loving family, it's probably not something you've had to deal with," she said, dumping a little sugar into her coffee and wading her spoon through the frothy layer on top. "I always felt like a misfit growing up. Like I didn't belong. I want someone who makes me feel like I *do* belong, like I'm wanted and cherished. And I want to be able to give him that feeling, too."

His chest tightened. So feeling alive was feeling wanted and understood. That was something he could get behind. But before he could respond, a familiar figure walked through from the back of the café and took a seat at the spot with the laptop.

"The eagle has landed," Jace said, stifling a laugh as he picked up his coffee. "I repeat, the eagle has landed."

"I never knew you were such a joker." Angie's gaze shifted to the bar, where Theo Hasikos sat by the espresso machine. Without him even having to ask, a coffee materialized in front of him, and his empty cup was whisked away. "Okay, research mode engaged."

"What are we going to do, watch him work all morning?"

"I want to see what he does, how he talks to people." Her eyes were still trained on Theo's back, and Jace shifted in his seat. He wanted her eyes back on him; he wanted that sunshine gaze making him warm on the inside. "You can learn a lot about a person by the way they speak to serving staff."

"And how are you going to tell if there's chemistry?"

She lifted one shoulder in a cheeky shrug. "I'll

have to make an excuse to go talk to him."

"Is this how people date?"

"No idea. I haven't been on a date in years before yesterday's disaster." Angie chuckled. "I am woefully inexperienced."

"Yeah, me too."

Why on earth did you tell her that? This isn't about you.

He leaned back in his chair and let his gaze drift around the café. There was a big table with five women and about as many small children. Another table held two women wearing the uniform of one of the local banks. There were several lone coffee drinkers, all with laptops set up in front of them. Free Wi-Fi tended to attract people with work to do who were looking for a change of scenery.

Theo chatted with the female barista. Jace had seen her the last few times he'd dropped in; she was a newer resident. Looking to make friends and fit in, like Angie. If he wasn't mistaken, her name was Felicity.

"When was the last time you went on a date?" Angie asked.

"Define date." Yeah, stalling was not going to work for this conversation. This would give her further proof that Jace was definitely not the kind of guy to put on her list. Not that she needed proof, mind you. She'd outright told him she wouldn't be knocking down his door to change his mind about marriage the night of the twilight party.

But that was before the almost kiss.

God, his subconscious was such a pain in the ass sometimes.

"Two adults going out with the purpose of getting to know each other in the hopes it might turn into something romantic." She narrowed her eyes at him. "How else would I define it? Unless you happen to be more of a casual-sex kind of guy."

Ha! If that wasn't the world's biggest joke, he didn't know what was. Most guys his age would have been happy to screw their way around the coast, but that wasn't Jace's style. Never had been. Until the Julia fiasco, he'd thought himself a relationship guy. Turned out that wasn't him, either.

So what did you call a guy who didn't want to sleep around but wasn't looking for a relationship?

Painfully celibate.

"It's been a while." He raked a hand through his hair, wanting to avoid the intense curiosity radiating off Angie while she looked at him. She appeared to have forgotten all about Theo. "I don't really date."

"But you've been in a relationship before?"

"Yeah, once."

"How long did it last?"

Too long. "Eight years."

Angie blinked. Clearly that wasn't the answer she'd anticipated. "Whoa. That's a serious long-term relationship."

If only she knew. He'd had the tux, the diamond, the vows written in his neat handwriting that were more personal than anything he'd ever

shared in his whole entire life. He'd known love…
at least he'd thought so at the time.

"Theo's leaving." Jace caught sight of Theo
packing up his things, a takeaway coffee cup in
hand. Saved by the bell! "That was quick."

"Should we follow him?"

"Doesn't that seem a little stalker-ish?"

Angie bit down on her lip. Her eyes sparkled,
and she drained half her coffee in one long swig.
"So long as we're outside, it's a public place,
right?"

Anything to stop the discussion about his own
dating habits. "Sounds legal to me."

He knocked his own coffee back and pushed
up from his chair. They made it out the front door
a few seconds after Theo, in time to see him round
a corner. "I feel like I should be wearing a fake
mustache and hiding behind a newspaper."

"Or we could be dressed like shrubs. That's
how they do it in *Scooby-Doo*." Angie grinned
and grabbed his hand, pulling him along. There
was laughter in her voice and in her eyes, and
damn if he wasn't having fun himself. Only she
could convince him to go on such a silly adventure
and make him actually enjoy himself.

They hurried along, keeping a few paces
behind the unsuspecting Theo. They walked past
the bank, past the Wattle & Oat bakery, past
the gourmet grocery store run by Mr. and Mrs.
Giannopoulos. Where was Theo going?

The street thinned out—bustling shop fronts
giving way to residential buildings. The houses
here were small and square, like a child's drawing

of a house. Two windows, triangle for a roof.

"If he turns around, he's going to see us," Jace said. "How far do you want to follow him?"

"A little longer. I know he's not going home, because he lives off Ocean View Drive." Angie chuckled when Jace raised a brow. "What? It's a fancy house, and it stands out. Everybody knows where everybody lives around here."

It was true. Patterson's Bluff was a typical Aussie coastal town—beautiful views, zero privacy.

"Wait, it looks like he's stopping." Angie laid a hand on Jace's arm.

Theo paused in front of a little place that was charming, if a little in need of some TLC. Peeling paint and cracked steps showed the property's age. But it had been decorated with cheerful pots of flowers and a funny statue of a gnome. He opened his satchel and pulled out an envelope. It wasn't a business envelope, more like the kind that would contain a card, since it was red and large. He slipped the envelope into the mailbox and then turned around, causing Jace and Angie to hurry along as though they hadn't been watching. But Theo didn't even seem to notice them.

"It would be bad of me to snoop, wouldn't it?" Angie said, her mischievous eyes glowing bright. "For research purposes, of course."

"Stealing people's mail is a crime."

"But it's not a crime to look, is it?" She waited until the coast was clear, and then she scuttled over to the mailbox like some giddy schoolgirl.

"Keep a look out."

Rolling his eyes, Jace awkwardly kept watch. What the hell was he supposed to do if someone came past? Flap his arms and create a diversion?

Angie peered into the mailbox and tried to angle her head to see better. After a moment, she stood up. "Who's Felicity?"

"The barista at Bright Bluff Café." He sighed. "Now I know why he goes there so often. She was working today."

Jace would bet his last ten dollars that it was Felicity's regular shift. Theo Hasikos was writing love letters.

"I can't very well chase a guy who's in love with someone else," Angie said with a sigh.

"It could be anything. Maybe it's her birthday?"

"Then why not give her the card in person if he just saw her?" She shook her head. "I know a secret crush when I see one. I have to strike him off the list."

Two down. Both Theo and Elijah were cut. "Who's next?"

Angie shifted on the spot and wouldn't meet his eyes. The evasion made him suddenly nervous, like intuition had wrapped a cold hand around his heart. There weren't *that* many eligible bachelors in Patterson's Bluff. Not the kind of guys who were the settling-down type anyway.

"Angie? Who's next?"

"I don't know." Her big whisky brown eyes tilted up to his, and it was like a fist to his solar plexus. "Well…your brother seemed interested when he invited me to the twilight party."

Shit. What the hell was he supposed to say to that?

Bloody Trent. He loved his brother, he really did. But the guy seemed destined to get anything that Jace wanted for himself…without even trying. That was possibly the worst part about it—there wasn't a bad bone in Trent's body. Every time he won, it was without any sweat. *Everybody* loved him. Old ladies, babies, animals of all descriptions. Hell, even the mean old cat that lived down the street had loved Trent when they were growing up.

But how would things fare for Angie? Her affections would be returned, of course. But not in the way she wanted. Not in the way she *needed*. Trent wasn't really the settling-down kind. He was all about living life to the max, and enjoying every moment like it was his last, and whatever other crap was likely to be printed on the side of an energy drink.

That didn't include a committed relationship and speedy trip down the aisle.

And if Trent screwed her around, promising more than he was willing to give…then what? He'd have to stop talking to his own brother, be exiled from the family, become the town pariah, and live out the rest of his days with his cacti.

A sick feeling settled in his stomach. He couldn't let the two of them get together—it was a disaster waiting to happen. But what was the alternative? She had six weeks to go. Who the heck fell in love and got married that quickly?

Nobody.

"We should change the subject," Angie said. The air felt as though it had thickened around them—filled with the kind of tension that was like an itch in a hard-to-reach place.

It burrowed under his skin. Jace's mind spun as he searched for a safe topic.

"So, uh…we've got a celebration next week." He kept his gaze ahead of him, trying to make sure he didn't give too much away to Angie. If she really *was* interested in his brother, then he had to keep his jealousy to himself. No way would he let her see it. "It's the last weekend before school starts."

"What's the significance of that?"

"Well, one, it's a long weekend. But two, it's something that we've always celebrated as a family. Like one last hurrah before 'real life' starts again."

"Enjoying summer until the very last bit." Angie smiled. "Very Australian. What do you usually do?"

"Catch some sun, drink beer, and have a barbecue. Then we play backyard sports because my brothers can't handle a day without some kind of competition."

"Sounds fun. So it's a family thing?"

Hmm. An innocent question, or was this all about her scoring an invite so she could hang out with Trent?

Wow, cynical. Maybe she doesn't want to spend a long weekend on her own? Don't be an asshole.

"Would you like to join us?" he asked. "We get the whole family together at my parents' house every year. It's a tradition."

Was it his imagination or did she blush at the last part about the "whole family" being there? "I don't want to impose."

"You've met my family, right? Open-door policy."

She laughed. "Your parents are always taking in strays."

"You're not a stray, Angie." He hated her thinking of herself that way. "And you're officially invited."

The smile that lit up her face could have powered a rocket to the moon. "Really?"

"Absolutely. It's a Walters rule—nobody is allowed to be left out."

She nudged him gently with her elbow. "Thank you."

"For what?"

She looked at him for a long moment, as if thinking carefully about what she wanted to say next. "For being you."

As they walked home, he thought about the plans for the long weekend. Maybe it would be good for Angie to come and spend more time with Trent, and then she would see for herself that they weren't a good match.

Either that, or she'd fall totally head over heels, and his invite would blow up in his face.

CHAPTER THIRTEEN

The last weekend of summer seemed to have a few traditions associated with it, at least in the Walters family. Of course, there was a barbecue involved—although Angie learned pretty quickly after arriving in Australia that "throwing a shrimp on the barbie" wasn't a thing, because Australians didn't use the word "shrimp."

They called them "prawns."

Unsure what to wear, Angie had thrown on a pair of denim shorts and a T-shirt she'd picked up while traveling earlier in her trip. It was pale blue and had a sun printed across the front, which felt very on theme. Now she was walking down the street toward Jace's parents' house. He'd gone over earlier with the dogs to help set up for the day's festivities.

And while he'd said his parents had an open-door policy, she wondered for a moment if maybe she was intruding. But hanging out with Jace's big, lovable family was the kind of thing she'd been chasing since forever. She couldn't pass it up.

Or should that be Trent's *big, lovable family?*

Everything was so tangled up. *Why* had she even said that to Jace? It wasn't like Trent really did anything for her. But part of her had wanted to see how he'd react—would he crack and admit that he was attracted to her? She'd been *sure* he would kiss her and then…poof! The man gave enough mixed signals for a Katy Perry song.

Sucking in a breath, she headed up to the front door and pushed the doorbell. There was a commotion inside—dogs barking and people laughing and music playing and feet running around. A second later, the door swung open, and Angie was greeted by Olivia, Jace's younger sister.

"Hello! Welcome to the Walters family home." Olivia gave her a quick squeeze. Like the rest of the Walters siblings, she had bright-blue eyes and tanned skin. Only her hair was darker than her brothers'. "I was so happy when Jace mentioned you were coming! It's always nice to have another woman in this house, helps even out the testosterone a bit."

This was exactly what she loved about Jace's family—how kind and open they were. They would have done this for anyone, because whoever came into their home was considered one of them.

"Mum usually picks up a few things each year from the Reject Shop to make us laugh. One year we had this giant inflatable beach ball, but we thought that might scare the dogs. Oh, and she always bakes something amazing." Olivia accompanied Angie through the house. "This year she outdid herself."

The house was totally empty, but a big sliding door led out to a huge yard. Jace's dad, Frank, and his oldest brother Adam stood by the grill. His mother, Melanie, was fussing with the table settings, while Nick and Jace chatted off to the side. Trent was playing with Truffle, tossing around a yellow tennis ball that was almost too big to fit in the little dog's mouth. Not that it stopped him trying, mind you.

"Have you met Soraya before?" Olivia asked.

"I don't think so."

Olivia waved Soraya over. "Hi, Angie. Nice to meet you."

Soraya was married to Adam, and they were the most adorable couple ever — university sweethearts and business partners. They ran Bluff View Inn, a gorgeous little bed-and-breakfast on the edge of the town. She was stunning. Tall, with deep olive skin, dark eyes, and long black hair that was swept back into a full ponytail.

"Thanks for including me. It really means a lot." Angie wished she'd brought some food or a bottle of wine along, but she'd been under strict instructions not to bring anything.

"Angie!" Mrs. Walters came over and bundled her up in a big hug.

If dictionaries had pictures, Mrs. Walters would be smiling next to the definition of "mother." She was warm, affectionate, and always fussed over people like she was a hen taking care of her chicks.

"We're so happy to see you, love." Mrs. Walters pulled back and then ushered Angie over to the table. "Grab a drink from the Esky. We've got beer, soft drink, or sparkling water. There's a bottle of white open on the table. And don't forget the sunscreen — it's blistering today, and we don't want any sunburned noses!"

"Jeez, Mum. She's not a little kid." Olivia

rolled her eyes. "I think she knows how the sun works."

"Well, we have a great big hole in the ozone layer here. Everybody could do with the reminder." Mrs. Walters shot her daughter a look. "Especially you, Miss Sun Bunny."

Angie caught Jace's eye across the yard, and she held up her hand in greeting. His face went from serious to something much warmer and more open when he waved back. Seeing him change like that—knowing she'd caused the smile that seemed to be rare for him—made something shift in her chest.

"You know, it's been a million years since my brother brought a friend over," Olivia said. "Now suddenly he's going to twilight parties, too. I could barely believe it!"

"He did. *And* he killed it at beach cricket."

"You're a good influence," Soraya said. "He really went into his shell after Julia."

Angie racked her brain, but the name didn't sound familiar. Not that Jace had ever talked about his dating life other than the single piece of information he'd shared about dating someone for eight years. Was Julia the woman he'd been with for *eight years*?

Curiosity niggled at her. It was his business, and she really shouldn't pry…

"Julia?" Angie asked, innocently.

So much for not prying.

Olivia and Soraya exchanged looks. Then Olivia reached for a beer nestled in ice and popped it open before handing it to Angie—as if the story might require a drink to wash it down. That wasn't a good sign.

Soraya clasped her hands together tightly. "Julia was Jace's fiancée."

Fiancée? Holy moly, *that* was a surprise. "I had no idea he was engaged."

"Yeah, it, uh…it didn't end well." Olivia snorted and reached for a beer for herself. She offered one to Soraya, but she shook her head. "Understatement of the year. Julia wasn't right for Jace. She didn't appreciate him for how awesome he is because she was too busy trying to turn him into someone else. Like he's not already great *exactly* the way he is."

"It was so sad," Soraya continued quietly. "He really cared about her."

"We thought she cared about him, too, until it turned out that Julia was a complete heartless monster." The anger radiating from Olivia was fresh, as if the breakup had only just happened. She took a swig of her drink. "I mean, who leaves their partner hanging at a wedding rehearsal dinner? Well, she's gone now, and good riddance, too. If I never see her again it'll be too soon."

Angie blinked. The story was so much worse than she'd imagined. "She just…left?"

"Yep." Olivia shook her head. She looked as though she wanted to say more, but the guys were headed over, so the conversation was quickly switched to the day's festivities.

Seeing the brothers all in one place, it was no wonder Chloe made a joke about the hotness genes running strong in this family. While they each had their own separate and unique look—there was no denying a family full of strong jaws, cut bodies, and tanned skin was something to be admired.

"Our guest of honor has arrived." Trent made the statement loudly. "I hope you're prepared for battle."

"Battle?" Angie widened her eyes. What had she gotten herself into?

Trent leaned in and gave her a hug. He smelled like wood smoke and the ocean, and it was a pleasing combination. But there wasn't even the barest hint of a spark from the physical touch.

When Angie caught Jace's gaze, he immediately looked down at his phone.

"Today's festivities include: a traditional Walters family feast cooked by the fastest man on a grill this side of the country." Trent pointed to his father. The older man laughed and raised his drink in salute. "Then a treacherous water gun fight. And yes, it's a battle. To the death."

"To the death, huh? Sounds intimidating," Angie said with a laugh.

"Some members of this family can be a little… competitive." Soraya looked up at her husband with a saccharine smile.

"A little?" Adam brushed the hair back from her forehead and looked utterly smitten. "How dare you insult my family name like that."

Soraya wriggled out of his grip and went to help Mr. Walters bring the delicious-smelling meat and char-grilled veggies to the table. "I was trying to be polite. What I should have said was the competitive nature is hard-coded into your family DNA."

Adam nodded. "Better."

"Following the water gun fight, there will be dessert. Mum makes a cake every year, and we're under threat of banishment if we peek before the big reveal. But there will also be fruit, pav, and *nammoura*, which is possibly the best thing I've ever eaten." Trent nodded.

"It's a really sweet cake with syrup," Soraya explained. "I use my mum's recipe."

"Then most of us young folk generally head to a house party afterward while Dad snores on the couch," Nick added.

"I heard that." Mr. Walters made a huffing sound. He was still in his apron and carrying a large platter of deliciously grilled veggie skewers. "I need my rest after doing all the bloody work around here."

"Don't let Mum hear you say that," Olivia said, herding everyone toward the table. "Or there won't be cake for anyone."

Angie got a crash course in Walters family politics when it came to the seating order at the big outdoor table. The dogs were put inside with their own tasty treats so everyone could have a break from Truffle's food scavenging. Angie ended up being seated between Jace and Trent, which felt like some kind of middle finger from the universe.

There was no pausing when the family sat down. Immediately, plates were passed around and food doled out in generous quantities—the boys ate like horses, piling their plates high. The second Angie bit down into one of the lamb chops she knew why—the taste was rich and savory. The perfect amount of char-grilled sharpness mixed with the delicious, tender meat.

"I think I've died and gone to heaven," she said through a mouthful.

Frank pressed a hand to his heart. "You're welcome back *anytime,* dear."

She indulged in plenty of grilled prawns, some *kibbeh* that Soraya had made, Olivia's favorite watermelon and feta salad, and sausages purchased from a local farm. It might have been the best meal she'd ever eaten.

The conversation was loud, jokes flying back and forth. Angie didn't understand them all, since it was clear this family had their own language. They were tight-knit, closer than any family she'd ever seen. God, what must it have been like growing up with so much love, it felt like her heart might burst from witnessing it?

"You're so lucky," she said to Jace as she paused after inhaling her lamb. "Your family is… perfect."

"I wouldn't say perfect," he replied with a dry laugh. "But I think I'll keep them."

"Oh yeah, what's not to love? Everybody's joking and smiling; the food is good. The weather is perfect. You're all ridiculously good-looking."

Jace raised an eyebrow. "Did you just call me good-looking?"

Yeah, oops. "You all are. There's some A-plus genetics here. Your parents should be proud."

"Ah. So it's a scientific observation, then?" He reached forward and grabbed the water, which had pieces of pineapple and cucumber bobbing in it, and refilled her glass like a true gentleman. "Nothing personal?"

Why on earth was he asking her *that*? Did he really want to know if she found him attractive? What purpose would that serve?

"I guess all taste is personal." She dropped her gaze back down to her plate, unsure what to say next.

"I'm still trying to figure yours out." Jace sliced into a big hunk of red onion that had been blackened around its edges.

"What do you mean?"

"Elijah, Theo…others." He left his brother's name off the list, but Angie caught his meaning. Jace was speaking low enough that only she would hear, but Angie had no idea why he'd decided now was the time to have this conversation. Beer confidence, maybe? "What do they have in common?"

"They're good people." The words stuck in her throat, and she found her face feeling a little warmer than it had a moment ago. "They're attractive."

"Not exactly a high bar."

Should she be insulted by that statement? It was delivered in Jace's standard way—as an unemotional fact. Bare bones honesty. Before she could respond, Angie felt a gentle pressure at her right arm. Trent was leaning over. "What are you two talking about? If I have to listen to Olivia crapping on about how good city life is, I'm going to throw her on the barbecue next."

Jace muttered something under his breath and went back to his meal.

"Someone's in a mood today," Trent said. "He's probably pissed because I called dibs on you."

Angie's eyebrows shot up, and she almost choked on her lettuce. "Excuse me?"

"For the water gun fight. I want you on my team." He grinned. Whereas Jace's grin was always delightfully crooked, Trent had the kind of smile that was so bright, it should be accompanied by its own *ping* sound effect. "Nick and I are team captains, and we've already squabbled over everyone. Jace is on the losing side, I'm afraid."

"You know nothing about my water gun fight abilities. I might be a terrible shot." Angie sipped her drink. "For all you know, you might be better off with Truffle."

"Oh, I didn't even think of that." Trent snapped his fingers at Nick across the table. "Dibs on the little dog!"

"We're *not* putting the dogs in the water gun fight." Jace shook his head. "I'm responsible for those animals, and I'm going to take them home in one piece."

His devotion to the role of doggy dad was adorable.

But Trent winked at Angie. "He never said he was going to take them home *dry*…"

"You're bad." She shot him a look, but Trent was unabashed in his mischief-making.

"Bad is fun, don't you think?" A lock of

golden hair flopped over his forehead, and Angie now understood the full extent of Jace's comments the night of the twilight party. Trent knew *exactly* how good-looking he was, and he'd honed his flirting skills to a professional degree. "Mum and Dad used up all their serious parenting with Adam, Nick and Jace, and by the time they had me, they'd given up."

"I doubt that."

"True story. Once, they went out to a restaurant when I was a baby, and they were so preoccupied with the other kids that they left me in my carrier under the table and got all the way to the car before they remembered I was still inside."

Angie clamped a hand over her mouth. "Oh no."

"Don't you tell her horrible stories about us," Mrs. Walters said from across the table, her cheeks pink. She had a glass of wine in one hand and pressed her other hand to her face in embarrassment. "That was one time, and I've never gotten over the guilt."

"Oh yeah, what about the time at the Royal Melbourne Show? You came back from the Bertie Beetle stand with three show bags instead of four."

His mother shot him a look across the table and then turned to Angie. "We are not horrible parents, despite what he says."

"You're certainly not. I would have killed to have a family like this growing up."

The words slipped out before she could think too much about them, and she wanted to slap herself for being so stupid. Crap. The whole table was looking at her now, like they expected some kind of explanation.

"I…" She shook her head, her brain refusing to get into gear and give her a solution.

"I'm sure being an only child would have its perks." Jace saved the day.

"Yes, that's right. No siblings for me, sadly. No big family occasions." She wanted to sigh in relief, but instead she mouthed a subtle "thank-you" once the conversation had resumed.

She really needed to be more careful. One Google search would illuminate everything she'd been trying to hide. She'd go back to being a freak show. A conversation piece. A morsel of gossip.

And there was no way she could let herself be that ever again.

CHAPTER FOURTEEN

Jace had hoped Trent's competitive nature and ability to dominate the conversation would be a turnoff for Angie. But instead, she'd giggled at his stories all through lunch, and they now appeared to be discussing strategies for the water gun fight, heads bowed and arms touching.

"Hey. Eyes over here." Nick waved a water pistol in front of him. "Time to get your head in the game, Red Team."

Their team consisted of Nick, Jace, Olivia, and their dad. Soraya was sitting the fight out so the teams could be even and also because she was a much better referee than she was at any competitive sport. The water guns—which ranged in size from smaller pistols to larger models— were filled with water and natural food coloring.

Everyone had changed into the white T-shirts Melanie had picked up, so any shots they received would be captured. The food dye would color the T-shirt, and at the end of a frantic ten-minute fight, Soraya would judge which team had taken the most shots.

"Mum went all out this year," Olivia said with a laugh. "I love how she gets so into it."

"Try being married to her," Frank grumbled, his mustache bobbing up and down. "She's a sore loser."

"We *want* you to be sleeping on the couch

tonight." Nick slapped his hand down on his father's back. "Winning is our goal."

Jace's eyes drifted back over to the blue team for a minute, where Trent was helping Angie aim her gun. His hands were on hers, and they were both laughing. If he were any more in her space, he'd be dry humping her in front of everyone.

"Jace! Man, can you pay attention for, like, five minutes?" Nick had on his *I must be number one* face. The whole family might be competitive, but Nick made the rest of them look like amateurs. "Okay, so we need to be strategic about this. How are the others likely to play it?"

"Trent will go in all guns blazing…pun most *definitely* intended." Olivia grinned. "But that will leave him open. I reckon Mum will be sneakier and so will Adam. Not sure about Angie; she's the dark horse in this race."

"What does our resident Angie expert say?" Nick turned to Jace.

"Since when am I the Angie expert?"

"You know her better than anyone here. How do you think she'll play it?"

Jace thought for a minute. "She's chaos. She loves the fun of things, so I think she'll run in and get right into the middle. No worry for her own safety."

That was how she was with a lot of things—jumping in with two feet. Not thinking about the consequences. Hell, if she was chasing after Trent, then that's *exactly* what she was doing.

"Right. So we'll want to position two people with some cover. You can try to get a few shots in from behind the trees back there." Nick gestured with his pistol to farther down the massive yard. "Jace and Olivia, you guys can do that. Dad and I will stay up here. There's less cover, but we'll be able to soak them when they come up from behind the shed."

"Got it." Olivia nodded.

Everyone broke away into their positions as Soraya got out of her seat and blew the "official" ref's whistle. "Two minutes, and then the timer starts."

From Jace's vantage point behind the Grevilleas, he watched Angie and Trent sneaking behind the shed. He was starting to wonder why he'd invited her here today.

Because you wanted to see her.

It was true. In fact, there hadn't been a day go past in the last week where he hadn't thought about Angie. He'd spent time thinking about when he was going to see her next, whether he could make up an excuse to drop by.

But then he'd opened his big fat mouth and agreed to help her. And why? Because he was too scared to go after what he wanted? Too worried she'd eventually reject him?

You know she will.

Of course he knew it. She wanted all the things he didn't…or rather, she *needed* what he was trying to avoid: commitment. Marriage. Their goals didn't align.

Because even if she knew all his idiosyncrasies and thought they were adorable now…he knew from experience that eventually she would find him frustrating and too rigid. And she would leave. He wasn't sure he had it in him to deal with that a second time. Change was tough for him. And losing someone after being with her for so long was one way to take his need for stability and rip it to shreds.

"I saw Angie and Trent go back there, and Mum is skulking around by the barbecue." Olivia had her back pressed to the tree and her water gun up by her chest like she was some kind of Jason Bourne. "Did you see Adam?"

"No."

"Too busy mooning over Angie?"

Jace's eyes snapped up to his sister's cheeky face. "What?"

"You've been giving her puppy-dog eyes all afternoon. If she hasn't noticed it, then I'll be sending her straight to Dr. Holt to get her eyes checked."

"You're full of it." Jace huffed.

"Nope. *You're* acting like a thirteen-year-old boy." Olivia jabbed him with her water gun.

Great. The last thing he needed was his family speculating on his love life. After the whole Julia debacle, he should have known they were biding their time for someone else to come along. Never mind the fact that nobody seemed to worry about Nick or Trent being single. But oh no, because Jace the Introvert wasn't banging his way around town, then he must need help to change his life.

"Liv," he warned. "I don't want to hear it."

"Why not? You can't stay locked up in your house forever. Just because—"

"I said *enough*."

Olivia blinked at him, taken aback by the harsh tone. "Wow. No need to get your jocks in a bunch. I was only saying—"

"How about everyone stops talking about me, huh? I'm perfectly happy living my life the way *I* want to live it." He took a breath to calm the frustration racing through his veins. He felt like a dick; it wasn't his sister's fault. Wrong place, wrong time and all that.

"You're happy being alone, are you? I get being single, trust me. But until recently I felt like we barely even got to see you anymore." Her blue eyes were brimming with worry. "You were starting to become like the character in your comics."

Before Jace had the chance to retort, Soraya blew her whistle and announced the game's ten-minute timer had started. Olivia shot him a look that said their conversation most definitely wasn't over. Peeking around the side of the tree, Jace could see his mother skirting the fence.

"I think Adam is up around the house," Olivia said. "I'm going to sneak past the table and try to catch him from behind."

Jace nodded. "I'll stay low and take the shed."

"Of course you will." She smirked. "See you on the other side."

Leaving the shelter of the tree, Jace crouched and followed a line of shrubs along the back of the garden. The shed sat in the other corner, and there was quite a bit of bare space to cross. From the other side of the yard, there was a shriek and laughter and Adam and his mum open fired on each other. The once-pristine white T-shirts were now streaked with watery lines of red and blue.

The hot sun beat down relentlessly, and sweat beaded along Jace's spine. In true Australian summer fashion, the day had started warm and was steadily progressing toward the fiery depths of hell. A few more minutes outside, and he'd welcome an encounter with a water gun. Hell, at this rate he might shoot himself.

"Hands up, sucker." Angie had her gun trained on him as she came creeping out from behind the shed. Her lips were curled up into a wide grin, and it looked like she was having a hell of a time. "I could hear those big feet coming a mile away."

"Big feet?" Jace stretched to his full height and brought his pistol up to face her. "That's no way to speak to your landlord."

"Oh, so it's landlord now? I see, *that's* how you want to play this."

"Makes it easier to shoot if there are no personal ties."

Angie laughed, and the sound ran like glitter through his veins. "You're a coldhearted man, Jace Walters."

"That's Mr. Walters to you." He couldn't keep a straight face for too long. Something about the water guns and the hot sun and Angie's smile had him feeling…calm—like she didn't make him want to be alone. At least maybe not always.

Sure, he needed his alone time. Time to think and process. Time to come back down to earth when the outside world got a little too much.

But that was the weird thing about Angie: being around her was like standing in the eye of a hurricane. There was a small space of calm in the swirling chaos. She made everything in the outside world fade away, leaving only them.

"Then prepare to eat my watery bullets, *Mr. Walters*." She raised her gun a little higher, both feet planted firmly on the ground.

They both fired at once. Streams of red- and blue-tinged water shot out, and Jace tried to twist away, but she managed to get him on the right shoulder and across the side of his rib cage. The cold water was a pleasant kiss of relief from the heat. Angie turned and ran back behind the shed. Grinning, Jace followed her, gun aimed in front of him.

But he was ambushed by Trent, his T-shirt quickly turning blue as the food dye spread. "You're going down, big brother."

Jace managed to hold his own, soaking Angie and Trent as much as he could while having the two of them on him. "Man down!"

His father appeared, a bandanna wrapped around his head Rambo-style. "Say hello to my little friend."

Trent made a break for it, but Angie got caught in the cross fire. Her shriek cut through the yard as she was cornered, thoroughly soaked and looking like she was loving every minute of it. The shenanigans went on for several more minutes as Jace jogged back out into the yard and rescued Olivia from Trent and Adam.

The fight went on until everyone was mostly

out of "ammo," and then eventually Soraya blew the whistle. "That's ten minutes!"

How could it only have been ten minutes? It had felt like hours. Everyone was laughing and slapping one another on the back. When was the last time he'd had so much fun with his family? Last year, he'd left early to go back to work. He'd skipped Adam and Soraya's annual Boxing Day bash because of a deadline, too. And he'd declined family dinners left and right, because sometimes the thought of having to answer everyone's questions about where he'd been was just…too much.

But now he saw what he'd been missing out on. Angie was right—he *was* lucky. More fortunate than so many people who were estranged from their families or had parents who brought them down. What's the worst thing he could say about his parents? That they forced dog-sitting on him? That they wanted to spend time with him?

A guilty little lump settled in the back of his throat.

But that guilty little lump promptly vanished when the entire family went silent for a heartbeat. The Walters family was *never* quiet. Not without a very good reason.

"Oh my God." Soraya clamped her hand over her mouth, and all heads swung in the direction of the back door.

Jace blinked. What on earth…?

Truffle trotted happily toward the group, totally unaware that he'd caused the entire family to come to a standstill.

"What the fuck?" Jace rushed forward to pick up the little dog, whose fur was damp.

And hot freaking *pink*.

"Oh no." Jace's mother clamped her hands down on either side of her face. "The extra dyed water...I left it sitting on the breakfast bar. But how...?"

"What exactly is in the dye?" His brain spun like a tire in mud—what if it contained something harmful? What if the dog went into toxic shock? Or what if he couldn't be cleaned?

What if he'd dyed Eugenie's dog forever?

"It's natural food dye. Organic. I knew the dogs were coming, so I picked something safe in case they got in the way of the fight."

"Or in case they decided to take a bath in it." Nick snorted.

"This isn't funny," Jace said, turning the dog around to inspect him. Every damn inch of him was pink—from the tip of his tail, down each of his four spindly legs, to his pointed, bat-like ears. "I'm supposed to be taking care of him."

"He's fine." Adam waved a hand. "You've... decorated him."

"I'd better check the kitchen," his mother said. "Where's Tilly?"

As if on cue, the older dog came out to the backyard, tail wagging and a bucket in her mouth. Given there was pink water sloshing out the side of it, Jace was pretty sure the mystery of the pink dog had been solved. Tilly had probably found something on the bench, so she jumped up and knocked the bucket over, drenching and dyeing the unsuspecting Truffle.

"And I was thinking a minute ago how I should come around here more often," Jace muttered.

Angie came to his side. "We'll get him cleaned up—it'll be fine. Come on, we'll do it now before the dye sits on there too long and hopefully it won't stain his skin, too."

"Just hose him down," Nick suggested unhelpfully. "Water pressure might dislodge the bulk of it."

Angie looked at his brother in horror, and Jace cut in before she could say anything. "Please never have children, Nick. We'll find them lined up in the backyard getting their nightly hose-down instead of having a shower."

Olivia snorted. "That's *totally* something he'd do."

"What? Sounds efficient to me," Nick said with a shrug.

"You can use the big sink in the laundry," Jace's mother said.

He picked up Truffle and cradled the dog against his chest. Red dye began to mix with the blue already on his T-shirt, making a purple splotch in the middle. Angie followed along behind, asking Olivia if she would keep an eye on Tilly in the meantime.

"You don't have to help. Go, have fun." He placed Truffle into the big metal sink. The dog jumped around, his toenails making sharp clicking noises against the sink's surface.

"I feel like the little guy is my responsibility, too," Angie replied, giving Truffle a scratch as

Jace turned the water on and tested the temperature on his hand. "What do you think about co-parenting?"

"I don't think I'm good at co-anything," Jace said.

"You're a lot warmer and fuzzier than you think." She leaned against the side of the house, her damp hair curling adorably around one cheek. Her T-shirt was soaked through, and it clung to every curve of her body—hugging the smooth roundness of her breasts and the flat plane of her stomach. She wore a bikini underneath, and the floral fabric showed through the semitransparent cotton.

Jace averted his gaze and concentrated on Truffle. The dog did not seem to enjoy the running tap and tried to squirm away, but they *had* to get some of the dye out. Otherwise Truffle was going to be returned to Eugenie, either looking like a Barbie accessory or with a brand-new buzz cut.

"Aw, he doesn't like it." Angie held her hands up to the side of the sink to stop Truffle from scrambling out. "Funny how he's fine with the beach and yet he hates the tap."

Truffle's nails scratched against the side of the sink, but Jace finally got him under the spray, and the water turned pink beneath him. The dye ran, and Jace gave his back a little massage, trying to dislodge as much color as he could from the fur. That seemed to settle Truffle down, at least a bit.

"How are you enjoying your first Walters family event?"

"It's great," Angie replied. "Your family is so

lovely for letting me come. The games are fun, although everyone is pretty darn competitive."

"Story of my childhood."

"You keep up fine." She reached out and tucked a wet strand of hair behind her ears. "Despite what you think."

"And what do I think, huh?" He turned to look at her for a moment. Water dotted her cheeks and nose, and a trail of it ran down the side of her face from her wet hair.

She looked like a sprite—or some kind of water fairy sent to put him under a spell. And he was, totally and utterly under her spell. Annoyingly under her spell. Her warm brown eyes were like handcuffs around his wrists, and the way her full lips parted was a whispered invitation to spin.

"You think you're so different than these people that you don't belong. But they love you, Jace. Different isn't bad."

Wasn't it? Sometimes it felt that way, like his needs bothered people. Like *he* was a bother.

"I happen to like different," she said.

"Do you?"

She bit down on her lip and nodded. "Yeah, I do."

Jace admittedly was the world's worst at reading social cues, but there was no mistaking the look in Angie's eyes right now. For some unknown reason, she wanted *him*.

Question was… What did he plan to do about it?

• • •

Um, what the hell was she doing? The plans for today did *not* include hitting on Jace—no matter how delectable he looked in his board shorts and that clingy white T-shirt.

His skin was glowing from the sun—beautifully bronzed and smooth, like a sculpture. His muscled arms looked strong enough to carry the world, and yet he handled Truffle as though the little guy was made of glass.

There was a gentleness to Jace that most guys didn't have. Kindness and softness beneath the undeniably honed, masculine exterior. And for a girl who'd grown up with men who were sharper than nails and harder than granite, she was deeply, deeply attracted to the parts of Jace that he seemed not to like about himself. Or at the very least, the parts he assumed others judged him for.

In fact, it was that perfect balance of hard and soft that was doing funny things to her insides, making them flip and twist and squirm.

Jace leaned in, and it felt like someone had lit a match inside her. Everything flickered and glowed, the pleasant warmth spreading through her limbs, and all he'd done was incline his head toward hers.

But up close, she could drown in the details of him—the strange little ring of gold that made his light-blue eyes totally unique. The tiny little scar that intersected the top of his lip and was barely visible unless you were close enough to kiss. The scent of soap and sea air and sun-drenched skin that grabbed her senses and squeezed, holding her totally and utterly captive.

His arms slid around her waist, tightening and pulling her close. Most guys went straight in for the kill—confident and sure—but Jace took his time. His was a slow seduction, like being lowered into a warm rose-petal-filled bath.

"You feel good." His voice was low and meant only for her. Like a secret.

She relaxed into him, totally aware of the heat charging the air. Of his hard arms around her, of the sturdiness of his thighs pressing against hers. Of the tiny flame of desire that was catching and spreading.

Who knew such a little flame could turn into an inferno?

She tilted her head up to look at him, to try to read him. His face was incredibly close to hers, the intensity of his stare melting her defenses. Warming her. Opening her.

He brushed a hand over her hair, sweeping it back from her face and tracing the shell of her ear with his thumb. Blood rushed in her ears, drowning out the sounds of the world. For a moment, everything shrank to them and only them.

Her lips parted because she felt the need to say something—anything—but no words came. Instead, his mouth dropped down to hers in a blissful contact that made her blood sing. His tongue drew a gentle line over her lower lip, a prelude to what they both wanted. What they'd both been dancing around.

When his tongue pushed inside her mouth, she tasted the mint on his lips, felt the tightening of his hands in her hair and the intensity of him seeping into her. When she kissed him back, it was with all the emotion she'd pent up inside her, all the fear and loathing and regret and desperation.

"Jace," she gasped into his mouth as her hands smoothed up his T-shirt. The hard ridges of his abs made her fingertips burn even with the layer of cotton between them. She wanted to touch him everywhere, to confirm that he was real and she hadn't spun out into some parallel world.

"You taste good," he murmured against her lips. "So sweet."

His hands dropped down to her back, sliding over the curve of her butt until his palms found purchase there. Fingers kneading her, he pressed her closer. Lined her up against the hard ridge of his erection.

Then Truffle let out a high-pitched yelp, startling them apart. Angie released her hold on Jace's T-shirt suddenly, as though he were a hot pan and she was about to get burned.

"I, uh…" Angie blinked, trying to right herself as the world swam beneath her feet. "Hmm."

"You're speechless," he said, a smile playing over his lips. "I didn't think that was possible."

"I didn't, either."

Jace. The quiet guy. The strong, silent, good guy who wasn't supposed to be right for her.

But God, if this wasn't right, then she had no sense of the word anymore. No sense of black or white or up or down. Because every cell in her body was screaming affirmations like *this* was where she was supposed to be. Not on a date with Elijah or Theo or Trent. Not looking around at every other man but the one who really lit her fire.

The one guy who'd made her feel like this place was home.

There wasn't much space between them. It would be so easy to step back into his arms. To step into his kiss. But she needed to think, needed to get her head straight because they had a lot of pain between them. A lot of baggage.

"I need a minute." She stepped back and cringed at the look of hurt sweeping across his face. But it was gone in an instant.

He turned and raked a hand through his hair, which looked considerably more mussed than it had before. Had she been tugging on it? Oh my God, she *had*. Angie rubbed her hands up and down her thighs as if trying to get the feeling of him off her skin. But judging by the throbbing heat that filled her body, forgetting that kiss wouldn't be so easy.

Then, like a coward, she turned and fled back to the party happening in the backyard.

CHAPTER FIFTEEN

The rest of the afternoon was an awkward dance between trying to act like she hadn't locked lips with Jace and thinking about it every damn second her brain wasn't actively engaged in a conversation. Now everyone was wrapping up and preparing for the continuing festivities in the evening—Olivia, Trent, and Nick were off to a big house party on the other side of Patterson's Bluff, and Adam and Soraya were hosting a small dinner party at their place.

Angie carried plates containing only the crumbs of Melanie's incredible cake—which was shaped to look *exactly* like the blue Esky that had been keeping their drinks cold all afternoon. Feeling full from all the decadent treats, she was looking forward to going home and putting her feet up.

"What are you up to now?" Trent asked as they walked into the house together.

"Well, I'm going to explode from everything I've eaten," she replied. "Jace will have to take me home so I can sleep it off."

The innocent statement caused a spark in her imagination—sweaty bodies and clothes floating to the floor. She almost choked on the spot but covered it by clearing her throat. One kiss and she was acting like they were going to jump straight into bed.

"You can't go home—it's only six. You should come to the house party with me." Trent took the dishes from her hands and stacked them into the sink. "It'll be fun."

"I think I'm fresh out of fun."

"No way. You practically run on the stuff; I can see that in your smile." He leaned against the breakfast bar, standing close to her in a way that should have had her heart racing. But all she could think about was Jace.

He stood outside, and she tried to catch his eye through the open double sliding doors. But he seemed to be studiously avoiding her. He'd been quiet ever since he deposited the freshly washed Truffle into the backyard to dry off. Was he regretting their kiss? How could he go from holding her one minute like she was the only woman on earth to not being able to even look at her the next?

What if this is another family competition thing? Oh my God.

She *must* be wrong. Jace wouldn't do something like that, would he? She was in full panic mode now. This happened anytime something felt good and right, because she'd been trained to assume those feelings would never last long.

"Well…"

"Come on." Trent grinned. "It's always a blast. The Fisher family hosts every year, and they have this *huge* house with the most amazing view of the ocean from the back deck. You'd love it."

I don't think I would. Not tonight.

"You could come as my date," he suggested

with a charming smile.

This was what she'd been wanting—a cute guy who could be everything. A guy who came from a good family, who had a good heart, an amazing sense of humor. Trent was the whole package. So why did her heart feel as though it was throwing up big, fat *no* signals?

You don't want him.

The second she thought those words, she knew it for certain in her gut—she *should* want to go with him, but she didn't. She couldn't. She wasn't attracted to Trent, not even a little bit. Because nobody made her feel like Jace did. And she was sure now that no matter how much "research" she did, no matter how many guys she investigated... there was only one Jace.

At that moment, Jace looked up from his phone and walked over. "Hey, what's up?"

"I'm trying to convince Angie to come to the party with me." Trent melodramatically clutched at his chest. "But she's dragging her heels and breaking my heart."

Jace's expression didn't reveal much. "You asked her out on a date?"

"Yeah, why the hell not?" He was so unashamed and unabashed that she had to laugh. Perhaps growing up the youngest of the four boys had given him the balls to take what he wanted instead of waiting for it to come to him.

"We're at a family function," Jace said, shaking his head.

"I asked her on a date. Not to join me for a drunken orgy at a sex dungeon, Jace." Trent looked at his brother strangely. Did he suspect anything?

The air in the kitchen was now thick with tension. So thick, Angie was sure the cake knife wouldn't even be able to make it all the way through. Jace's blue gaze caught hers, and he was stock-still as if waiting for her response. Oh God, what was the right thing to do? Go with Trent so Jace didn't think she was chasing him and then quietly feign a headache and slink back home by herself? Or go home with Jace and hope he wasn't regretting everything and that he wanted to pick up where they left off?

Now would be an amazing time for Jace to give her some kind of clue as to what he wanted.

"I, uh…" She swung her head back and forth between the two men—who looked so alike with their sandy hair and oceanic eyes but who couldn't be more different in personality.

"Anyway, I'm going." Jace held up a hand in a kind of non-wave and headed out toward the front door, but not before Angie saw the hurt flashing in his eyes. Crap. "Are you coming home, Angie, or are you heading off with Trent?"

"I'm coming home," she said, the air rushing out of her lungs. She gave Trent a quick, platonic hug. "Thank you for the sweet offer, but I'm seriously so ready for a night on the couch."

"No worries." He bobbed his head, a confused expression on his face. "Next time."

"Sure, absolutely. One hundred percent." She bounded out of the kitchen and said goodbye to Jace's parents, thanking them for including her in their family festivities.

Out the front, Jace was waiting for her. The dogs were ahead of him, Tilly and a very pretty pastel-pink Truffle. For a few heartbeats, they walked in silence, as though neither one of them knew how to start.

"I wasn't going to say yes," she said eventually.

"I thought he was on your list?"

"Maybe he was…I don't know." Except she *did* know. "He's not anymore. *That* I know for sure."

"For what it's worth, I think you'd be a terrible match." They were halfway down the street now, and Jace was barely looking at her. But he was still talking, so that was a good sign…right?

"Because he's not a seventy-year-old model-train builder?" She attempted to make a joke, but it fell flat.

"I know him better than most people do, and you won't be long-term for him."

"You don't think he'd see me as a long-term option?" She looked at the ground as they walked, mustering a half-hearted smile for Truffle, who turned back to look at her as he trotted — oblivious of Jace's hurt and Angie's mental anguish and the fact that he looked like a My Little Pony reject.

"Look, I know it's not what you want to hear, but you won't hold his attention. Nobody does. It's not how he operates."

"So I'm not good enough to be that special someone." She swallowed, her gaze trained on her feet.

"You *are* special, Angie. You'll find the right guy one day, but right now…" He looked at her briefly, and it was like being lanced through the heart. "I think you're playing a losing game."

Why, for once in her damn life, couldn't things go the way she wanted them to? Why had she kissed Jace this afternoon? If she hadn't, then she'd probably be going up to the house party with Trent now, blissfully unaware that her sexier-than-sin landlord and the object of her most ill-advised crush thought she was a giant dumb-ass.

Except you know it wouldn't have gone any-where, even if you did *go to the party. You know it in your gut.*

"I guess some people aren't meant to be win-ners."

"Who's going to win in this situation?" Jace sighed and raked his free hand through his hair. "You're looking for someone who's going to fall head over heels for you and then sign on the dotted line in what...five weeks?"

"Six," she whispered.

"Do you have any idea how unrealistic that sounds?"

She did. Of *course* she did—the whole batshit plan was denial hiding out in a new form. When she'd listened to Jean talk about her husband, she'd believed...hell, for a moment there she really *had* believed in miracles.

"Do you really watch those movies and think it could happen?" Jace asked. "Hollywood isn't selling the truth, because people are messy and relationships stumble and not everything works out in the end."

"Wow, I didn't know you were so cynical. I'd always assumed artists were dreamers."

Jace's jaw tightened. "I don't fit any of my labels neatly. I thought that was obvious."

She did. Heck, it was one of the things she liked most about him. He was a bit left of center, a bit out of step. Just like her.

"Is it really so bad to think that someone might fall in love with me?" Her voice wobbled. "Or am I the one who's lost my grip on reality, because I've been hoping for that very thing ever since I was a little girl? That *someone*, somewhere might want me."

Jace stayed silent. It was like she'd taken a knife and cut her chest open in front of him, and he'd suddenly turned into stone.

"You know, one of my foster mothers told me once that she thought my life would be easier if I smiled more. So I smiled. I smiled at every goddamn person who came my way, and I kept smiling when she took the money that was supposed to feed and clothe me and spent it getting high. I smiled through my fear when I tried to report her and her husband to Child Protective Services for chaining me up next to their dog to teach me a lesson for complaining that I was hungry. And I smiled through my tears when they sent me back there anyway because there was no proof." Her lip trembled. "And I'm still here, and I'm still trying to smile…trying to believe there's good in the world and that I might end up somewhere beautiful and calm."

"God, Angie." When Jace looked at her, he had

that look. The look that stopped her from telling people her story, because it was so brimming with pity it made her want to put a fist through a wall. "How did you get through that?"

"I kept hoping."

She was a survivor, at least that's what all the papers had said. She'd become the face of child neglect, after someone at Child Protective Services grew a conscience and decided to drop in after her report didn't go anywhere. They'd found her skinny and half-starved, with a chain thicker than her arm holding her captive, her face covered in so much grime, her tears left tracks in the filth. The picture she'd taken had been leaked, and Angie had spent every day since with the past around her neck. Squeezing. Ever-present.

"So yeah, my plan might be crazy but...a long shot is all I've got." Shame burned through her like wildfire. "Because I'm desperate, and I know the smell of it drives people away. So I try to be happy Angie, kooky Angie with her zany plans to make this town a better place. I stand up and I speak up and I keep trying because it's all I have in my control."

The house was in front of them now. She hadn't even realized they'd made it so far—she was lost in her own head and the soothing *slap-slap* rhythm of their steps and watching Truffle's pink furry butt.

"I don't expect you to understand, Jace. I'm sorry I kissed you... I felt..." What? Like the one guy who actually got her heart thumping and her pulse racing might *be* the one for her? Like they were both a shade different than the norm, and yet they fit together. "I felt something, and I thought you might have felt it, too."

She looked at him, searching his face for confirmation that she wasn't the only one putting herself out there. Her breath halted while she waited for him to say something—anything. To lean in and kiss her again.

But Jace was as immovable and strong as an old gum tree, stoic. Unreadable. Sharing nothing.

Shaking her head, she jogged toward the side of the house, slipping out of sight and down the path toward the little unit she wouldn't be able to call home in a few short weeks. Her vision blurred, making it tough to see the lock, and she fumbled with her key.

Metal scratched over metal as she frantically tried to let herself inside so she could hide from the world. And start to make plans for the fact that life as she knew it was coming to an end.

Because one thing was for sure, her plan was officially obliterated, and she was going to have to not only leave the town she'd come to love but Jace, too.

• • •

Jace watched Angie bolt, his heart heavy and his mind mushy like scrambled eggs. Truffle and Tilly stood still for a moment, clearly confused by Angie's sudden departure, but Tilly looked back over her shoulder, her dark eyes narrowed as if she knew *exactly* how much of a jerk Jace had been.

He was the king of jerks. His royal highness of Jerkington Kingdom.

"I screwed up," he said to no one in particular.

Tilly made a snorting noise as if to say, *You sure did.*

He'd taken Angie's bubbly, yellow-balloon optimism and aimed a big, pointy needle at it. And why? Not even for anything as noble as keeping her best interests at heart or being honest that she and Trent would be a giant disaster — even though that *was* what he thought. There was his bluntness ruining everything again. His inability to read the room and lack of verbal filter making other people feel bad. He'd poured salt on the wounds made by her past.

Ass. Hole.

Worse, he didn't even know how to make it better. An apology wouldn't be enough. But what else was he supposed to do? Bring flowers? Chocolates? Or was that old-fashioned?

He led the dogs into the house and paced around his kitchen until he was sure he would wear a hole in the floor. *This* was why he wrote about a character who lived on his own — because solitary life was simple. He could have his surfing time, his working time, his relaxation time all uninterrupted. He could cruise through each day knowing exactly what he was going to get done and setting his goals with no one in mind but himself.

It was perfectly uncomplicated.

But the thought of it now felt hollow. Some of the best times he'd had in the past few weeks were doing things with Angie, Tilly, and Truffle—the beach party, fish and chips in the back of his car. Even "researching" Theo had been entertaining.

What would his life be like when Angie left and Eugenie came back to pick up the dogs?

Tilly whined and scratched at the back door, her big paws having already created some grooves in the wood. "You want to go out, girl?"

He flicked the lock on the door and let it swing open. She immediately bounded across the yard and went straight to Angie's door, whining and scratching. It wasn't possible she knew they were fighting…was it?

"Tilly!" He clapped his hands together, but the dog ignored him. Jace strode out into the yard, shaking his head. "Stop that now!"

Before he could make it all the way over, Angie's door swung open, and she tensed up at the sight of the big dog standing on her doorstep. His heart twisted in his chest, because now he knew why she reacted that way.

But Tilly nuzzled her head straight into Angie's palm, making a soft crying noise as if offering her version of canine sympathy. Angie's eyes were red and watery—and somehow, even crying, she was the most beautiful woman Jace had ever seen.

Yeah, she was sailing on a hope and a prayer… and what she needed was a friend to fill her sails. Not deflate them.

"I don't know what she's looking for," Angie said, obliging the dog by scratching behind her ear.

"I'm pretty sure she's here in female solidarity." Jace jammed his hands into his pockets. "She was looking at me like I'd kicked a puppy."

Despite her tears, Angie laughed. "Glad to know I've got someone on my side."

"I *am* on your side." He took a step forward, and when she didn't retreat, he took another. "My practical nature gets the best of me sometimes, and when you pair that with a big mouth and a missing mental filter..."

Angie leaned against the door, watching him. Her gaze was so intense, he seemed to want to look anywhere but directly at her—hey, was that a crack in the frame above her head?

Focus. And don't screw this up. Not again.

He wanted to make amends, but he didn't have any flowers or chocolates in his house. He didn't know how to do the grand gesture thing, like they did in those movies she loved to watch.

Think, dammit. What else have you got?

Angie was still observing him, her hair kinked from when it had air-dried in the sun after the water gun fight. Having her watch him made it harder for his brain to work. It felt like an old machine that was turned on for the first time... sluggish and dusty.

Dusty! He was sure there was a bottle of gin back in the house. Jace wasn't much of a spirits drinker, as he had his preferred brand of beer and never deviated, but someone had given him a bottle once. People in movies had drinks. Maybe that would work?

"So...uh. I have gin," he said. It wasn't the best start to an invitation, but usually he liked to rehearse these kind of things and now he was totally winging it, flying out of his comfort zone like a paraglider over a volcano. "It's a bit dusty, though."

She raised a brow. "The gin is dusty?"

"Well, the bottle is dusty. I assume they seal them well enough to keep the dust on the outside." *Holy awkwardness, Batman!* "I'm sure it's fine to drink."

He chanced a quick glance at her, and her expression shifted, but he wasn't sure exactly what it meant. Angie's face was like looking at the sky sometimes—a person better at reading people than him would have been able to identify her feelings like watching shapes in clouds as they blew by.

"Okay." She stretched the word out like toffee. "Why are you telling me this?"

"I thought maybe we should drink it." He cleared his throat. "Together."

"And why would we do that?"

Jace let out a long breath. He'd been hoping the invite might be enough, but... This was one of those times where he needed to push past the things that made him uncomfortable, for the other person. Like he did with his family sometimes, because he cared about them.

And you care about Angie?

He looked up, meeting her eyes and watching the change in her face. Watching the pink come to her cheeks and the blacks in her eyes grow a little wider. God, she was beautiful.

"Sometimes I do things..." He sighed. "I would like to have a drink with you and listen to whatever you have to say."

"Do you even know how to make drinks?" she asked, a soft smile on her lips.

"Step one, open gin. Step two, pour gin."

"Let me guess. Step three, drink gin?" She laughed. The sound carried on the night air and filled his heart. "I hope you've got something to go with that gin because I am not a straight liquor kind of woman."

"We'll find something," he said.

Angie followed him back into his house, still dressed in her oversize dye-colored T-shirt and bikini. She could have been wearing a shopping bag from Woolies and she would have looked a million bucks. He'd been denying it for too long—at first because that was his MO, and then because he knew he wasn't the kind of man she was looking for. But dammit, he was attracted to Angie. More than that, he liked her…a lot. She made him happy, made him question things. Made him want to attempt things outside his comfort zone.

And then she told him she felt something when they kissed.

Everything was muddled now. Because he'd started to wonder if maybe they were a good fit. But he'd have to tell her everything first. She deserved to know he wasn't changeable. He was born this way, for better or for worse.

CHAPTER SIXTEEN

Angie watched as Jace made their drinks, his fingers deft and capable as he handled the two fancy crystal tumblers that looked like they were older than he was. The way those hands had threaded into her hair and kneaded her ass when they'd kissed had made her think they could do anything.

A shiver ran the length of her spine. She hadn't been kissed like that in a while. A *long* while. And it made her wonder why. For the last few years, the dates she'd been on never ended in a kiss. Not for a lack of trying for some of them, but every time one of the guys leaned in…

She'd never been able to pull the trigger.

Except Jace.

When he'd put his lips to hers, it was like her world had suddenly been blessed by the sun for the first time. Every dried-up, hollowed-out, aching part of her had been comforted by him. He made her feel whole and good. *So* good.

Jace carried the glasses over to the couch, where Angie was settled into the corner. Tilly lay protectively at her feet and Truffle was curled up in her lap. "Don't I look like the perfect dog mama?"

The genuine smile that lit up his face was like a knife twisting in her heart. "You've had a change of heart with Tilly?"

"It dawned on me that maybe she's a little misunderstood like the rest of us. And she took my side this afternoon, so I had to give her points for that."

"You girls always stick together."

"To drowning our sorrows." She held up her glass.

His gaze held hers as they clinked glasses, and she almost melted into a puddle. Heavy lashes framed his eyes, so thick and lush and sexy. Stubble coated his jaw and made him look even more brutishly handsome. His sandy hair was messy, as usual. Jace was the kind of guy who could kiss like a champ, take care of dogs, and didn't mansplain things. It was unbelievable he hadn't been snapped up already.

Angie took a sip of the drink and her eyes immediately watered. "Jeez. You're a heavy pour."

He grinned and took a sip from his own glass, trying to hold back a cough. "Okay, so it's a little on the strong side."

"This might be the worst drink anyone has ever made me," she said with a laugh. "But I appreciate the gesture."

"So I should give up on my hopes of one day owning a bar?" He attempted another sip and pulled a face. Then he held his hand out to take hers and plonked them both on the coffee table. "Yeah, that's really bad."

"You can own a bar, but maybe don't tend it," Angie advised. Her stomach churned, because she had no idea where this was going and she really, *really* wanted it to go somewhere good. "Or maybe stick to those slushy drinks that look like something you get from a 7-Eleven. You could even have a little umbrella in them, let people think they're on a tropical vacation instead of just going to the local watering hole."

Shut. Up.

"You use a lot of words," Jace observed. But he didn't say it in a judgmental way, more like it was something he found interesting about her.

"And you don't use many at all." Something compelled her to try and understand this mystery man—to untangle the knot of details and imperfections. "I thought you didn't like me the first time we met."

She cringed at the memory. The first time she'd met Jace, she found him a little stuffy. Straitlaced. A little awkward. She'd tried to strike up a conversation and he did his best to evade her questions.

But slowly they'd gotten to know each other, and she'd come to understand he took his time letting people in. There were a lot of layers to him, and most people probably didn't get past the first few. But she had.

"Is that your way of saying I've grown on you?" he asked.

"Maybe it is."

"I think you've grown on me, too."

She gasped. "I was charming from the beginning, thank you very much."

He chuckled, and the sound ran down her spine like a caress. Heat spread through her, slowly tracking along her limbs and pooling low in her belly. Would she be acting like this if he hadn't kissed her? If she didn't know how skilled he was with his mouth?

Get a friggin' grip, Angie. It was one kiss, and you're making out like it's going somewhere.

"I'm not good with people. With change," he muttered, running a hand through his hair. "I, um…I'm on the autism spectrum."

Angie held her breath. This new information was like a puzzle piece clicking into place—and now some of his behavior made more sense. She didn't dare move, dare speak, in case he clammed up. Because she felt the weight of importance in him sharing this part of himself. Knowing how intensely private he was, for him to open up about something so personal was a big deal.

"The doctors said I was 'high-functioning,' so a lot of people can't tell just by looking, but I have trouble making eye contact. I need my routine to feel like I can breathe. I sometimes say the wrong thing or I don't say anything at all when I should say something." He raked a hand through his hair. "I'm not the best at reading a room, either."

Now she knew why her knees turned to jelly when he *did* look her dead in the eye—it was so intense, because usually his gaze was a little off. Focused on something behind or to the side or above. It was as if she'd sensed how important that connection was with him, that it wasn't something he doled out easily.

He nodded, as if choosing his words carefully. "I was engaged once. I don't know if you knew that."

Raising a brow, Angie watched him. She hadn't expected him to come out with that detail. "I'd heard."

He paused for a moment. "Julia and I had been together ever since the end of high school. I got the courage to ask her out the night before our graduation ceremony, and when she said yes, I nearly fell over."

"You loved her?"

"I was going to marry her, so yeah. But looking back, there were a lot of problems." He picked at a loose thread on the couch, worrying it back and forth with his nail. "She knew about my autism, and for a while it wasn't a problem, especially when we were younger. But I guess as the years went by, she finally understood there were some things I couldn't change. My need for routine upset her, because she always wanted to do different things without planning beforehand. Sometimes I really needed to be alone, and she acted like it was because I didn't love her. Well, I guess it was too much in the end. All those things don't make me a very attractive fiancé."

Her heart ached for this wonderful man — for the pain he must have felt being rejected for something about him that was out of his control. No wonder he had acted so strongly when she'd made that joke about him marrying her.

"I was at the wedding rehearsal dinner, waiting for her," he said. "We were *all* waiting for her. It was two days out, and she never showed up. I was worried. I thought she'd been in a car accident or something. When I got home, all her things were gone. There was a note on the kitchen bench."

"What did it say?" she whispered.

Jace wouldn't look at her now. He was lost in his thoughts, perhaps playing the past like a film reel in his head. She sat, waiting, giving him the time he needed. Maybe she shouldn't have asked. This was so personal. So heartbreaking.

"That she thought…" He swallowed, his Adam's apple bobbing. "That she thought she was in love with Trent."

Oh no. The look on Jace's face from the moment in his parents' kitchen today made so much more sense now—the razor-edged hurt, the darkness. It must have been like a tiny little section of his history replaying. That comparison must have killed him.

"She said she cared about me but that she knew it wasn't love. She wanted the kind of passion that made her heart sing and no matter how I tried, I could never give her that feeling. I was too closed-off, too logical…too rigid."

Angie shook her head, her heart exploding with emotion on Jace's behalf—anger, frustration, disbelief. How was it possible someone who was going to marry him didn't see all the amazing parts of his personality? Sure, he might not be a hearts and flowers kinda guy—but he showed he cared in so many other ways. "I'm so sorry."

"Don't be." His voice was rough. She'd never heard him speak like that before. "It's not like they had an affair. As far as I know, Trent was totally oblivious to it all. Julia wanted him from afar, but she never did anything about it."

"And then I poured a whole bunch of salt in that wound, didn't I?"

"It's an old wound."

"But it's not healed."

His gaze was still averted as if the conversation was embarrassing him. "No, it's not."

"I can't believe I did that."

"You didn't know." He stretched his arm along the back of the chair, his fingers tangling where her hair lay in slightly wild sun-drenched waves, kinked and textured from the summer air. The touch was so tender, so familiar, and it made her heart sing. "Hardly anyone does. I never told Trent because I didn't want him to have to shoulder that burden. He didn't encourage Julia by doing anything more than being himself."

"He steals the spotlight, doesn't he?"

"Since he was old enough to sit upright." Jace laughed. "I guess since you never had siblings, you might not know this, but we're *always* compared to one another. No matter how old we get, people like to put us in categories and rank us against one another."

"Really? I wondered if that only happened between the 'real kids' and the foster ones."

"It's practically sport." Jace's expression had a faraway look to it—like he was sifting through all the moments that had led him here. In many ways, they had a lot in common. They'd both struggled to fit in, only it had taken them in different directions. Jace had curled in on himself, and Angie had worn a mask most of her life, trying to bend and twist and jump through whatever hoops people set in front of her.

"I envy you, you know," she said. "You're so…
yourself."

"I don't have it in me to be anyone else." His
lip quirked. "I can't spend my life trying to be
someone I'm not."

"That's very mature."

He chuckled. "I can be, at times. Well, for a guy
who makes a living drawing cartoons."

"Don't downplay it like that. *Hermit vs. World*
is brilliant. It's funny and relatable and somehow
you manage to get these important things across
in such a small amount of space. You're talented."

"And you're going to make my head so big
it won't fit through the doorframe." He paused,
glancing over her right shoulder. "I had no idea
you read my comics."

"Well, I had to do my due diligence when I
moved in."

He quirked a brow. "You looked me up?"

"Of course. Single girl traveling on her own
and all that…you can't be too careful." She
grinned. "I had to make sure you weren't an ax
murderer."

"As opposed to some other type of murderer?
Would it be less of an issue if I didn't use an ax?"
The question seemed like a serious one until
Angie detected the barest hint of a twinkle in his
eye. "I've always wondered that."

"Maybe you should write a comic about it."

"*Ax Murderer vs. World*? Doesn't have quite
the same ring to it."

"I have no doubt you'd make it work."

"Your faith is misplaced."

She searched his face, noting the way his eyes shifted away from hers when she complimented him. But they returned quickly, as though he wanted to make sure she wasn't about to run away. He didn't need to worry—this was *exactly* where Angie wanted to be right now. Not at a house party with his brother, not chasing down some local hottie for whom she felt nothing more than the barest of *snap, crackle, pop*. No, she wanted to be here with Jace—the one guy who definitely wasn't going to solve her problems but who made her feel like she could power a whole fireworks display.

The one guy she wanted at the top of her list from the start.

"I don't think it is." She shifted on the couch, moving closer to him. Truffle grumbled and changed positions between them, but Jace slipped his big hands under the little dog's body and moved him to the floor. "What I *do* think is that you've become a world-class champion at shutting people out, because it's easier than taking the risk of having them reject you."

"A world-class champion in avoidance, huh?" The light shifted in his eyes. "Worst Olympic sport ever."

"You've turned being the lone wolf of Patterson's Bluff into a full-time job." Her hand came up to his face, her fingertips feeling for the prickle of stubble along his jaw. It was rough and soft at the same time, a perfect contradiction, much like the man in front of her. "Hell, you're so good at it, you made a whole comic about it."

"And what about you, Angie? Why are you here if I only shut people out?"

"That's the biggest question in my head right now," she whispered. "I have no idea. Maybe you got lonely."

"You're not just a warm body." His tone was deadly serious. "I wasn't looking for anyone right now. Or ever."

God, how she wanted to believe it. All her life she'd had this craving to be someone's "special one." To be the person they sought out, who they leaned on. But it was never in the cards for her. Only her illogical lovesick heart kept ripping open the stitches and begging for another chance, no matter how likely that she'd end up hurt and disappointed.

"If it wasn't you here…" He leaned closer. "This couch would be empty. I don't want anyone else. Only you."

She swallowed against the dueling mix of hope and fear. "I want to believe it."

"But you can't?"

"I don't trust anyone." Truer words had never been spoken.

She couldn't help touching him—tracing the curve of his biceps and the rounded thigh beneath a frayed patch of denim, hard muscle twitching beneath her fingertip. He caught her hand and kissed the center of her palm, jacking up her pulse. It was such a simple gesture, but he filled it with simmering heat.

"Maybe I could help," he said, tugging her

toward him.

"Help me with trusting people?"

"Yeah." Jace's eyes were like blue fire—shimmering and beautiful and she knew she shouldn't get too close. "I...want to help."

The memory of their kiss swirled in her mind. The taste of him, the scent of sunshine on his skin. The firm hands pulling her impossibly close, melting her body to his. She clamped her thighs together, trying to quell the insistent throbbing between her legs.

What about tomorrow? What about my plans?

Being with Jace now meant she would have to leave Australia, because he couldn't give her what she needed: the chance to stay. He didn't make decisions quickly. They wouldn't fall in love hard and fast and end up married by her deadline. This was a fork in the road. A choice.

Sleeping with Jace would mean giving up her dream home. Did she want him that much?

Yes.

"Just touch me," she said, sinking into her swirling desire and need.

His hands coasted over her knees, his thumbs rubbing insistent circles higher and higher until they brushed the edge of her T-shirt. She still had only her bikini underneath, and her body felt hot and heavy.

Her worries from earlier were drowning under his touch, the protests fizzling out like dead fireworks. How could something that already felt so good be bad for her? Sure, this wasn't part of her plan to stay in Australia, but that plan suddenly seemed wrong and pointless and this... this felt real and right. And so damn good.

When his thumbs brushed under the hem of her T-shirt, grazing the edge of her bikini bottoms, she gasped.

He hauled her into his lap as though she weighed no more than a feather. She'd never been the kind of woman who wanted to feel small and delicate—because those things had been a liability in her life—but right now, Jace made those parts of her feel beautiful and feminine. He made those parts feel right.

His fingers stroked her skin, his lips possessing hers. Her knees dug into the couch on either side of his hips, and when she lowered herself down, rubbing against him, they both moaned. Their breaths came hard and fast, mingling together as they kissed. The gentle slide of his tongue stole the breath right from her lungs.

"God, Angie," he moaned into her mouth. "I've been thinking about this for so damn long."

CHAPTER SEVENTEEN

Jace didn't know what was going on. It was like he was a pendulum swinging from one extreme to the other. Thoughts swirled in his head. They were wrong for each other, their goals didn't align now—*or* for the future.

But his body was aching for her; his hands couldn't be full enough of her.

And he wanted nothing more than to throw her down on the couch and lose himself in that tangled chestnut hair and those wide whiskey eyes and lush lips. But this wasn't something to be rushed. He shifted forward on the couch, lifting her and encouraging her to wrap her legs around him. Then he turned them both and laid her down. Her hair spilled around her, and her chest rose and fell with her quickened breath.

"How long?" she asked.

"Too long." He pressed his face to her neck and inhaled the scent of faded perfume and sunscreen on her skin. "You captivated me from the moment you walked up to my front door."

"The first day?"

"The first second." He'd never been the kind of guy to be swept away by looks—because Jace was far too logical for that. Love at first sight was *not* a thing. But Angie's spirit had been so loud and so clear—that hopeful, expectant smile socking him like a clenched fist straight to his chest. She was everything carefree he wished he could be. "You demanded that I pay attention to you with all your questions. All your words. I never stood a chance."

"I thought you weren't interested in getting to know me." Her hands curved around his face, and she pulled his mouth down to hers. "You seemed to keep your distance."

"I thought life was easier if I stuck to myself." He brushed the hair back from her eyes and tucked it behind her ear. "But maybe I was wrong."

"Why?"

"Because I like you. A lot."

The smile that lit her face could have powered him for the rest of his life. "I like you, too."

When she kissed him this time, there was no hesitation. There was no gentle exploration. Her arms looped around his neck, and she held him tight as if they were swaying in the ocean and he was her life raft and *God*, it felt good. Being wanted by someone like Angie—someone so kind and sweet and true—was like coming home after being away too damn long.

"Uh, Jace?" She pulled away for a second. "How do you feel about having an audience?"

He turned to the side and was met with two pairs of doggy eyes that were a little too close for comfort. "We should take this to the bedroom."

"Given Truffle has trouble controlling his animal urges...uh, yeah." She laughed.

Jace pushed up from the couch and swept Angie into his arms, her legs dangling as she shrieked and clutched his neck. The noise turned to laughter when he strode through his house, kicking the bedroom door shut behind them and leaving two disappointed pooches in his wake.

"Privacy achieved." He laid Angie down on his bed.

Outside, the sun was sinking on the horizon, and it bathed the room in a rich golden glow. For a moment, he could only stare.

"Are you changing your mind?" she whispered.

"No." He stood at the end of the bed, letting his eyes feast on her. "Just making sure I remember every single detail of this."

Excitement flickered across her face as he sank to his knees on the mattress, capturing her ankle in his palms, his thumbs tracing the small protruding bone there.

"I want to remember this bit." His hands slid up her calf to the bend in her knee. "And this bit." Then farther up still over the gentle curve of her hip. "And this bit."

His fingers curled into the waistband of her bikini bottoms, and he tugged the fabric down her legs. Soon her T-shirt and bikini top followed. She didn't try to cover herself; instead she stretched out, arching her back off the bed and thrusting her small pink-tipped breasts in the air.

"You're perfect," he said, coming down over her and taking one in his mouth. Her skin was sweet and smooth, her nipple hard as he rolled it against his tongue.

Her hand fisted in his hair, tugging sharply. So there *was* a bit of sting with the sweetness. Jace returned in kind, scraping his teeth over the peak of her breast and eliciting a pleasure-filled sound from her.

"Yes," she gasped, but she pulled his head to her other breast. He worshipped her skin, sucking and nipping and tugging until pink marks peppered her. Her hands smoothed up his chest, driving under the cotton of his T-shirt. "You need to get rid of this now."

It came off in one fluid motion, and he pushed down his shorts and underwear together. Heat swelled within him as her eyes took him in, slowly and languidly. Her gaze burned a path from his chest all the way down. Reaching out, she caught the tip of him with her fingertips, and his whole body tensed, the muscles in his shoulders bunching up around his neck as he tried to control the excitement racing through him.

Stepping out of her reach, he lowered his head to her stomach. Her skin was hot against his cheek but smooth—the opposite of his stubble-roughened jaw. A soft sigh came from her lips, and the gentle pressure of her hand against his head told him what she wanted. His lips blazed a trail down her stomach, and he pressed a chaste kiss at her hip.

"Please, Jace." Her voice trembled as he nuzzled the sensitive spot at the apex of her sex, reveling in the scent of her. So musky and intoxicating.

He had an ounce of control left—a mere thread—but he was going to cling to it. His tongue flicked over her, gentle at first. Teasing.

"Please…" The rest of her words dissolved

into a string of pleasure sounds as he blew against her heated skin. Goose bumps rippled across her thighs and stomach. "Oh God."

He couldn't hold back anymore. As he sucked at her most sensitive part, her fingernails dug into his shoulders, and knowing there'd be marks tomorrow got him all hot and bothered. Her hips rolled against his mouth, and she cried his name. Softly at first. Then louder.

He felt the pressure building inside her, and when she was close, he slipped a finger between the lips of her sex, pressing it inside her. She came hard against his mouth. When the tremors subsided and her legs fell away, her fingers moved from tugging to something far softer.

"Best long weekend ever," she said, her breathing shallow.

A laugh rumbled deep in his chest. "How's that for a little holiday magic?"

"Hmm." She reached for him lazily. "I certainly saw fireworks."

"Is this the part where I make a joke about something down under?"

She flung an arm over her eyes and laughed. "The jokes basically write themselves here."

Running his hands under the hollow of her back, he lifted her up to him, and she wound her arms around his neck. If he didn't have her soon, he was going to burst. They lay in a tangle of limbs for several heartbeats, and he had to tear himself away to dig out a condom from the still unopened box in his bathroom.

She watched from the bed with hungry eyes

as he tore the foil and rolled the rubber down his length. But this, too, wasn't to be rushed. Since neither of them had any idea where this was going, he would take his sweet time and enjoy the flare of her pupils as she watched him handle himself.

His pulse raced. Damn, she excited him. She made his blood rush in his ears and heart pound heavy and hard in his chest. He had to hold back the desire to race to the finish line. Her hand stretched out, and he slid his cock into her palm. "Mm, yes."

The bed shifted as he knelt between her legs, spreading her apart with his hands. The smokiness in her eyes urged him on, and he was desperate to hear her moan again. To feel her clench around him as he took her. His skin tingled. He felt so... alive.

So that's *what that saying means.*

He understood it now—that breathing and a heartbeat weren't the only things required to feel alive. Being with her made him feel so much more.

"No more waiting." Her legs came around his waist, her ankles crossing behind his back. "Please, I want this."

He pressed against the entrance to her sex, waiting for her to shift into position before he pushed inside. Her hot muscles clamped around him as he buried himself to the hilt.

"Oh, Jace," she sighed. "Yes."

His face pressed against the sweet curve of her neck as he gave her a moment to adjust to him. "You feel so good. So tight. So perfect."

She urged him on by rolling her hips and

meeting him thrust for thrust. Their bodies fused together, he slid his arms under her, pressing her to him so that no air could get between them. He had to be as close to her as possible.

"Yes." She arched in his arms, her head lolling on the pillow as she rubbed against him.

He could feel her orgasm gathering again, tightening her, tensing her. The second she broke, it pushed him over and he pounded into her, eyes clamped shut, until he found his own release.

After, when Angie had slumped against him and pressed her face to the base of his neck, he felt incredibly at ease. Peaceful, even. What he'd been missing all this time was human contact. Being here alone every day and avoiding neighbors and trying to pretend he *was* the protagonist of his comic had left him feeling…like a shell.

And it was Angie who'd given him what he hadn't even known he was missing.

Outside, the sound of the trees rustling in the evening breeze was a soothing soundtrack. It mingled with the gentle in-out *whoosh* of Angie's breath and warm puffs of air that heated his skin. She was curled into him, her cheek at his chest and her eyes heavy-lidded and her arms tucked between them.

She was going to leave soon.

The thought, which should have been the ultimate *get out of jail free* card—no expectations, no awkward conversations—left him with a rock in his stomach. Knowing they were over before they'd even started had him wanting to hold her tighter.

Eventually the silence was broken by the scratch of doggy paws at the bedroom door. Angie lifted her head—looking groggy and sleepy and sexy as all get out. "They're wondering what happened to us."

"Tell 'em we're busy." He kissed her temple.

"That's mean. We shouldn't keep them locked out."

"You want to let them in?" He chuckled when a smile immediately lit up her face. "Go on."

Angie got off the bed and went to Jace's chest of drawers, pulling each one open until she found what she was looking for. After liberating a clean T-shirt, she slipped it over her head, and it hung down to her knees. Jace tugged his underwear on and then hopped back into bed. A second later, she pushed the door open and two excitable creatures burst into the room.

"They were worried." Angie bent down and scooped Truffle up into her arms. Never one to be left out of the action, Tilly nudged Angie's leg until she was rewarded with a head scratch of her own.

Then the three of them piled up onto Jace's bed in one big, messy, furry tangle, and he wondered if maybe a life with a little more fuss wasn't so bad after all.

CHAPTER EIGHTEEN

Angie lay on the bed with Jace, her head resting against his chest and her belly full of the delicious peanut butter toast they'd made, trying—and failing—not to give too much away to the dogs. Carbohydrates were important, she'd come to understand, to sustain marathon sex sessions. There'd been a long-weekend fireworks show on the beach, and they had a great view from the deck while they ate, and then they'd napped on the bed, woken, shooed the dogs out, and then he'd made her come twice more before they'd gotten in the shower for another round. Eventually they'd fallen into an exhausted sleep around three a.m.

Now the sun was up and buttery morning light filtered into the bedroom. She watched the clouds shift in the breeze and listened to the sound of Jace's heavy breathing while Tilly and Truffle curled up at their feet.

Was this torture?

The perfect image of a life she'd never have—a loving husband, fur babies, sunshine, and anonymity to live freely and separately from her past. A home. A sweet, sweet home with a comfy bed and a sprawling backyard and a kitchen with that one cupboard that wouldn't close right but that she would love anyway.

Tears pricked the backs of Angie's eyes. She

knew Jace's story—knew that he wouldn't let her get too close or let this thing get too far. And by sleeping with him now—no matter how much she'd wanted it—she'd shot her Expedited Love plans in the foot. Because there was no one else on her list...only him.

A friend had given her some advice before she left—*be safe and make some better memories*, she'd said.

This probably wasn't what she'd had in mind...or maybe it was? Reckless, potentially heartbreaking sex counted as a good memory, right? It would only hurt if she let it.

He'd almost married a woman who was in love with his brother. Who didn't accept him as he was. Why would he want to be with her, knowing she had something to gain from the relationship? Trust couldn't exist in such a situation.

Still, the talk last night had led her to one conclusion: She deserved happiness. She deserved that night with him, no matter where it might—or might not—lead. The important stuff was the here and now, the present. Because who knew whether there would be a tomorrow?

"My feet are going to sleep," Jace said, his voice sleep-heavy and sexier than ever. "I'm going to have serious pins and needles when Tilly decides to move."

"You softie," she said. "You love that dog so much."

"I don't know about love." He cocked his head. "But she *is* awesome. They both are."

"I've come around to her." Angie's hands

brushed Tilly's soft fur, and the dog rolled over to expose her belly. "Look at that level of trust."

"If you rub her belly, she'll love you forever."

"I think I can handle that."

A pause filled the air, and Angie found herself wondering what would happen when their bubble burst. She wasn't eager to retreat to her place now that there was something developing between them, something unexpected and wonderful. Something she wanted to explore.

Still, their time together had an expiration date. She couldn't forget that.

"My nan would have liked you," he said out of nowhere.

She swallowed, keeping her face toward the dogs so he couldn't see how much that statement made her feel warm and fuzzy inside. "Yeah?"

"She liked people who didn't shy away from difficult things. Who were resilient."

A lump lodged itself in her throat. How could his ex have ever thought he wasn't a passionate person? That he was too logical? Too rigid? The scary thing was Jace had *so* much passion inside him, when he trusted someone enough to let it out. She had a feeling she'd caught a rare glimpse of who he *really* was. And he was even more perfect to her now than he had been yesterday.

But at the moment, all those feelings were a little too much. She needed time to sift through all the swirling thoughts in her head and figure out how to tackle the royal mess she'd made.

"Was that too much?" He let out a laugh and rubbed the morning scruff on his jaw—somehow managing to look adorably awkward and charming all at once. "I told you I don't always know the right thing to say."

"It was very sweet." She bit down on her lower lip. "A lack of filter can be a good thing."

"My teachers never appreciated it." His hands drifted lazily over where her arm peeked out from the sleeve of the T-shirt she'd stolen from his drawer. "They always thought I was causing trouble when I was expressing myself. I guess that's why I started drawing. It got me into less trouble."

Angie smiled at the thought of a younger Jace doodling away in the back of his school notebook. She could picture it vividly—his mop of sandy-colored hair flopping over his forehead, blue eyes narrowed in concentration.

"Can I see what you're working on now?" she asked, sitting up.

"You want to see my comic?" He sounded so surprised, a laugh burst out of Angie.

"I do. Is that weird?"

"It's not, I guess." He got out of the bed, quickly pulled up his jeans from last night, and ducked into the studio, which was next to the bedroom and also faced the backyard. He returned with a notebook. "It's just not a request I get very often."

"Well, *I'm* interested. I've never known an artist before, and it's a pretty cool job, if you ask me." Angie looked through the notebook with sketches. "You gave Hermit a pet!"

"I didn't mean to, but I was having a day where

I couldn't move the story along and…well, a dog seemed like a good idea at the time."

The little character was big-eyed and scruffy, with pointy ears. Little thought bubbles showed the dog's wisecrack comments to Hermit's antics. "Oh my God, I love it. He's hilarious!"

"I made him a mash-up of Tilly and Truffle." He leaned over, and the heat from his body sent a little shiver down Angie's spine. "He's got Truffle's energy and what I imagine is Tilly's sarcastic running commentary."

"Funny, that's exactly how I imagined she'd sound if dogs could talk, too." The latest strip showed Hermit shaking his fist at a man with a round belly, who was holding a fistful of money. "This is about the bridge, right?"

"You're up to date. I'm impressed."

"I told you, I'm a big Jace Walters fan." She cocked her head. "I also love that you totally made the mayor a caricature of Glen Powell. He's perfect, right down to that ridiculous oversize mustache."

"It's got me in trouble more than once," he admitted. "That's why you should never piss off an artist—they'll write you into their work and it won't be flattering."

"So I should look out, huh?"

"Nah. You've got nothing to worry about." He nudged her. "At this rate, I'm never going to finish the damn storyline anyway."

"How come?"

"I don't know. I don't usually get writer's block, but ever since I started writing this plotline about the bridge to the mainland, I keep getting stuck. So I detoured and wrote T the Dog and we had a few funny moments with him." Jace shook his head. "But I can't figure out how to resolve the bridge issue. I had thought about Hermit having some foiled attempts to delay the bridge's production, *Pinky and the Brain*–style. Maybe trying to blow it up. But that seemed a bit extreme."

"And he doesn't want the bridge to be built because it will bring more people to his island."

"Exactly. He's trying to keep his life quiet and stable, and the bridge will bring tourism and noise and all the other things he hates." Jace reached over to the notebook and flipped a few pages back. "I did a 'nightmare' sequence, where the town is overrun with children, that was pretty funny."

"So he's all about keeping the status quo?"

"Yeah. He has life the way he wants it, and the mayor wants to grow and expand the town to make more money."

Angie snorted. "Sounds familiar."

"I certainly take inspiration from real life."

"The thing I always wondered was how you were going to keep the story going if Hermit never changes." Angie traced a fingertip over one of the drawings of Hermit. The character was tall and had delightfully spiky hair and wore a pair of round glasses. Jace had worked a cute little detail into the drawings where Hermit's T-shirts always said something funny that related to the strip. Sometimes they were riffs on brand slogans—*Just don't do it.* Other time they were funny sayings—*I can't people today.*

"What do you mean?" he asked.

"I mean, Hermit always wants the same things. He's constantly battling changes to his town—"

"I would say he's preserving what he sees as important."

"Sure. But it's always the same thing, right? If he's always chasing the status quo, then what happens in the long term? Do you keep coming up with scenarios to have him fighting off the next big bad without ever changing?"

Jace leaned back against the headboard and blinked. "I never thought about it like that before."

"Maybe it's all the romantic comedies I've watched—the person has to change at the end of the story. They have to sacrifice something they care about to show how they've grown." She lifted a shoulder into a shrug. "But what do I know about comics? Probably nothing."

"You're smarter than you think." He was looking at her with fresh eyes now—like he'd seen something that wasn't there before.

Her heart skipped a beat. "Maybe if I was smarter, then I would have found a lawyer I could trust."

There it was—the dark cloud hovering on the horizon that threatened all the perfection of her night with Jace. It would rain all over the day if she let it. Maybe the best thing she could do now was create some distance. Try to figure out her next move.

"I should get going," she said, climbing off the bed carefully so she didn't disturb the snoozing dogs.

"Why don't you stay? We could grab lunch."

It was tempting. *So* tempting.

Jace looked like hot buttered toast and cinnamon sticks and all things cozy and right with the world. He had a pair of jeans riding low on his hips, his obscenely perfect chest on display in all its sculpted glory. His hair stuck out in every direction—coaxed by her fingers and his. But the worst thing—slash *best* thing—was the glimmer in his eyes. The anticipation. He wanted her to stay.

Angie hadn't exactly been with many guys in her life; her past and messy relationship with trust made abstinence the easier option. But on the few occasions she *had* slept with someone, there'd always been this awkward dance the morning after where she'd never quite felt welcome. Where there'd always been some niggling feeling like she needed to get out of dodge. With Jace, that feeling wasn't there. He was an open book, for better or worse. Which meant he was happy to have her here, knowing it went against her plans.

And she wasn't sure how to feel about that.

"I, uh…I promised I'd check in at work." She backed away from the bed. "And aren't you usually heading to the beach by now?"

He glanced at the clock. "Yeah."

"I don't want to disrupt your plans." She smoothed her hands down the front of the borrowed T-shirt and tugged on the hem. It came to mid-thigh, yet she still felt naked. "Thanks for last night. I had a good time."

"So did I."

Bobbing her head, she scooped up her bikini and T-shirt from the floor and headed out into the main room of the house. The throw pillows were on the ground and two barely touched Worst Cocktails Ever sat on the coffee table. It looked so…homey. Comforting.

This isn't your home. You've made damn sure of that.

Swallowing past the sense of uneasiness in her throat, she headed out Jace's back door and strode across the lawn to her place. An afternoon with her favorite poker-playing ladies should help her get her head on straight—they always had good advice. Maybe they would know what her next steps should be.

• • •

After Angie left, Jace couldn't get his head back in the game. Not even his morning surf helped, and that *always* made him feel good. Was it the amazing, mind-blowing sex? Or was it that Angie had totally zeroed in on Jace's fears about *Hermit vs. World*? That his comic was stagnating. That *he* was stagnating.

Shaking off the troubling thought, he pulled on a T-shirt and decided to head down to the pub on his lunch break. There was a tradition in Patterson's Bluff after Australia Day, where long-term residents headed to the White Crest for some good old-fashioned "hair of the dog."

Hangover cure for the true-blue Aussie.

By the time he got to the pub, it was scorching. He pushed the door open and was blasted with frosty air-conditioned air and the scent of beers and salty hangover-reducing foods. Immediately, he spotted Adam and Nick at the bar with two of their friends—brothers Leigh and Kellen.

"Hey! It's been a while." Kellen went to fetch an extra barstool to squeeze him onto their small high table. It was loaded with half-empty foamy beers and two baskets of what looked to be chips and calamari rings. "How've you been?"

"Busy." Jace took a seat. "I've been working a lot. You?"

"Same. The gym is starting to take off, but you know what it's like around here." Kellen sighed. "The true test will be how many people come through the door beyond February."

Anyone who lived in a town like Patterson's Bluff knew that dance—high season could bring money in like waves crashing on a sandy beach, but the second school started and the tourists went away…*poof!* A business could vanish quicker than it had appeared. People got cocky during the on season, made one too many risky decisions, and then didn't make it through the wet, financially barren winter.

"You should talk to Angie," Jace said. "She's putting programs together for the residents at the retirement home. It's good publicity, might be a way to make sure the locals are supporting you. She's getting Chloe in to teach a yoga class."

Leigh raised a brow. "The bendy bunnies got

an invite and we didn't?"

"Bendy bunnies?" Adam shook his head and took a long swig of his beer. "Now I've heard everything."

"Because they're always hopping around full of energy from their bloody wheat juice and kale smoothies." Leigh pulled a face. "I bumped into one of the instructors and she literally told me to have a 'namaste day.' What does that even *mean*?"

Kellen was the muscle in their gym business, and Leigh was the business brains. When they'd first opened the gym, there had been a little "disagreement" over parking space, given the gym and Chloe's yoga studio shared a lot out back. Looked like they hadn't quite patched things up.

"She was probably yanking your chain." Nick shrugged. "You don't exactly make it difficult."

"You saying I'm uptight?" Leigh frowned and went to take a sip of his beer but noticed his glass was bone dry. "Actually, don't answer that. I'm going to do the very *not* uptight thing and get the next round. Jace, you want in?"

"Thanks, man."

"So." Adam leaned back in his stool, folded his arms across his barrel of a chest, and cocked his head. It was his favorite interrogation pose, which could mean only one thing. "What happened to you last night?"

"After the barbecue? I went home."

"With Angie."

Suddenly all eyes at the table were on him, and Jace felt like the room had shot up a few hundred degrees. He hated being the center of attention—especially over something he couldn't classify properly in his head. He and Angie hadn't discussed terms or figured out next steps or put any boundaries in place. It was *not* how he liked to operate. The fuzzy gray would only lead to trouble.

But she'd bolted out of his room all of a sudden that morning and had totally shot him down when he'd invited her to stay. Though he might not be the best at reading between the lines, he *was* getting better at reading Angie.

"Well, she is currently living on my property so…not exactly a coincidence." Yeah, he sounded guilty as all hell. He was like a giant piece of tasty steak tossed into the middle of some circling sharks. "We decided to walk home together."

Adam grinned like a cat that got the cream. "That's not what Trent said."

Bloody Trent. "What *did* he say?"

"Only that he asked Angie to go to the house party with him, and you looked pissed."

"Angie the American girl?" Kellen nodded. "She's cute. Real sweet, too."

"There's nothing there." But even as Jace said the words, he knew it was bullshit. Angie had slipped past his defenses and stirred up all kinds of things he wasn't sure how to deal with. Now he was questioning everything. "Trent's story is more interesting than reality."

"Ain't that the truth." Kellen chuckled.

But reality took a sudden turn toward the interesting—well, for everyone *except* Jace— when the door of the pub swung open and the one person he'd hoped never to see again walked inside: Julia.

It was like the whole place went dead silent for a moment. If Jace had been feeling the heat of the spotlight a moment ago, it was nothing compared to this. All heads swung in his direction, including hers.

"Ho-ly shit." Adam reached out and clamped a hand down on Jace's shoulder.

His brothers might tease him and they might fight and debate and argue, but there was no doubt in his mind they had his back. Especially when it came to the source of his one and only heartbreak.

"You want me to run interference?" Adam asked.

"You don't have to talk to her," Nick added.

But Julia's small hand lifted in a kind of half wave, and there was a tightness in her face. It struck Jace that this would be *way* more unpleasant for her than it would be for him. No matter how ashamed and embarrassed he'd felt after Julia's no-show at the rehearsal dinner...*she* was the one coming back to the town who'd stood by him.

There must have been a pretty good reason for her to come back.

"It's fine." Jace slid off his stool as Leigh returned to the table with their beers. He grabbed his pint and took a fortifying sip.

Julia still hovered by the door, looking like she wanted to approach him. No doubt the curious glances of everyone in the pub—not to mention the fact that Adam was giving his patented penetrating stare that could make even the biggest of blokes break out in a sweat—was keeping her rooted to the ground. Maybe it would be good karma to put her out of her misery.

"You're really going to talk to her...after what she did?" Nick shook his head. "You're a saint, Jace. And a bigger man than I would be in your situation."

"Let's see how the conversation goes before you start the canonization process," Jace muttered.

He crossed the pub floor, trying not to notice how everyone had their eyes on him. This was small-town gossip fodder—jilted groom and the girl who crushed his heart reuniting in public. Well, he wouldn't be giving them a show, no matter what she had to say for herself.

"Hey," she said softly. "Thanks for coming over."

She looked different than he remembered—and not because he'd drawn horns and a pitchfork onto the memory of her. Her reddish hair was shorter now, feathery layers dancing around her shoulders rather than falling in a heavy sheet to her waist, like how she used to wear it. Her eyes were harder, her lips tighter. She seemed guarded and more remote.

Makes two of us.

"You're back." He took another sip of his beer, relishing the slide of the cold brew down the back of his throat.

"For now." She toyed with the hem of her dress, which had a soft trimming of lace around the edge. *That* hadn't changed—she'd always loved whimsical things. "My dad is sick. I came home to help around the house."

"Is he going to be okay?"

Despite what had happened, Jace had never held anything against Julia's father. He'd always liked the older guy, because he'd never made Jace feel uncomfortable or rude when he blurted things out at their dinner table.

"I don't know." Julia's eyes glimmered. "The doctors are hopeful, but we've got a long road ahead. He's moving very slowly at the moment, and he needs someone with him at all times."

"Lucky he's got you."

Something flickered across Julia's face—an emotion he wasn't quite sure how to label. "I wanted you to hear it from me, anyway. That I was home and that I'll probably be here for a while."

"You don't owe me an explanation," he said. The truth was, as much as the past had hurt, seeing Julia now...well, maybe the memory of what happened was worse than the reality. He'd expected to feel something stronger—a twisting in his gut, a clench in his chest. Some kind of remnant of what they'd shared. But he had nothing.

Maybe he *had* moved on after all.

"I feel like I do," she said. "I was hoping you'd be here today, because I've tried three times to walk up to your front door, and I kept chickening out."

"So you thought it would be better to have this

conversation in public?" He raised a brow.

"I don't know if there *is* a better way to do it."
She wrung her hands in front of her. "I feel like
everyone's watching us."

"That's because they are."

A quick sweep of the room sent people's
gazes skittering back to their own tables, but not
before Jace had caught every last person looking.
He loved Patterson's Bluff. But gossip reigned
supreme here. And right now, he and Julia were a
prime source of entertainment.

"Let's head out back." Jace motioned for Julia
to follow him outside to the beer garden.

The air was heavy and hot, the summer
sunshine beating down in dry, relentless waves. It
made the air full of the scent of jasmine, which
crept around the wrought-iron fence enclosing
the space. There were a few people dotted outside,
sitting at the small round tables and chugging cold
drinks. But they, at least, seemed engrossed in
their own conversations.

"I thought I should clear the air," Julia said,
taking a seat at one of the free tables tucked away
in the corner of the beer garden. "I mean, I know
I can't undo what I did, but…"

"But?"

"I owe you an apology." She bit down on her
lip. "I treated you appallingly. Leaving a note and
then running away was a terrible thing to do."

"Yeah," he said. "It was really shitty."

"I can't justify it. And I wish I had some grand
explanation that made sense of it all, but the fact
is I was scared. I knew I cared about you, but

something felt wrong and the closer we got to the wedding…I was worried we were both making a huge mistake."

"You were in love with my brother."

The words held no emotion, because Jace didn't even know how to feel about it anymore. It was a fact—something she'd confessed in a cowardly way. Something that had made Jace doubt himself. Doubt his worth. Made him believe the best life he could create for himself was one of solitude.

"I thought I was, and I felt so guilty about it. But, looking back, I wonder if I simply knew we weren't right for each other and that was my brain's way of trying to come up with a reason. Because we *should* have worked…on paper." Her eyes searched his. "We had history; we cared about the same things in life."

"Did we really?" Because now he remembered something else. Something he'd locked away deep down into a part he didn't often access: the fact that he'd *also* been dreading the wedding.

The night before the rehearsal dinner, he'd tossed and turned until dawn, trying to figure out why he wasn't more excited at the prospect of getting married. Trying to figure out why, instead of picturing his bride-to-be in flowing white satin, he was wondering if it was possible to drive all the way out of town with the headlights off.

Rather than anticipation, he'd only had anxiety and a deep, sinking sensation in his gut. But the invites had been sent, the flowers ordered, the tuxedos fitted. Everyone was expecting a wedding.

So he'd told himself not to be rash—it was cold feet. Marital jitters. Nothing more.

He'd told himself they had to go through with it because everything would work itself out.

But he'd never told anyone that when he found out Julia was gone, Jace had felt the briefest flash of relief. That was, until he'd read the note. Only then had he felt the shame and humiliation of being jilted by his would-be bride. It had taken him four lonely years to make that connection.

Julia's actions had probably saved them both a lot of pain in the future.

"I don't know why it didn't work," she said, shaking her head. "All I know is that you were nothing but kind to me. You treated me well…but we didn't mesh."

"I had doubts about marrying you, too," he admitted.

"Really?" Her shoulders sagged a little as if he'd lifted something heavy from them. "Is it weird that makes me feel a bit better?"

"Life is weird." He brought his beer up to his lips and tipped his head back. "I was still hurt that you left…" God, this was awkward. But it needed to be said. Maybe getting it out in the open was the best thing possible. "And by what you put in that note. But I've moved on."

"I'm glad. I knew it would be awkward coming home, but I told myself that if I could at least face you, then maybe I wasn't quite the same person as when I left." She sucked in a breath. "So I'm sorry I ran away and didn't confront the problem like I should have."

"And I'm sorry I let you think you were the only one having doubts."

Silence settled between them like a leaf drifting down to the ground, and then the world started to filter back into their sphere—laughter and conversation, the sound of squawking gulls overhead, music floating from the open window of a car. Jace wrapped his palms around his pint glass, absorbing the last of the cool, refreshing feeling into his skin.

He stared into the foamy depths, not quite sure what to say now. Small talk was *not* his strong suit. "Are you happy to be back home?" he asked.

Julia laughed and tucked a strand of hair behind her ears. "Am I happy to come back to the place where everyone thinks I'm an evil bitch because I ran out on the town's most beloved family? Uh, no. Not really. I'm happy to be spending time with my dad, but everyone is looking at me like I've got the plague."

"I hope your dad is doing better soon," he said.

"I hope so, too." She offered a watery smile and pulled the sunglasses that were perched on her head down over her eyes.

Julia let herself out of the beer garden through a small side gate, and Jace stayed at the table, staring into space. His beer tasted like nothing now, and it had lost its cool, crisp edge. Sweat beaded along his hairline, prickling his scalp. But he couldn't move. It was like his body was glued to the chair, unable to move until he'd adequately sifted through the conversation that had just taken place.

He'd never wanted to marry Julia.

How had he buried that thought for so long? Maybe because it was easier to be angry. Easier to be the guy who got left behind because it fit with his view of who he was—a loner, a misunderstood creative. A guy who was too rigid and too in his own head for anyone else to have a chance of knowing him. Of accepting him.

But Angie seemed to accept him. Last night had been…everything. And it had been so effortless. They'd talked about so many things— from his comics to her deep love of romantic movies, to the plans she had for Patterson's Bluff and how she loved to bake and that chocolate chip cookies were her specialty. The feeling of her body curled into his side, her hair spilling over his chest, while colors exploded in the distance, was the most at ease he'd felt in a long time.

Maybe *that* was the guy he was supposed to be.

He liked her. He wanted her to stay. And there was only one way for that to happen.

CHAPTER NINETEEN

By the time Angie pedaled home from her volunteer shift, she had a much clearer head. Riding through the quiet tree-lined streets tended to do that. She'd stopped past the Wattle & Oat bakery on the way home and picked up some vanilla slices because she knew they were Jace's favorite.

She'd give herself one more night to indulge what made her feel good before she had to face reality. Because if being with him for a short while meant enough to give up on finding lasting love in Australia, then she was going to enjoy it. She was going to make those happy memories and, hopefully, one day the good would outnumber the bad.

As she got to the front of Jace's house, she hopped off her bike and wheeled it down the path alongside his house. Bright yellow fluffs of wattle dotted the ground and gumnuts were strewn everywhere, no doubt from where the birds had been scratching for worms. The yard was quiet, but she immediately spotted Jace sitting out on his deck, sketch pad in hand. And was that…?

Angie clamped a hand over her mouth. "What the hell? Did you put Truffle in a baby sling?"

Jace looked up from his drawing and grinned. Truffle was snuggled against his chest, held in place by what appeared to be a length of cotton material wrapped around both him and Jace's torso. Angie had seen people carry babies like that, but not dogs.

"He was being super needy, and I had to get some work done. The only time he would shut up was if I let him sit on my lap, but then he got in the way." He moved his hands around as if to say, *Voila!* "So I improvised."

"He looks less pink than yesterday." Angie leaned her bike against the fence and grabbed her things from the basket hanging off the front handles. "Did you wash him again?"

"I gave him a little scrub." He eyed the bag from the bakery with its telltale flower stamp. "What have you got there?"

"Wouldn't you like to know?" She came up the small set of steps leading to the deck and saucily opened the bag so he could see inside. "A little birdie told me you like vanilla slices. And…well, I wanted an excuse to come over."

"You ran out of here like a bat out of hell this morning. I thought I must have put my foot in it."

Her heart squeezed. "It was all me."

"Do you want to come inside now?"

Usually, when Jace invited her in, there was no subtext in his words because that's the kind of guy he was—straightforward. To the point. But now… oh boy. Now, his eyes were burning her up. It was like they were channeling the hot Aussie sun and sending it straight her way.

Did he want this as much as she did? He certainly looked like it.

"You might want to ditch the doggy sling," she

said. Her voice was a little husky, a little uncertain. But 100 percent excited.

Laughing, he cradled Truffle with one big hand and set about unwinding the sling with another. It was *far* too easy to picture him as a dad, doing this very thing with a tiny bundle of joy cradled in his arms. Hell, she was cluckier than a bossy mother hen and that *wasn't* normal.

This isn't about making babies or getting married or any of that. This is about what feels good. You deserve it.

Jace released Truffle to the ground and tossed the material onto the wicker chair behind him. Then he walked straight toward her and cupped her face with his long fingers, dipping his head straight down to her mouth. Holy. Moly.

His lips coaxed her open, and his tongue drove straight into her mouth, stroking. Teasing. She almost dropped the bag of pastries while clinging to his T-shirt for dear life. Because this kiss was like having the rug pulled out from under her—he wanted her. It was written all over that intense, hot gaze and the firmness of his lips and the way his hips pressed against her and...oh yes. It was written *everywhere.*

"Wow," she breathed when he pulled away. "That's quite a greeting."

"I've been thinking about it all day," he admitted with a shy smile. "And since I mess up words, I figured action might be safer."

"I'm not here to judge you," she said. "Especially not when I was the chicken this morning."

He took her hand and led her into the house,

his fingers entwined with hers like they'd done this a thousand times before. Words jostled in her head—should they set out some kind of agreement? Some boundaries? Or were they already on the same page and would her trying to negotiate ruin this sparkling, sexy bubble?

Angie put the treats down on the counter, her other hand still in Jace's. Her appetite was being driven by only one thing—and it wasn't delicious vanilla-y custard-based snacks. Jace pulled her close, settling his butt back against the kitchen counter. She stepped between his legs and draped her arms around his neck.

"Why did you run out?" he asked.

"I needed some space to think," she admitted. "Everything you told me last night…it was a lot."

"Too much?"

"No. I'm so glad you trusted me with it. I feel like we have this connection…"

"We do."

"I wasn't prepared for it. I mean, I knew I liked you…but it was something else." She lowered her eyes for a moment, feeling exposed by the truth. Should they really be getting into this? Wouldn't it hurt less if they stuck to the physical? "I had a really good time getting to know you better."

"I did, too, Angie. You're so…everything." His hand skimmed down her back. "I haven't been able to concentrate on work. I kept drawing you over and over."

"You did?"

"Yeah." He tilted her face up to his. "You've captured me."

"And you think you don't know what to say."
She pressed up on her tiptoes and kissed him.
Softly at first. Tiny fluttering kisses. Then harder.
Deeper.

He spun her around and hoisted her up onto
the breakfast bar, nudging her legs open with
his hips. It felt like something out of a movie—
they moved seamlessly together, like it was all
choreographed. Like it had been predetermined.
Angie slid her fingers into his hair and pulled his
face close to hers, taking control of their kiss. She
felt powerful with Jace. She felt beautiful and
wanted and free.

His hands braced against her thighs, sliding
up her bare skin toward the hem of her skirt. His
fingertips traced the white flowers embroidered
into the edge of the pale-blue fabric. It matched
the cupboards in Jace's kitchen as a costume
designer had chosen it specially.

He pushed her skirt up, revealing more of
her thighs, which had turned a deep tan over the
summer. Each touch stirred something inside
her—a desperate, needy wanting that coiled low
in her stomach like a snake.

"Higher," she whispered in his ear. Jace let out
a soft moan, and his fingers tightened around her
thigh in response, denting her soft skin. "Harder
is good, too."

His lips were hot against her neck, teeth scraping her skin in a way that had every cylinder in
her body firing at maximum *oh yes!* speed. He
kissed and sucked, and all the while his palms
worked their way up and in. Opening her. The pad

of his thumb traced the seam of her sex through her underwear, and she had to bite down on her lip to keep a cry from rushing out.

She let her head roll back against the upper cabinets with a soft *thunk* as he continued the sensual exploration. His knuckles rubbed against the tight bundle of nerves before he slipped one finger behind the elastic edge of her underwear and felt the slick heat there.

"This good?" He stroked her more boldly, rubbing moisture over her clit. The sensation made Angie's back bow, her hips almost launching into the air, and she gasped.

"You don't speak pre-orgasmic moaning?" she teased. "Let's me translate: hell yes, yes please, and yes, yes, yes!"

He crouched down and placed a kiss on the inside of her knee. "That's a lot of yeses."

"I can't help myself when it comes to you."

He looked up at her and grinned.

The sight of his sandy brown head moving between her legs was possibly the most erotic thing Angie had ever seen. She waded her fingers through his hair, loving the way the stubborn strands sprang back into place and slowly melting into an Angie-shaped puddle of lust as he kissed the inside of her thigh.

"You're going to ruin your appetite."

Something darkly sexy flashed in Jace's eyes. "If there was a person on earth who'd give this up for a vanilla slice, I would be *very* surprised."

He slid her to the edge of the countertop, encouraging her to drape her legs over his shoulders.

When he set his mouth on her sex, sucking through the soaked cotton, fireworks exploded behind Angie's shuttered lids. It was like New Year's and Christmas and the Fourth of July and Australia Day and every other goddamn holiday rolled into one.

He teased her through her underwear, giving her almost enough...but not quite. "Please," she whimpered. "Is this punishment for leaving this morning?"

"Not punishment." He toyed with the leg hole on her underwear, dragging it to one side so there was no barrier between them. "Encouragement."

"An encouragement?" she panted. She curled her hands over the edge of the counter as he swiped his tongue along her, sending arrows of pleasure driving through her body. She was so close...oh, so close.

"That maybe you might wanna stay a while."

His words drew a groan from her mouth. She knew he didn't mean stay forever, but was it terrible if her heart interpreted it that way?

She shifted, trying to give him better access. Showing him what she wanted. Then he sucked her clit between his lips, his tongue doing some amazing flicking thing that had her screwing her eyes shut and making soundless cries. Yes, yes, yes. Then she was flying, shaking, trembling. Actually freaking trembling like it was her first time having an orgasm. She'd never had one so strong before.

Jace was gifted with his mouth, even if its best use *wasn't* talking. She slumped back against the upper counters and watched as he rested his cheek against her thigh. Warm breath puffed over her skin, and when he blinked, his lashes tickled her skin.

She'd never thought of oral sex as particularly romantic. Hot? Yeah. Pleasurable? Of course. But never...sweet. Yet here they were. That tended to happen with Jace; he caused her to flip her opinions on their head.

"You're really good at that," she said shyly.

He straightened up and helped her down from the countertop. She smoothed her skirt down over her legs.

"Don't fuss with that too much." His voice was as gravelly as the roads leading to the beach. "It's going to get pretty wrinkled when I throw it on the floor."

"And what about this?" She brought her hands to the fine mother-of-pearl buttons on her cami top. She pushed one through the hole and then another. And another. "Are we throwing this on the floor, too?"

"All of it," he growled.

She backed through the kitchen, working the buttons loose. But when she went to turn into the bedroom, he changed their course, steering her into his bathroom. She caught a glimpse of herself in the mirror above the white vanity—hair coming loose from her ponytail, eyes wide, lips pink and swollen. She looked every bit like a woman in charge of her sexuality.

He came up behind her, catching her gaze in the mirror. Without breaking eye contact, he slipped the camisole's straps from her shoulders and let it slither to the ground. Underneath, she had on one of those barely there bras. The kind that was more for the visual than for the function—with generous sections of lace that showed her nipples through the fabric. He slid his hands up over her ribs and cupped her, his thumbs brushing the sensitive peaks.

Brushing his hands away, she unhooked the front closure and tossed the bra to the ground, relishing in the appreciative sound Jace let out behind her. Then she bent forward, shimmying out of her skirt and underwear. She took a good minute undoing the straps on her sandals and kicking them off, knowing he was getting quite the eyeful.

"You are putting on one hell of a show," he said, letting his eyes roam over her naked form.

She reached into the shower and turned the knob until water started flowing. "Now it's your turn."

"Want to give me a hand?"

She yanked the T-shirt out of his jeans and whipped it over his head…well, as much over his head as she could with their mismatched height. He had to finish the job, and they both laughed, not caring about any little awkward moments. Because that was life. Sex *wasn't* choreographed and this felt so…real.

So right.

Jace was staring flames down at her as she ran her hand over the fly of his jeans, gently grazing the bulge that pressed hard against his zipper. When she squeezed him, he let out a *whoosh* of air. Good Lord, he was thick. She'd been so swept away last time, she hadn't given herself a moment to appreciate him. Every detail was perfect.

Swallowing against the slight tightness in her throat, Angie pulled Jace's zipper down and shoved the soft fabric over his hips. His boxer briefs went, too, and he toed off his sneakers and socks, leaving him naked.

"Wow," she said. He was a sight to behold—all six foot four, lean and bronzed surfer goodness. "You are *literally* muscled everywhere."

To Angie's absolute delight, Jace ducked his head, and a faint wash of pink colored his cheeks. Who knew a bashful guy could be the hottest thing of all? A guy who looked like that— with sculpted pecs and strong arms and those superhero-movie V muscles—shouldn't be so modest.

"Don't be embarrassed," she said, coming up to him and grabbing his hand. "You work hard, and it shows. I know you don't do it for the looks, but I'm still going to enjoy the fruits of your labor."

He fisted her half-fallen-out ponytail in his hand and tipped her head back for a searing kiss. "Water should be good now."

"Condom?"

He broke away and grabbed one from his cupboard and tore at the foil, getting frustrated when it didn't open immediately. "Glad to see I'm still smooth as sandpaper underneath it all."

"I love it. *And* it balances out all this." She waved her hand up and down him. "Less intimidating that way."

"Thanks…I think?" He raised a brow.

"It's a compliment, trust me."

Angie took the foil packet from his hands and got it open. Then she rolled the rubber down the thick, curved length of him, and suddenly the teasing mood evaporated like steam. Teasing was comfortable and easy, but a quick scratch at the surface revealed that she was very, *very* hot for Jace. Like, *about to spontaneously combust* hot for him.

"I happen to think *you're* the intimidating one." He stalked forward, backing her right into the shower and under the steady stream of deliciously warm water.

"Bullshit."

"Seriously." He pressed her against the tiles, and the shock of the cold at her back with his hot body at her front was enough to temporarily freeze her brain. "You're the kind of girl I never thought I'd stand a chance with. Beautiful, funny, smart, kind."

"I like the way I look through your eyes."

"It's the truth."

He grabbed her wrists in one big hand and pinned them above her head, his body easily moving hers into position. Using his free hand, he hoisted her leg over his hip. The hard length of his cock pressed at her entrance, and he rubbed back and forth, coating himself in her. Warming her up.

"I want you inside me," she whispered, but the drumming water swallowed her words. She grabbed his head and yanked it down to hers. "Jace, please. I can't wait any longer."

Letting out one of the most incredible sounds Angie had ever heard, Jace turned to the shelf on the back wall of the shower stall that held a small collection of shampoo bottles and body wash. Sweeping one hand across the lot, he knocked all the bottles to the ground and then hoisted Angie onto it. The ledge was small, not really made for a human backside, but with his large body in front of her, she was totally secure.

Jace ran his hands along her legs and pulled her ankles behind his back. Water streamed over them, and it ran in rivulets down his magnificent chest. She imagined this was how he looked emerging from the ocean—like a sea god coming to claim the land before him.

"I love it when you look at me like that," he breathed. He positioned himself at her entrance, one hand braced against the tiles.

When his eyes connected with hers, strong and steady, her stomach filled with butterflies. Thousands and thousands of beating wings, making sure she'd remember this forever.

"Ready?"

"I was ready an hour ago."

When he pushed inside her, the sensation exploded through her body, sending champagne bubbles racing along her veins and making every muscle coil tight in anticipation. Jace swore against her neck, moving slowly at first as if savoring the moment. But Angie didn't want sweet and slow. Her body was so wound up, she needed to know he was as uncontrolled with passion as she was.

So she raked her nails along his back, and Jace's eyes flew to hers, the blue of his irises eaten away by arousal. This time when he pushed into her, it was hard. Hot. Angie clung to him as he thrust into her over and over, whispering all kinds of dirty things in her ear. Each slamming heartbeat brought them closer together, and she was panting his name within minutes.

Who knew sex could be as good as in the movies?

Another orgasm curled deep inside her, building and building and building...

"Oh my God," she cried, arching into him. Her teeth scraped along his shoulder and when she came, shuddering hard in his arms, it was like she'd launched straight up into heaven. "Jace!"

"I'm with you." He pumped into her once more, long and smooth, and then his hips jerked. His arms tightened around her as he tipped over the edge, following her into the foggy cloud of pleasure.

CHAPTER TWENTY

They didn't move until the hot water ran out, and then it was a mad scramble to freedom. Laughing, they tumbled out of the glass stall and reached for the fluffy towels hanging on a rack by the door. Jace couldn't believe how lucky he was to have Angie here with him again. Her cheeks were flushed pink, and her eyes were sparkly and wide.

"They're doing it again," she said, covering her face with her hands. "We've got to start locking them out if we're going to get busy."

Tilly and Truffle stood in the doorway, looking up at their half-naked babysitters. Jace pulled the towel tighter over his crotch. "Not cool, guys. It's starting to get creepy."

Angie flashed him a wicked smile. "Not into voyeurism?"

"What can I say, I'm a selfish guy." He pulled her close and wrapped his arms around her waist. "I don't like to share."

"Neither do I." She tipped her face up to his. "I want every bit of you all to myself."

"For how long?"

The question seemed to suck the life out of the room, but Jace had decided that he didn't want to go any further before they talked about what it all meant. If his chance meeting with Julia had taught him anything that afternoon, it was that ignoring an issue wasn't helpful. He could have saved them both a lot of heartache if he'd voiced his opinions and wants instead of letting the doubt fester silently.

He wasn't going to make that same mistake with Angie.

"What do you mean?" she asked.

"You want every bit of me…for how long?"

Her eyes suddenly became closed off, as if she'd shuttered part of herself away. "Is that a rhetorical question?"

"No, it's a serious one."

"I…I don't know. I have no idea what this is." She shook her head. "I'm having fun."

Jace frowned. It wasn't exactly the response he'd been hoping for. Had Angie changed her mind about wanting to stay? Was this a last hurrah to her? "I'm having fun, too."

She toyed with the knot holding her towel closed and glanced awkwardly down at her feet.

Wow. Way to kill the mood. Maybe you should have let the good feelings roll for a whole minute before you started infecting them with your awkwardness.

"I wish I was better at this," he said with a sigh.

"At what? The extraction?"

"Huh? No. I mean the 'after' bit." This was *not* going how he'd wanted it to. "I'm not trying to extract anything. I thought maybe it was a good time to…"

What *did* he think?

"It's fine, Jace." She walked into the hallway and started making her way through to the kitchen, scooping up her clothing as she went. "I promise I'm not going to get all stage-five clinger on you."

"I don't even know what that means." He scrubbed a hand over his face.

"It's been clear from the start that we want different things…and then we fell into bed. I don't regret it at all." Her cheeks turned a deeper shade of pink as she clutched her clothing to her chest. "But I'm telling you not to worry, because I'm not expecting you to change your stance. I understand why now."

Was this more about his failed attempt at marriage with Julia or because he shared that he was on the spectrum?

"So based on that," she continued, "I know that two nights of great sex won't magically solve all our problems. We shared something amazing and that's it. I'm going to lock that happy memory away."

"You're already viewing it as a memory?"

She talked like it was over and done with, a check in the box. Like they weren't still together right now.

"I didn't want to make this difficult on either one of us." She bit down on her lip. "I thought if I focused on the good…"

"Isn't it all good?"

She made a noise that sounded a hell of a lot like his family did when they were frustrated with him. "What I'm saying is that I'm trying not to expect things that will leave me disappointed."

The conversation was going south quicker than a newbie wiping out on a heavy wave. "We haven't even had a chance to discuss expectations."

Jace was certainly not an expert in reading subtext—*that* had been proven many times over. But nothing coming out of Angie's mouth was ringing true, not even a little bit. She was trying to shut him down before he had the chance to say what he was thinking, like she assumed he was going to be a jerk about it. That stung, if he was being honest. But Angie must be trying to protect herself, and he had to respect that.

"I'm not trying to kick you out," he said, closing a hand over hers. "But you're not even giving me a chance to say what's on my mind."

She eyed him warily. "Is this a conversation where I should be dressed?"

"I honestly don't know. The more I talk, the less I understand how communication works."

That seemed to slow down Angie's spiral, and the corner of her lip twitched. "You and me both."

It was times like this that Jace wished he'd been better blessed with the gift of gab like every other person in his family. Clearly, he'd been standing in another line when God was handing out interpersonal skills.

But he was going to try. Because that's all that was in his power.

"I like you, Angie," he began.

"But?" Her eyes glimmered.

"But this isn't a normal situation." He raked a hand through his damp hair. "There's a clock ticking."

"Tell me something I don't know." She looked away from him.

"I feel terrible that you're in this position because of someone else's ineptitude. It's not fair." He paused for a minute to select the words as carefully as he could. This was not a time to stuff things up. "I want to help."

There was only one way he *could* help. Only one way he could keep Angie here, with him, so they could keep exploring each other. Keep learning. The thought of her leaving now— thinking they were nothing but a memory—it felt so wrong, he wanted to scream.

He'd been looking at everything with the lens of his failed relationship with Julia, but talking to her had changed his perspective. Marriage wasn't the problem. It was communication, or lack thereof. And with Angie, he felt like maybe he could be better.

Frowning, she looked back at him. Something he couldn't quite read was swimming in her eyes. "How?"

"I'll marry you."

She blinked. "Excuse me."

"I'll marry you so you can stay. I can fix your problem."

He'd expected her to show some reaction to his offer, but instead her face was a mask. Dammit. He *hated* being like this. He hated feeling like he was messing things up when he was trying to make them better. He wanted her to stay more than anything.

"It's what you wanted, right?"

She blinked slowly. Once, twice, three times. "No, it's not what I wanted."

Shit.

"Jace…" Her expression was definitely somewhere in the gray area, and Jace suddenly found it hard to breathe. "I know you probably think you're doing the right thing, but I said from the start I didn't want a fake marriage. I'd hoped I might be able to find love and get married and have a chance at finding a home here, a *real* happy life."

"That's what I'm offering."

"No it's not. You're offering to help. You're… fixing my problem, like it doesn't even have anything to do with what *you* want." To his horror, her face went white. "This wasn't a pity screw, was it?"

"What? No! Were we not experiencing the same thing in there?" He gestured to the bathroom. "I like you, Angie. A lot, in fact."

"But you've made it clear that you don't want to get married. You want to be the hermit from your comics and live alone in your quiet, unmessy little world." She pressed her hands over her face, but her towel slipped and she swore. She sounded as though she was spiraling inside—he knew that because that's often how he felt when things went wrong. He knew that tornado of thoughts, each one worse than the last. "This conversation definitely needed us to be fully clothed."

He was digging a hole, and now he couldn't see the way out. "I thought that's what I wanted, but the foundation of that entire belief was based on something false."

"Which was?"

"I never wanted to marry Julia in the first place. I had doubts, but I kept them quiet, and then when she left and I was hurt by what she wrote in the note...so I focused on that. I knew it was wrong at the time, but I couldn't admit it to myself."

"So you're telling me that you know you want to marry me because you were about to marry someone else who you actually didn't want to marry...only you were going to do it because you felt obligated?" She stared at him like he was an alien species. "That makes no sense."

"It made sense in my head," he replied with a sigh.

"Even the non-proposal?"

Was that what this was about? Because he hadn't gotten down on one knee? "Can we start this conversation again? It went in a direction that I didn't want it to, and I'd like to try again."

Angie bit down on her lip. "I don't think that's a good idea."

"I want you to stay." He stepped closer to her. "I like you and I want you to stay here. The only way for that to happen is for me to marry you."

"And how will I know that the night before the wedding, you're not silently regretting your decision, hoping I'll back out so you don't have to?"

Ouch. "I don't make the same mistake twice."

"Neither do I, usually." Her eyes fluttered shut for a moment. "I shouldn't have come over."

She headed for the door, going straight outside

in his towel. Jace wasn't sure how long he stood there, watching her cross the lawn and wondering what the hell had happened. How did he manage to screw everything up even when he had the right intentions?

Tilly trotted out to the main room and plopped down by his side. But when she looked up at him, he got the distinct impression she was judging him.

• • •

Angie avoided Jace all day on Thursday and for most of the day on Friday, but not because she was annoyed with him. She was more annoyed with herself. They'd had amazing sex where she'd felt this deep connection, only for the moment to be ruined by both their baggage the second things got real.

It wasn't his fault. She'd started to wrap her head around the fact that the thing between them wasn't going anywhere, and then he'd thrown a wrench in it by suddenly wanting to swoop in and save the day like some kind of matrimonial superhero.

It's a bird… It's a plane… It's marriage man!

Ugh. He wanted to "fix her problem"…not exactly what all her little-girl fantasies had been building up toward. She'd hoped one day that a man might be so enraptured by her that he'd fall to one knee and profess his love. Was it old-fashioned? Maybe. But it's what she wanted. The whole twinkling fairy tale complete with a big red-bow-style happily ever after. The passionate love that couldn't be tamed.

Not a pity proposal.

In a fit of disgust at her own pathetic-ness, she'd boxed up the VHS player and all the rom-com tapes. She would return the player to him, and if he didn't want the tapes, she'd ride them down to the charity store next week. She had no use for them now.

After being with Jace, she knew there was no way anyone else in this town—or possibly anywhere else—would compare. Sure, he didn't always say the thing she wanted to hear, but there was no denying he made her heart flutter. That was the worst part of it all—she *really* liked him. Liked the way he made her feel, liked the fact that he listened to all her grand plans for the retirement home and offered thoughtful suggestions. She liked that he was creative and good with dogs and a total family guy. He wanted to help her…but she needed more than that. If she was going to marry someone, it would be for the right reasons.

You're asking for too much.

But was she? Hadn't her childhood taught her that she was responsible for finding her own path, her own happiness? That if she didn't think herself worthy of a good life, then nobody else would be lining up to give it to her? She had to seize it. Demand it.

And as much as Jace was everything she could have wanted, she wouldn't settle.

She stood in the middle of her cozy little

granny flat and looked around. When she'd moved in six months ago, she'd done her best to make it feel like home.

She loved this little place. Never mind that she could reach the kettle from the dining table or that her bedroom was barely more than a ruler's length around the double bed. It was the first place to ever make her happy. The first place she'd looked forward to coming home to.

"Maybe you should be grateful you had it, even if for a short time," she said to herself.

There were people who'd come out of the foster system a lot worse than her—people whose scars were external as well as internal, who had more to worry about than living their life in a fishbowl. Angie *was* grateful to have had the opportunity to come to Australia, even if it felt like her heart was breaking knowing she'd have to leave.

Jace popped into her head. Whenever she thought about the future, he was there. That crooked, sexy smile. Those bluer-than-blue eyes.

"Stop it," she cursed herself. What kind of self-inflicted torture was this?

A *thump* on her front door startled Angie out of her reverie. She was supposed to be working on her proposal for the retirement home board today, making plans to call local businesses and get their agreement to donate classes.

She headed to the front door and pulled it open.

"Hey." Jace stood there, a crinkle between his brows and his hands shoved into the pockets of his jeans. "Can we talk?"

"I'm working." *Liar, liar, pants on fire.*

She wasn't ready to deal with this yet, mainly because she still hadn't figured out how to protect her heart around him.

"Please."

She hesitated a moment longer, but he looked so earnest that eventually she stepped back and allowed him to come inside. God, what was she supposed to say? Or maybe she shouldn't say anything at all.

This was *just* like all those times she'd been shuffled to a new home. That period of awkwardness got shorter every time, once she learned how to quickly insert herself into people's lives. But even though she didn't let that weirdness show, it didn't mean it wasn't there on the inside.

"What did you want to talk about?" she asked.

Jace walked over to the couch and dropped down on it, his long legs needing to bend so they didn't hit the coffee table. "I didn't articulate myself very well the other day."

She took a seat on one of the chairs on the other side of the table. "Okay."

Jace dug into his pocket and pulled out a note—it looked like it had been folded and unfolded several times. The edges were bent, and there were crumple marks all over it. He drummed his fingers against his leg. That little sign made her relax—because it meant this at-ease exterior was simply that: a front. He was as nervous as she was.

"I wrote down what I wanted to say because I thought it might go better, since…well, you know," he said. Then he cleared his throat. "The marriage proposal wasn't only about helping you stay, because I know that if you were only looking for a piece of paper, you could have found that anywhere. The thought of you leaving makes me really sad. In fact, there's not a single reason in the pro column."

"Did you actually write a list of pros and cons about me leaving?" For some reason, that made her heart melt.

"Yeah, I did. And they were all cons." He looked so sincere, it made her want to throw her arms around his neck and kiss him silly. "If this were any normal situation, I wouldn't be proposing now. That's not romantic, but it's the truth. However, this isn't a normal situation and I've been viewing marriage for a long time tainted by something that shouldn't have tainted it. So if the only way that we get to explore this thing between us is for me to propose, then I want to do it. Because not having that chance to see where it goes is too high a price to pay."

"Wow," she breathed. "I was *not* expecting that."

"I wasn't, either. But if I put my logical cap on—"

"When did it ever come off?" She laughed.

"If I put my logical cap on," he repeated, ignoring her dig, "why not try? You have forty days remaining on your visa, right?"

"Forty-two, actually." Not that she was counting down every single second or anything.

"Why don't we trial it for a month? We'll get engaged, and we've got thirty days to see if it's working. If not, then you have almost two weeks to say goodbye and get everything in order."

Some part of her had thought that in the cold light of reality—rather than the rose-tinted post-sex haze—Jace would change his mind about his offer. Instead, he was here, asking her to reconsider. Showing he'd put a lot of thought into it. It wasn't romantic, sure. But it was Jace, through and through.

"Angie." He stood and walked around the coffee table to her, reaching down to her hands and pulling her up to standing. "I was too afraid to admit it before, because I let my own insecurities and fears get the better of me. But being with you...it meant I couldn't ignore how I felt anymore."

"I couldn't ignore it anymore, either," she said. "But?"

This was the time to be honest with him. He'd taken a leap, showed his cards, and laid everything on the table. She had to do the same. "I'm scared."

"Scared of what?"

"That you're going to regret asking me to marry you. That you're going to wake up in a month and think that what you thought you wanted—peace and quiet and solitude—*is* actually what you want."

That he would change his mind, like he'd done before.

And *that* would be like experiencing foster care all over again. The hopes dashed when inevitably people found her too difficult. Angie had tried so damn hard, but eventually the facade of the "perfect girl" was too difficult to keep up. She'd slip, let her imperfections show. Let the real Angie show. And that's when she'd find herself packing her bags, unwanted and unloved again.

Maybe she'd been chasing that mythical passionate "big" love because it wasn't real…and therefore she couldn't get hurt. But this thing with Jace, whatever it was, was fragile and delicate and honest.

And that scared the crap out of her.

You can make it work. You want this, and you want him. Everything you asked for is staring you right in the face, but you're too chickenshit to take it!

"I can't remember the last time I was so happy as the other morning when I had you and those two funny dogs all piled on the bed with me." He squeezed her hands. "It's the opposite of everything I thought I wanted. So let's try. Let's see where this goes."

"I never thought you'd be the kind of man to jump into something and 'see how it goes.' Don't you plan everything out?" She cocked her head, wondering if she pinched herself, she would wake up and be cuddling her pillow.

"I have planned everything out," he said. "We need to submit a Notice of Intended Marriage form to the Victorian Marriage Registry at least one month before the intended wedding date along with our birth certificates and IDs. Then we could get married at the registry office so we can put your application in for a spousal visa, and then we can have a non-legal ceremony with all the trimmings at whatever point we want."

Of *course* he'd done the research.

She laughed, shaking her head in wonder. "This is nuts."

"It was your idea," he pointed out.

"And I honestly wasn't sure I'd ever pull it off."

"Does that mean you don't want to take your chance with some other eligible Patterson's Bluff bachelor?" His tone was joking, but there was something serious and vulnerable glimmering in his eyes.

"No, I don't. Not even a little bit." She swallowed against the lump in the back of her throat. "The only reason you weren't on my list was because of the conversation we had when I first found out about the mistake with my visa extension. You made it clear what you thought of marriage."

"That was the only reason?"

She nodded. "Otherwise you would have been the entire list."

"Well, now that it's settled…" He dropped down to one knee and pulled a small box from his pocket. It was old and worn; the pretty blue flocking was totally rubbed off in patches. Inside was a small gold ring with a subtle pattern engraved on the band and a small but sparkly diamond in the center. "Angie Donovan, will you agree to a thirty-day trial engagement?"

Despite the warning prickle of tears in her eyes, she laughed. "Do I need to read a terms and conditions document before I accept?"

He frowned. "I didn't think of that."

"I trust you," she said. Jace was one of the only people she'd told about her past; he knew more of her real life than anyone. If that wasn't a sign he was special, then she didn't know what was. "And yes, I agree to a thirty-day trial engagement."

"I know the ring isn't much, but it belonged to my great-grandmother. If you want something different—"

"Stop." She shook her head, finding herself feeling a little overwhelmed. "I never had a family, so I never had heirlooms or history or anything like that. Which makes this the *most* perfect thing you could have given me."

He took her hand and slipped the ring onto her finger. It was a little snug, but Angie took that as a good sign. It was like the ring wanted to stay there.

"Thank you, Jace."

"For being the kind of guy who writes a list of pros and cons before proposing?" he teased.

"For being willing to be more."

CHAPTER TWENTY-ONE

Jace woke slowly, blinking at the bright sunshine streaming in through his window and the unfamiliar sound of someone pottering in his kitchen. Usually when he woke, the house was silent and dark, but for some reason...

He glanced at his alarm clock. Nine thirty? He was usually up for hours by now. Given it was a Saturday, the beach would be horrendously busy already and that was *not* how he liked to surf.

But he couldn't even feel grumpy about it—he was still reveling in the happiness from last night. After he'd proposed, they'd decided to celebrate with wine on the deck and a simple dinner of barbecued salmon and vegetables. The dogs had played in the yard, and they'd stayed outside in the balmy evening air until the sky turned from blue to orange to star-speckled navy. Eventually they'd fallen into bed, limbs entwined and mouths connected, and made love until God only knew when.

There was a thump on the other side of the wall, followed by what sounded like a curse and the excited yipping of Truffle the Troublemaker. A few seconds later, there was a soft knock at his door.

"Come in," Jace said. "And, for the record, if you're going to be staying here, you don't need to ask permission to come in the bedroom."

The door eased open slowly, and the two dogs bolted past Angie, who was moving slowly thanks to the tray balanced in her hands. Or rather…the cutting board?

"I wanted to make you breakfast in bed, but I couldn't find a good tray anywhere." She beamed as she came over to him, carefully setting the board down on the bed.

A plate was full to bursting with bacon, eggs, and toast. In a small dish was some precisely cubed apple and melon, a dollop of yogurt, and a full mug of coffee with a jug of milk on the side. It was easily enough to feed an entire footy team.

"I hope you're going to help me finish all this," he said in bewilderment. Usually, his breakfast was plain porridge, and that was *after* he'd worked up an appetite on the waves.

"Oh, I don't usually eat breakfast." She shooed the dogs away from the food. "But I'll sit with you after I've cleaned up in the kitchen."

"This is really sweet, Angie. But I don't expect you to make me breakfast in the morning." He caught her wrist.

"I know." She nodded. "It just…well, it's our first morning as an engaged couple, and I wanted to do something special."

"Thank you, I appreciate it."

Her smile returned, and she bounded out of the room, the clanging in the kitchen resuming a moment later. Truffle and Tilly were on his bed, all two sets of canine eyes trained intently on the feast. He'd made it a rule not to feed the dogs from his own plate, not wanting to send them back to Eugenie with any bad habits they didn't already possess. But this morning would have to be an exception.

As nice as it looked, the smell turned his stomach a little. He wasn't used to eating as soon as he woke, but he also didn't want to disappoint Angie. He'd learned that lesson the hard way with Julia—sometimes it was better to do what was expected.

He picked up a piece of bacon and bit down on it. The dogs' staring intensified.

Feeling more than a little guilty, he made the dogs get off the bed and told them to sit. Then he fed them each a piece of bacon, which they wolfed down in less than a second.

"You like that, huh?" he said softly.

Truffle jumped up against the bed, his paws slapping down on the side of the mattress.

"No. Down." The little dog obeyed, and then he gave them each a bit more bacon.

He forced himself to eat a piece of toast with some of the scrambled eggs, and then he hid some of the bacon under the other piece of toast. He'd have to make sure he was the one to throw it out, so it looked like he'd eaten more than he had. No way was he going to hurt Angie's feelings on day one of their trial engagement.

By the time he'd spent an appropriate amount of time feeding the dogs and rearranging his plate, Angie was done with the cleanup. Jace got out of bed and walked into the kitchen, plate in hand and dogs trailing after him like he was the Pied Piper.

"Wow." The kitchen was sparkling. Not that Jace was a messy kinda guy—not at all. But Angie had taken the cleaning to a new level. "I can see my own face in the backsplash."

"It's nothing." She wiped her hands on a tea towel. "Too much food?"

"It was amazing." He planted a kiss on her head and stealthily moved past her before she could see the mushrooms and extra bacon hiding under the remaining piece of toast. "I guess I was still a bit full from all that salmon last night."

He scraped the leftover food into the bin and quickly closed the lid.

"It was delicious. You're a great cook," she said. "Who taught you?"

"Both my parents are good in the kitchen, so I learned from them. Then when I moved in here, I wanted to be independent and I didn't have a lot of money at the time, so takeout wasn't a regular thing. Necessity breeds skill, I guess."

"This is your grandparents' house, right?" She leaned against the bench and reached for a mug of coffee.

In the bright morning light, Angie looked incredibly beautiful. She had on a loose white shirt that billowed around her slender body and a pair of denim shorts that exposed her long tanned legs. They'd spent the night exploring each other more slowly, like they were taking the time to indulge. To learn each other. But he was *still* hungry for her. Still found lust drilling into his bones and tightening his senses.

He couldn't get enough.

He nodded. "They'd lived here ever since we were kids. Back then we were closer to Melbourne, but we came here as a family when I started high school. I ended up moving in the flat you're staying in when I was seventeen."

"How come?"

It seemed silly now, looking back at it. But at the time it had felt like the most necessary thing in his life. "I needed to get out of the house. I was sharing a room with Trent, and he was driving me bananas. There was no privacy, and it was loud all the time. I couldn't be myself."

The light bounced off her eyes, highlighting the rich golden-brown tones. They crinkled ever so slightly when she smiled. "And your grandparents let you use it?"

"Yep. The place had been empty for a few years, after my great-grandmother passed away. When I confessed I was having a hard time at home, they offered to take me in." He remembered how hurt his parents had looked when they found out he wanted to move out—but they'd understood. They'd probably figured he'd never move out, given how much he struggled with a change in his environment. But *that's* how badly he wanted his own space. "I was pretty responsible with school and homework, so they didn't worry about that. The first night I moved in there, I felt so…free."

Something flickered across Angie's face, but it was gone before Jace could decipher it. "What made you decide to rent it out?"

"It's a good supplement to my comic income.

At least, it was at the time."

His income had grown steadier with *Hermit vs. World* amassing a hungry and loyal fan base. As with any creative job, there were drier spells. But if he signed a contract with the syndication company…well, he wouldn't have to worry about money at all.

"That's great. Not many people can make that sort of thing successful."

He nodded. "I'm very fortunate."

"No, you're very *talented*," she corrected.

Silence set between them a little awkwardly. It was like something had shifted since his proposal yesterday, but he wasn't sure what exactly had changed. It seemed like they could communicate perfectly fine in bed. There, they were in sync. In tune. But here in his exceptionally clean kitchen, his stomach protesting the heavy breakfast, something felt…off.

"Is everything okay?" he asked.

"Of course. Why would you ask that?" There was a flash of mild panic on her face, but she pasted a pretty smile over the top.

These were the times Jace doubted himself— doubted what he was reading in other people, doubted that he could trust his own intuition about his relationships.

It's just nerves about the whole marriage thing. Your life kind of changed overnight, so no wonder you're feeling a bit off-kilter.

But the mental pep talk didn't help.

"Why don't we go for a drive?" he suggested. "We can take the dogs, head along the coast, and get some fresh air. If you put some bathers on, then we can find a spot quiet enough to have a dip."

"I thought you hated going to the beach on the weekend?"

"I don't like crowds," he replied. "But we can get out of town, head over to the bay side, and find somewhere nice."

"Only if you want to," she said. But Jace could tell Angie *did* want it—though why she didn't come out and say that was beyond him.

Clearly, he still had a long way to go in navigating communications and relationships.

"I wouldn't have suggested it if I didn't want to do it." He offered what he hoped was a reassuring smile. "Come on, let's get changed and grab the dogs."

. . .

Angie couldn't shake the weird cocktail of feelings brewing inside her. She had this overwhelming sense that she was going to mess things up with Jace—that she'd do the wrong thing or say the wrong thing and he'd end up regretting his decision to propose.

His car whipped along the Nepean Highway, skirting the edge of Port Phillip Bay, with the windows down and wind rustling their hair. Truffle and Tilly were in the back—Tilly laying across the seat and Truffle in his padded booster so he could see out the window and avoid getting car sick. The weather was perfect—not too hot, not too cool, sunny with fluffy marshmallow clouds. A Goldilocks day.

But Angie's thoughts were like an itch that couldn't be scratched. She'd been here before—new opportunities, new promises so fragile, she was sure they had to be broken. History had made her wary of being excited in the face of something that seemed too good to be true. And this did.

She glanced over at Jace, who had a pair of wraparound sporty sunglasses covering his eyes. The sun hit his profile in the most spectacular way—highlighting his strong jaw and nose, bouncing off the golden hairs dusting his forearms, and making his skin look bronzed and smooth.

"I can feel you staring at me," he said without taking his eyes off the road.

"Just admiring the view," she quipped. Nestling back into her seat, she tore her gaze away and tried to relax.

You should be enjoying yourself. Not worrying about every little thing that could go wrong.

She rubbed her thumb over the ring sitting on her left hand. Ever since Jace had slipped it onto her finger with a reverence she'd never expected, Angie couldn't stop staring at it. The gold band was beautifully designed, the engraving giving a slight Art Deco feel. It was nothing like the OTT rocks many jewelry stores put in their windows—the whole bigger-is-better thing never resonated with Angie. But this…this was perfect. Sentimental, meaningful, honest.

It was the real deal. Only now, as an adult

who'd had her eyes opened by life, she truly understood the risk involved in such a gesture. The immense amount she had to lose.

Jace pulled off the highway where a sign pointed to a camping ground. "This spot is good. Shouldn't be too busy, since school starts back on Monday and most families have gone home to get prepared."

He was right. The small camping ground and caravan park was barely half-full—probably well less than half, in fact. There were a few clusters of people who looked to be in their twenties, mostly drinking and laughing. A group of guys played soccer in one of the grassy areas, and their friends cheered from the sidelines.

They continued through to a quiet road on the other side that led to a small parking lot. Jace pulled into one of the remaining spots and killed the engine. As soon as they opened their doors, the sound of the ocean flooded them. There were quite a few people on the beach, but it was nothing like the height of the holiday season where finding a spot big enough to lay your towels down was like hunting for a needle in a haystack.

Jace helped Tilly and Truffle out of the back seat. Truffle was on a leash with his harness, since he tended to be a bit skittish when first assessing a new place with other people. Tilly, however, was perfectly happy to lope beside them, unharnessed.

"Don't forget your SPF," Jace said.

"Thanks, Dad," she teased.

"Mock me all you want." He slung a beach bag over one shoulder and locked up the car.

Angie took Truffle's leash from him to free up his hand. "You haven't experienced the rite of passage where you think you're invincible and end up turning into a lobster. Many of the cafés and shops have sunscreen dispensers to encourage more people to protect themselves."

"I feel like that describes Patterson's Bluff in a nutshell," Angie said with a smile. "Everybody looks out for one another."

"Almost everybody," Jace corrected. "We've got our bad eggs like everywhere else."

"But those people are an anomaly. I've never felt so welcomed into a community like I did when I moved here. It's one of the reasons I was so desperate to stay." She felt the analytical slide of Jace's gaze over her skin.

"Speaking of which, we need to tell my parents about the engagement."

The statement cycled in her head, making her feel like she was hovering at the edge of a cliff. *This* was the element she hadn't considered when concocting her grand plan to fall in love hard and fast…what other people might say.

Who cares what other people say?

But Angie did care what Jace's family would say, because she liked them a lot. They were lovely people, the kind of family she'd always hoped to be a part of. And, of course, because she knew he cared, too. As someone who'd been at the mercy of other people's opinions her whole life, it worried her.

What if they questioned her motives? Would he want to be honest that her being able to stay in the country was a driving force for their getting married? Or would he want to hide that detail away? Keep it secret and hope that nobody ever found out?

Oh God, what if Paul Westerly decided to tell people about her visa issues when news of the engagement got out?

"And we should probably tell them soon." Jace said it as though it wasn't a big deal that Angie was currently doubt-spiraling over. "They'll have questions, no doubt."

"Questions?" she squeaked.

They were walking across the beach, looking for the perfect spot to stop and settle. But Angie's mind couldn't have been further from the blue skies and bluer waters. Even the enthusiastic wagging of Truffle's skinny little pink-tinged tail didn't make her smile like it usually did.

"Well, yeah." Jace looked at her strangely. "I mean, we're springing an engagement on them when they didn't even know we were dating."

"That's because we weren't dating." In true Angie fashion, she'd jumped in with both feet—no thought to the consequences.

Jace stopped and shook out the towels, laying them down carefully and then smoothing out the wrinkles with his palms. That little quirk always made her smile—he did it the same way every time. Shake, smooth. Shake, smooth. But today, the smile was not forthcoming. "Are you worried about telling them?"

"A little," she admitted.

"Sit down," he said.

Angie crouched and pulled Truffle into her lap, as though the small dog might provide a measure of comfort. Dammit. Why did she have to be so up in her own head about this? She liked Jace; he liked her back. That was all she should be worrying about.

"My family is probably going to be surprised," he said. "But they're always kind of surprised when it comes to me."

"Is that a good thing or a bad thing?"

"It's neither…or both. But I don't need their approval to do this. They think you're great already, and they'll get over the shock because they want me to be happy."

She swallowed. "But what if it all falls apart?"

"I handled it once before, and it sounds like you handled your life falling apart as well. We're both tough. No matter what happens at the end of the month, we'll keep swimming." He reached over and cupped her face, the touch bringing a moment of stillness to her frantic mind. "Do you still want to do this with me?"

"Yes." It was the only thing she *did* know at the moment—that she'd fallen for Jace and that she wanted so badly to make it work. "I absolutely want this."

"Then nothing else matters." He brought his lips down to hers, coaxing her mouth open and kissing her hard and deep. They pulled away a second later, and Angie reached for his hand, intertwining her fingers with his. "Because I sure as hell want it, too."

She *would* make this work. She would do her

utmost to make sure his parents were happy to welcome her into the family, and she would be the perfect fiancée.

You can do whatever you set your mind to—you've proven that.

All she had to do was be a little more confident in herself. She *was* fiancée material. She liked Jace a hell of a lot. And she was already playing her part in this town. For once in her life, everything was on her side.

CHAPTER TWENTY-TWO

Despite an awkward start to the morning, everything seemed to be on track. After their chat about the family situation, Jace saw a change in Angie. She seemed more relaxed, more herself.

After walking at the edge of the water with the dogs and trying to make sure Truffle didn't get swept away by any rogue waves—or stealthy children who seemed enamored with him—Jace had gotten them both an ice cream.

The water lapped at the sand, and Angie's white shirt flapped in the breeze, giving him tempting flashes of her backside in a skimpy-cut black bikini bottom. Her hair was mussed and curly, given texture by the salty water and wind, and her pink lips wrapped around the ice cream in the most enticing way.

He couldn't stop staring at her. Couldn't stop thinking about getting her back home and into his bed. Or maybe the shower…or the kitchen table. Heck, why even bother going inside when there was a perfectly good deck chair out back?

"I think you've turned me into a horny teenage boy," he said, leaning in and bringing his lips close to her ear.

She turned her head, and her mouth curved upward. "Have you got your mind in the gutter again?"

"Seems to be a constant thing around you."

They walked, content and eating their ice creams. Truffle trotted alongside them, off his leash now, and Tilly loped on ahead. She was sniffing everything, overturning shells with her nose and having a ball.

"I guess we should head back. I'm thinking movie night, fish and chips, lazy sex on the couch."

Jace chuckled. "Lazy sex?"

"Yeah, you know that kind where you're taking it slow and you're a little sleepy and it's delicious and…well, lazy."

"I'm not sure I've had that kind of sex before. But it sounds good to me."

"You're missing out." She bit into her ice-cream cone with a loud crunch. "Lazy sex is the best. Followed closely by shower sex, makeup sex, outdoor sex, and middle-of-the-night-am-I-dreaming sex."

"Are you trying to corrupt me?"

"One hundred percent."

He was about to pull Angie in for a kiss when a loud yelping noise broke them apart. A child's cry up ahead drew their eyes, and that's when he saw Tilly retching all over the sand. She was making an awful noise, and a small child near her was waving his arms.

"Shit." Jace handed Angie the remainder of his ice cream and jogged over, panic mounting in the back of his throat. "What happened?"

But the kid didn't need to say anything, since as soon as Jace saw it he knew *exactly* what had happened. A translucent blob was lying still in the sand, half-buried. It was a common sight around here. Dead jellyfish littered the beaches at certain times of year, and everyone knew to keep their distance. Even dead, their stingers could do damage for several weeks afterward.

"Tilly." He crouched down beside the dog and placed a reassuring hand on her back. She looked up at him with those soulful amber eyes as if to say, *Please help me.* "You poor thing."

Then she vomited again, her body wracking. That wasn't a good sign. If she'd tried to eat the jellyfish and swallowed the stinger… Panic started to coil around his bones like a vine, squeezing until his vision narrowed. If anything happened to her because he hadn't been paying attention—hadn't been treating his responsibility with the care it required—he'd never forgive himself.

"Oh my God." Angie was beside him now, with Truffle securely in her arms. "What happened?"

"Jellyfish." He couldn't see where she'd been stung, which was an issue. Usually, the first thing you did was ensure the tentacles were off the skin. Then you had to wash the area in the ocean—saltwater helped.

The offender looked like a jelly blubber, which weren't poisonous to humans, but they stung like a bitch. But for dogs? He wasn't so sure. Tilly was old, and he couldn't find the stingers.

He tried to open Tilly's mouth, but she snarled at him in warning. "We need to get her to the vet. Now."

Angie looked at him with wide, unblinking eyes. "Is she going to be okay?"

"I don't know. I hope so."

He looked at the older dog and prayed she wouldn't sink her teeth into him. But when he slid his hands under her body and scooped her up, she only whined. They'd drawn a crowd now, with the kid who'd found Tilly crying so hard his mother was holding him.

"She'll be okay," he reassured the child, hoping to hell he wasn't lying.

He walked as quickly as he could across the beach, his bare feet sinking into the sand with each step. It was no easy feat carrying a dog her size, but he would do anything to make sure she was okay. She'd buried her face against his chest and made an awful sound.

"Please don't vomit on me, girl. We'll get you to the vet." When he got to the car, Angie was right behind him, and she pulled the keys from the beach bag. "Can you sit in the back with her?"

"Of course." There was no fear in her eyes—not like there had been that first day when they'd tried to rescue the dogs from the hailstorm. She even reached out and stroked Tilly's fur, her eyes full of worry.

Within minutes they were on the road, speeding back toward Patterson's Bluff. There might have been a vet in a town closer to them, but Jace trusted only one person when it came to animals.

He drove as quickly as he could without being dangerous and pulled into the parking lot in front of Happy Paws in record time. He left Angie in the dust as he grabbed Tilly and took her straight into the vet.

"How can I...?" The vet's receptionist, an

older woman named Fran, frowned. "Oh no, what happened?"

"Jellyfish. I think she might have swallowed the stinger." Thankfully there was no one else waiting to be seen.

"Mira! We've got an emergency." Fran jumped up from her chair and scurried out the back, knocking on a door marked Staff Only.

Mira Holland came rushing out, her hair in disarray. "Bring her into room three."

Mira grabbed her lab coat from a hook by the door and slipped it on over her black pants and the bright-yellow polo top with the Happy Paws logo embroidered at her chest.

"Should I come in?" Angie asked. She had Truffle on his leash.

"Might be best to keep the little guy out here," Mira said. "We don't want him getting distressed, and Tilly will probably be in some pain while we assess her."

Angie nodded. Her brows were knitted above her nose, and she was biting down hard on her lower lip. When she swiped her tongue along it, there was a streak of red.

"I'll be out soon," Jace reassured her, hoping to hell he sounded calmer than he felt. Then he followed Mira into the assessment room.

• • •

Angie sat in the waiting room, feeling like her heart was about to leap out of her body. The receptionist sat behind her desk, tapping away at her computer and asking Angie every so often if she needed something—water, a cup of tea, a mint.

But Angie couldn't bear the thought of eating or drinking anything. She wouldn't be able to swallow a damn thing until she knew Tilly was okay. Funny how frightened she'd been of the big beast on their first fateful meeting, but they'd come to like each other. Tilly was a little grouchy, but she was also *seventy* in dog years. They'd come to an understanding—Angie scratched behind her ears and Tilly would keep her feet warm.

The thought of not having either one of the dogs around made Angie sad. They'd slotted into her life in Patterson's Bluff, keeping her company and making her laugh and generally bringing joy into her life. She loved the four-legged critters with all her heart.

Truffle looked up at her with his big buggy eyes as if to say, *I love you, too.*

Sighing, she wrapped her arms around the small dog and held him close to her chest. "I hope your sister is okay," she whispered.

At that moment, the bell over the front door tinkled and Angie's stomach dropped as Jace's mother strode in. Melanie Walters rushed straight over to her.

"What happened? I was driving past on my way home from the shops and I saw Jace's car." She clamped a hand over her mouth. "It's not the older dog, is it?"

Angie nodded. "We went to the beach, and there was a jellyfish on the sand…"

"Oh no. Is she going to be okay?" She dropped down into the empty plastic seat beside Angie. "Oh God, Eugenie will be devastated if anything happens to her while she's away."

"I'm still waiting to find out."

"I'll wait with you." Melanie reached out to grab Angie's hand, and the world decelerated into slow motion.

The engagement ring. Would she notice it? Angie wasn't sure she could handle any more drama on top of what was already going on. But she knew from past experience that's when the universe was most likely to strike.

"Pretty ring," Melanie said absently; then she looked away. Angie barely had time to breathe a sigh of relief before Jace's mother did a double-take. "Familiar ring."

Oh no. What was she supposed to say? They hadn't worked out the exact story they were going to tell his parents, and it was still so new and so unreal and so…inexplicable.

Melanie looked at Angie. She had the same blue eyes as her son—pale and rimmed with the most unique hint of gold. "Is this what I think it is?"

Angie gulped. "Yes, ma'am."

"On your wedding finger."

"Well, I guess technically speaking it's my engagement finger at the moment."

The older woman didn't react. She simply stared, dumbfounded, at Angie. Then she shook her head and laughed, raking a hand through her frizzy blond curls. "That dark horse! No wonder he brought you to the long weekend family event."

Angie breathed out the rest of her sigh of relief. "It all happened very suddenly, and we hadn't figured out how to tell people yet."

At least she could say *that* with her hand on her heart. It probably wasn't a good idea to start off a relationship with her future mother-in-law by lying.

Um, except you're forgetting that whole thing about your past.

"I didn't even know you were dating."

"We've been friends since I arrived." Kinda. Well, maybe not exactly from the moment she arrived. Jace had taken a while to warm up to her. "There was a spark there right from the beginning. I had a giant crush on him."

All 100 percent true.

"I can't believe he didn't tell us." She shook her head. "That's my middle son for you—always keeping his cards close to his chest. Well, I'm thrilled, frankly."

Angie's heart soared. "Really?"

"Absolutely. He had a rough time after his last breakup, and I felt like he was retreating more and more into his shell. He needs someone to remind him why relationships are important."

"I can certainly do that."

"And I couldn't have picked a better match myself. All the work you've done at the retirement home, volunteering every week and putting a smile on people's faces—it's wonderful. I heard all about how you were calling local businesses to get them to volunteer classes."

Wow, news traveled fast in this town.

"It's a very noble thing, Angie. You're making a big difference in their lives."

"Thank you."

Mrs. Walters reached over and gave Angie a hug. "I'm so happy for you both."

A great big weight had been lifted off her shoulders.

"I guess this means you'll have to fly your mother out to Australia. How exciting! I can't wait to meet her."

And like that, Angie's heart sank. The lies of omission that had built up since she arrived in Patterson's Bluff had been designed to protect her from her past—a cocoon of vague stories. But now she'd have to woman up. She'd have to admit that she led people to believe things that weren't true.

They'd want to know more, to dig. Her past might follow her here if too many people gossiped about it. Anxiety curled like a fist around her heart. Would there be people here who said those horrible things like they had back home? That she was lying about what her foster parents did? That the picture of her in chains was staged so she could cash in?

"Are you okay, love?" Mrs. Walters frowned and touched the back of her hand to Angie's forehead in such a motherly way, it made her want to cry for how guilty she felt.

"I'm worried," she said. Her eyes drifted to the closed door hiding Jace and Tilly away. "I hope Tilly is going to be okay."

"Me too."

The sounds of a vet clinic filled their silence—
Fran's fingers flying over the keys of her computer,
the whirr of the air-conditioning, and intermittent
ringing of the telephone. A woman came in with
her daughter and their adorable kitten that was
small enough to fit in the teenager's pocket. They
sat down in the empty plastic chairs, and Truffle
eyed the kitten with disdain but otherwise didn't
cause any trouble.

A few minutes later, the door to the assessment room swung open, and Jace strode out. He
still had a crease between his brows, but some of
the color had come back to his cheeks. That was,
until he saw his mother sitting there.

"What are you doing here?"

Mrs. Walters stood and rushed over to give her
son a hug. "I saw the car sitting in the parking lot
as I was driving past, and I knew something must
have happened to one of the dogs. Is she going to
be okay?"

"Mira says she should be fine. We couldn't
find the stinger, so it's likely that Tilly got it out
when she vomited on the beach. She's got some
nasty blisters inside her mouth that will irritate
her whenever she tries to eat or drink. So Mira
suggested leaving her overnight—if not for a few
days—to make sure she can get her fluids in."

"Oh good." Angie sighed and pressed a hand
to her chest. "What a relief."

"She's not out of the woods yet, but with some
supervision, she should be feeling better soon."

Mira walked out into the main area. "I've

set her up in our emergency care section, and I'll keep an eye on her personally. It's a good thing you brought her right in. With older dogs, they can sometimes react more severely than a younger dog might. We'll take very good care of her."

Mira bid them all a good afternoon and went to greet her other clients with the kitten. Jace's eyes strayed to the room where Tilly was being kept, as though he hated to be away from her, even if only for one evening. For a man who hadn't wanted to dog-sit in the first place, he was certainly becoming quite the doting pet owner.

After Jace left his contact information with Fran and fixed up Tilly's bill, the three of them went outside.

"So," Mrs. Walters said with a coy smile on her face. "I heard you have some good news."

"She saw the ring," Angie explained.

"We'd wanted to tell you together." Jace sighed. "It's not that we were hiding it. Please don't tell the others, okay? We want to do it properly."

"You want me to keep the most exciting news our family has had in some time a secret?" His mother gasped. "Your father will take one look at me and know I'm harboring important information."

Jace rolled his eyes. "We're not talking about the key to eternal life. Just keep it quiet until we can get everyone together."

"I will do my best. But you know your dad, Jace…" She shook her head. "He's got a sixth sense for that stuff."

"Please try. I don't want anyone to feel left out."

Angie's heart skipped a beat. He really was the sweetest guy, especially when it came to his family. Could she picture herself spending the rest of her life with Jace? Yeah, she totally could. That was, if she didn't mess things up.

They all climbed into their respective vehicles, and Angie took a moment to settle Truffle into his seat. He kept looking around as though trying to figure out where his big sister was.

"She'll be back soon, I promise." She gave the little guy a hug and then closed the door gently before climbing into the passenger seat. "I feel so bad; he keeps looking for her."

"We should probably keep a close eye on him tonight." Jace started the engine and waited for his mother to pull out of the parking lot before he backed out. "So, busted, huh?"

"I didn't stand a chance." Angie scrubbed her hands over her face. "Will she keep it quiet?"

"Not likely. She has the world's worst poker face." Jace shook his head. "So we should probably sit them all down as soon as possible."

Angie chewed on her thumbnail. It was a habit she'd kicked years ago but that sometimes reared its head when she was stressed. "She wanted to know when I was going to bring my mother over so they could meet."

Jace glanced at her as they paused at the exit to the Happy Paws parking lot, waiting for a gap in the traffic. His expression was difficult to read. "Right."

Ah, the response that wasn't really a response. He was waiting to hear what she had to say. Angie sucked in a big breath. "I'm going to have to tell everyone about my past, aren't I?"

"Only if you want to."

"I can't keep lying. It's hardly the right way to build a foundation as a family." That fist was back again, squeezing and squeezing. "And besides, it's going to be quite the one-sided wedding guest list."

It occurred to her then that she was bringing very little to this relationship beside the fact that she had a fat bank account thanks to her legal settlements. That was also something she'd kept quiet from everyone except Jace. If anyone had ever asked her how she managed to fund a trip to Australia for a year without working, she'd claim it was inheritance left to her by a dead relative.

"You only have to tell them as much as you want," he said.

"But they'll ask questions."

"So?"

She sighed. "I'm worried they won't accept me. That they'll look at me differently."

"You're not giving them enough credit. Have *I* treated you differently?"

"No." Now that she thought about it, he'd left that conversation well enough alone after their talk. "Won't they ask questions?"

"Yes. I want to know everything about you, too. But that doesn't mean it's right to ask." He reached his free hand over and placed it on her bare thigh. "If you ever want to talk, then I'm all ears. But until that point, it's your decision to make."

"How did someone not marry you already?" She slipped her hand over his and interlocked their fingers.

"I thought we went through that already," he deadpanned.

"But seriously." She stared at him as he drove them back home. "The ladies of Patterson's Bluff have been missing out, and their loss is totally my gain."

They sat quietly for a moment, trying to sift through everything in her head.

"You never even looked my name up online?" she asked eventually.

"Did I Google you?" He snorted. "Isn't that kind of…stalker-ish?"

"Everybody does it."

"Doesn't make it right." They paused at a red light. "And no, I didn't Google you, Angie. Jesus."

"What?"

"I get you've had some people treat you badly in the past, but you can't go around expecting the worst of everyone." He sounded hurt.

"Says you. You thought marriage was a sham because the person you didn't even want to marry walked out on you." The words sounded *way* more defensive than she'd wanted them to. But everything was so close to the surface right now—her fears about the future, her feelings of inadequacy, all the wounds she *thought* she'd stitched up for good…

Clearly not.

"It's been a long day," Jace said quietly. "Let's go home and watch a movie, okay?"

"Okay, sure." Angie twisted the engagement ring around her finger, still not used to the feeling of it.

This should have been the happiest time of her life—but her brain seemed to be locked into the thirty-day part of Jace's proposal. Like it was a hurdle mocking her at the finish line. Would she be able to clear it? Or would she fail to measure up like she always did?

"Stop worrying, Angie," Jace said, as if he could read her mind. "Everything will work itself out."

Somehow, she couldn't bring herself to believe it.

CHAPTER TWENTY-THREE

Ever since the day they took Tilly to the vet, Jace had been doing his utmost to show Angie that he wanted her...and it was taking a toll. He was so far behind on his work that he was scrambling to make his deadline at the end of the week. *That* was a first.

Not to mention the fact that he'd barely surfed, and without the calming vastness of the ocean to start his day, he felt...off. Instead, he "slept in," better known as lying in bed watching Angie sleep—*not* in a creepy way—and wanting to be there for her when she woke up. He'd forced down the breakfasts she made him, not having the heart to tell her he didn't like them. And every time she suggested a spontaneous activity—going out for coffee or an extra-long walk with the dogs to explore a different part of the beach—he said yes.

After all, the last thing he wanted to do was repeat his mistakes. Julia hadn't been able to handle his rigidity and his need for alone time... so he was working on those things. He wanted Angie to be happy.

And, in the process, he was wearing himself down. Each time he varied from his routine, it felt like he chipped away another piece of himself.

"So I was thinking," Angie said. "Why don't we go out for brunch this morning?"

She was standing at the end of the bed in a white bra and undies, her long dark hair hanging down her back in glossy waves. Yeah, sure, she'd screwed his routine into oblivion. But man…he could watch her all day. It wasn't only her body—incredible as it was—it was the sparkle in her eyes, the way she took such care with things like picking the perfect flowers for the dining room table and how she *never* dog-eared the pages in her books.

"Brunch?" His stomach churned at the suggestion.

"Yeah, I was chatting with one of the staff members at the retirement home, and she was telling me about a new place that opened up. It sounds cute." She pulled a breezy yellow sundress from his cupboard—which was now their cupboard—and pulled it over her head. "Unless you've got work to do?"

"I'd love to do brunch." The words came automatically, as though his "say yes" training had taken root. "That sounds great."

His eyes coasted to the clock on his nightstand. It was past eight thirty already, and he was usually getting ready to settle into the studio by now. When he looked back up, he caught Angie observing him.

"You sure?" she asked, a frown causing a delicate crease in between her eyebrows. "We can totally go another day if you've got stuff to do. No pressure."

Julia used to say stuff like that—*no pressure. No worries. Whatever you want.* Words he'd taken at face value when he shouldn't have.

"I want to go everywhere with you." He got out of bed and stalked over to her, pulling her into his arms and lowering his head down to hers. Even with his body coiled tight from feeling so out of his element, holding her was like a balm over it all.

"What if I'd suggested we go shoe shopping, huh?" she teased. "Would you have come then?"

"Yep." Okay, now he was lying through his teeth, and they both knew it.

"What about…getting facials?" She tapped a fingertip to her chin, her nose crinkled with mischief. "Would you sit there for an hour with cucumber on your eyes?"

"Anything for you."

"What if I asked you to watch a whole marathon of Drew Barrymore movies with me?"

He snorted. "Okay, now you're pushing it."

"Even you have limits." She tapped his cheek and planted a kiss on his nose. "Good to know."

Jace released her so he could get dressed. As he was pulling up his jeans, watching intently as Angie bent in half to fasten her sandals—giving him a *glorious* view—he reminded himself of how lucky he was.

"Oh hey, I've got an idea. Why don't you bring your sketchbook?" she suggested. "We can chill at the café for a bit. I'll bring a book and we can sit and be quiet."

He knew she was only suggesting that for his benefit—Angie could *literally* talk all day. But it was clear she was doing her best to respect his needs, even if what he actually wanted was to stay home and lock himself away for several hours so he could create.

But relationships had to come before work. They would grow apart otherwise. And the fear of that was like a presence in the room, a gloomy third wheel.

"That sounds great," he said with a nod. "I'm sure I'll get lots done."

• • •

Jace did *not* get lots done. In fact, he speculated that "brunch" was some secret term for *bring all the screaming babies to one place*. The noise level would rival that of an AC/DC concert—groups of women chattering, kids yelling, some generic bass-heavy pop song playing over the speakers.

He and Angie were jammed into a tiny table in the corner of the café where his sketchbook took up so much of the space, he had to hold it at an angle—half in his lap, half on the table—to get anything done. At first, he hadn't even bothered to pull it out. But Angie had insisted. So now, he was pretending to draw while she pretended to read.

He could feel her eyes flicking up to his at regular intervals. "Are you having fun?" she asked.

I have the worst case of writer's block ever.

The problem was, his head was too noisy. It was like his brain was stuck on a loop, reminding him every thirty seconds that there was something else he was supposed to be doing. Reminding him that he didn't have time for brunch when he should be working. It was like an alarm that refused to turn off.

"Sure," he said, arranging his face into the best *I'm having fun* expression he could think off. But Angie didn't seem convinced.

"Can I see what you're working on?"

Shit. He looked down at the page, which was totally blank, save for a doodle of Hermit with his hands over his ears while five babies screamed around him. If she saw that, then she would *know* he wasn't having fun.

"I, uh...don't like to show my work at such an early stage," he said, flipping the book shut.

A waitress was heading toward them with a notepad, and Jace had scanned the menu over and over in the hopes he'd find something simple to eat. He was pretty sure if he ate another piece of bacon, all his arteries would clog simultaneously.

"What can I get you?" she asked.

"I'll have the sourdough with avocado and a poached egg. Oh, and a flat white, please." Angie smiled and handed her menu back to the waitress.

Jace scanned the menu again, hoping that something appealing might suddenly appear, as if by magic. "You don't happen to have plain porridge, do you?"

The waitress cocked her head. "We have some oats out back that we use for the Bircher muesli, so I'm sure the chef wouldn't mind cooking them up for you. How do you like them?"

"With regular milk," he said, feeling relieved. Jace didn't mind being adventurous with his meals at other parts of the day, but there was something about breakfast that needed to be simple—as if it was a promise that the rest of the day could be easy and uncomplicated.

"Okay, and for toppings? We've got strawberries and banana fresh in today, as well as blackberries. Plus any of the condiments: honey, golden syrup—"

"Just plain. Thanks."

For a moment, the waitress looked at him as if she hadn't heard right, and Jace got that awful feeling that he was being judged. It was funny how he'd never been great at reading people, but *that* was always one thing he felt down to the very marrow of his bones. He had an urge to cover it up with a joke or to feign a bit of an upset stomach or lie and tell them he was entering a body-building contest and was on a strict diet of oats, chicken breast, and broccoli—but dammit, why should he?

What was so wrong with wanting to eat something boring for breakfast?

"Coming right up," she said with a nod.

Angie was watching him with a concerned expression. "Everything okay?"

"Everything's fine." But the muscle in his jaw was twitching.

It was like his need for normalcy was a balloon growing inside him, pushing on his heart and lungs, filling up every cavity until he was almost bursting with it. But he didn't want to expose Angie to this side of him—the side that would never go away no matter how much he tried.

She's going to see it eventually.

His stomach sank. It felt like his world was unraveling, and he didn't know how to fix it. Why couldn't he be like other guys and shrug things off? He had a beautiful fiancée sitting in front of him and...dammit, she was so important to him. Already. Why couldn't he be what she wanted?

He glanced at the clock across the room. They'd been here for half an hour already and they hadn't even eaten. No doubt, she'd want a leisurely stroll back to the house and then...

She's got a volunteer shift this afternoon. You can work then.

How was he going to keep this up for thirty days, let alone the rest of his life? Eventually she would see what he was like and...she would leave.

"Jace, if I ask you that question it's because I'm genuinely interested in how you're doing," she said. "Not because I want you to dismiss me with 'fine,' okay?"

She saw way too much. Either that or he was the world's shittiest actor...probably a little of both.

"I know this must be a big upheaval for you—"

"I said I'm fine."

Don't let her see it; don't let her see it; don't let her see it.

"You can let me in. I promise I won't judge you." Her voice sounded like she was telling the truth, and Jace guessed that her face did, too.

But he'd thought the same thing about Julia, and he'd been wrong. It would be fine; he would simply have to try harder...and maybe sneak out of bed to get his work done at night while the house was quiet.

But a little voice in the back of his head whispered words of dissent. How much longer could he play the role of Husband Material Jace before it all blew up in his face?

• • •

"*What* on earth is going on?" One of the Patterson's Bluff retirement home residents peered at Angie through thick-rimmed glasses.

"A surprise," Angie said. "You'll have to wait and see."

After brunch with Jace ended in a verbal stand-off—cue them heading home in silence—Angie decided to distract herself with work for the retirement home. Her meeting with the board was approaching, where she would present her plans.

She'd collected research on how learning new skills worked to combat degenerative brain disease and created a case study of a retirement home overseas that had used a similar approach to improve the mental health of residents. But today was putting her theory into action—a test case of what she hoped would win over the board.

With permission from the facility manager, the recreation room had been converted for this special event. Last week, Angie had put in a call to Chloe and asked if she could take her up on the offer of free yoga instruction for an hour…but with one fun twist.

The residents of the retirement home wouldn't

be taking the yoga class alone.

Chloe bounced on the balls of her feet at the front of the room, excited as a bag full of jumping beans. Her dark hair was twisted up into a messy knot, and she wore cute galaxy-print leggings and a fitted tank top advertising her yoga studio. Angie stood beside her, waiting for the go-ahead from Nadesha. They'd had ten people sign up for the mystery class, and all had turned up as instructed—barefoot and wearing comfortable clothing. Betty, Jean, and Meredith occupied the back row like a band of naughty schoolgirls, giggling and chatting among themselves.

What made the whole thing better, however, was that Marcus was in the row ahead of Jean… which she suspected was not a mistake.

"We almost ready to start?" Chloe asked.

Angie looked over to the door, where Nadesha had appeared and was giving them the thumbs-up. Showtime.

"Thank you all for coming along today. For anyone who doesn't know me, I'm Angie Donovan. I'm a volunteer here at the Patterson's Bluff retirement home, and I truly believe that learning new things and having new life experiences is so important for keeping people happy and healthy. So…" Angie couldn't keep the grin off her face. "I've enlisted the generous support of a great local business to bring the fun to you."

Chloe stepped forward on cue and introduced herself, then explained how the yoga class would work. They were doing her "yoga for seniors" class, which focused on gently building strength and flexibility and could easily be modified for different mobility requirements.

"But," Angie said, "we have some extra-special guests who are very excited to join you today."

She signaled to Nadesha to open the doors, and in came a group of people with a small army of dogs trotting by their feet. Two of the staff from the local animal shelter were also carrying some very fluffy puppies. Excited gasps rose up from all around the room, and Angie's heart soared. This was exactly the reaction she'd been hoping for. It hadn't been easy gathering the dogs to attend the session—the shelter didn't have a lot of extra staff, and she'd had to reach out personally to people she knew who owned small, well-behaved dogs. But every single one of them had come.

Including Jace.

Her eyes caught his across the recreation room, and a zap of something hot and sparkly shot through her. Butterflies stirred in her tummy. The last few days had been tense—and the more Angie tried to be perky and play the role of perfect fiancée, the more Jace seemed to pull away.

Regardless, he was here now, supporting her and shooting her an encouraging smile across the room. The second she saw it, her nerves instantly eased.

"Look at this cute little guy!" Betty bent down to pat a scruffy black dog that could barely see out of the shaggy hair covering it's eyes. A pink tongue darted out to swipe her hand, and she laughed.

"Each dog has a handler," Chloe explained. "Just in case they get rowdy or you need a break. But otherwise, I'll guide you through how to encourage the dogs to be part of the routine so that we all have a fantastic time."

The dogs were in their element, sniffing and exploring and greeting the residents. Truffle bounced straight over to Angie and jumped up, slapping his tiny paws against her leg and letting out an excited *yip!*

"Looks like someone has a favorite." Jace came over. He looked incredible—his hair still slightly damp, as though he'd come straight from his morning surf, and a black T-shirt that outlined his broad shoulders and washboard stomach.

"Take him for a wander around and see if he bonds with any of the other participants, otherwise I'll take him." She reached out and touched Jace's arm. "And thanks for coming. I really appreciate it."

"Of course." He scooped up the white Chihuahua. "I wouldn't miss this for anything."

• • •

"Exhale and hinge forward at the hips. Bend down to meet your yoga partner." The room was mostly quiet, broken only by the sounds of Chloe's instructions and the occasional excited noise from a four-legged participant. "Take a moment to engage with the dog and make them feel part of your practice."

Jace didn't have a dog to engage with, as Truffle

was happily playing along with a charming older woman named Meredith. He didn't know her at all, but it sounded like she'd spent most of her life in Melbourne rather than in Patterson's Bluff. She'd totally charmed Truffle, anyway. And he was looking more relaxed than ever, lying on his back with his legs unabashedly spread.

Like a canine centerfold.

At the front of the class, Angie was doing yoga as well. She was keeping an eye on a hyperactive little French bulldog named Cosmo. But as she bent forward, the charcoal material of her leggings stretching tight across her butt, Jace had to force himself not to topple over.

He wasn't the kind of guy who objectified women, but there must have been some male gene inside him that turned his brain to goo at the sight of her perfect ass. Besides, they were engaged. So it was perfectly okay to ogle. Even if they *still* hadn't told people.

For some reason, every time he tried to bring it up, Angie would go into some silent panic. He could see it in her eyes, though she would plaster on the same irritatingly fake smile as if that might fool him. Well, he'd clearly gotten better at reading expressions when it came to her—because he knew the difference between her real smile and a fake one.

The whole thing had made a little kernel of doubt unfurl inside him—was he heading straight for a repeat of history? Would Angie leave him with a note on the kitchen table like Julia had? Or was it simply nerves about telling the truth about her past?

"Now we're going to do a little partner work," Chloe said. "Pair up…"

Before Jace even had a chance to figure out who he would partner up with, a hand landed on his shoulder. It was Meredith, the woman behind him.

"Let's be partners," she said with a wide smile.

It didn't take long to figure out why she'd been quick to claim him. The woman next to Meredith, with the white curly hair, was looking around. Both her friends had quickly leaped to work with other people. When the tall Italian man next to Jace also ended up alone, he turned and extended a hand out to the white-haired woman. Jace tried to remember her name…was it Jane? No, Jean.

Jean's face was rosy pink, and she could barely make eye contact with the Italian man. But she shuffled over to his mat, shooting a glare at her friends on the way.

Ah, so this was a setup.

At the front of the room, Angie was paired with a woman with dark hair and red glasses. They were both smiling, looking like they were having a great time.

"Please go back-to-back with your partner," Chloe said from the front of the room. "We're going to lean against each other, finding balance by both parties working to support the other person. Then we're going to take a gentle bend at the knees and keep backs pressed together. Let your dogs relax or play at your feet."

Jace and Meredith got into the pose. He didn't

```

usually like getting up close and personal with people he didn't know, but he distracted himself by watching Jean and her partner. They were sweet and a little shy around each other, and Jean spent the entire pose shooting daggers at her friends.

"I know what you're doing," she whispered.

Behind him, Jace felt Meredith shrug. He'd been around enough wannabe matchmakers in his time to see the tricks a mile off. It was sweet. From all Angie had told him about the residents at the retirement home, these three ladies were her favorites. "The poker gang," she called them. She'd said it was like having three awesome grandmas.

"Now raise your arms up toward the ceiling and press the backs of your hands together."

This was a little awkward, and everyone laughed as they tried to find their partner's hands. His rudimentary understanding of yoga being some hippie-dippy activity full of self-appraising chants and uncomfortable positions had been thwarted. Around him, dogs were jumping up and generally getting in the way and nobody minded a damn bit. Truffle danced at his feet, yipping before going off to play with another dog.

"Now we're going to turn around and face our partners."

Jace turned, and Meredith winked at him before inclining her head slightly toward the Italian and Jean. "She's had a crush on Marcus ever since he arrived," she whispers. "But she won't do anything about it."
```

"Maybe she's shy."

"That's why you need friends to give you a push in the right direction."

Chloe clapped her hands together at the front of the room. "Okay, now hold hands. We're going to softly lean away from each other, creating a slight tension in the arms. Only go as far as your joints will allow. This is a gentle session, so don't push beyond your limits."

Jace's eyes strayed to Jean and Marcus. Every time they looked at each other, she'd quickly glance away, her face growing increasingly pink. In the row ahead of him, Jace spied Angie watching the older couple, too, a delighted smile on her face. When Jace caught her eye, she grinned.

Even when she should have been focused on herself, she was caring for those around her. Trying to bring sunshine into everyone's world. It wasn't often that he met someone who cared so deeply about the community around them. She would fit right in with his family—their values were aligned, their view in the same direction.

The rest of the yoga—or *doga* as they'd starting calling it—session went smoothly. After a few more partner poses, they went back to their individual mats for some gentle movement and stretching.

"I'd like everyone to slowly ease down onto your mat," Chloe said from the front of the room. "If you feel comfortable, bring your dogs onto your chest or keep them close by your sides. We're going to settle into corpse pose or a comfortable seated position for a few minutes to finish the session."

Jace stopped to give Marcus a hand to move to the side of the room, since he wasn't able to get down on the ground. There was laughter from all across the room as the dogs tried to take over the class, licking faces and generally being mischievous. Within a few minutes, everyone settled.

"Breathe to my count," Chloe instructed. "In, two, three, four and out, two, three, four."

Jace tried to relax, but his body was tighter than a new couch spring. This whole situation with Angie had him totally confused and on edge... which was affecting his work. This morning's sketching session had been less than productive, and he couldn't seem to figure out how to move the story forward. Which was becoming a problem. He had to get his folio together for the syndication group, and he needed a complete storyline.

He'd *never* had this kind of writer's block before. But lately his concentration was no better than a goldfish's. It was all this disruption to his routine, and he needed to get himself together or he might lose this important opportunity.

"Let your mind go blank," Chloe said.

Ha! Fat chance of that happening.

"If any thoughts come along, acknowledge them and then send them on their way."

What was he supposed to acknowledge? That his engagement was starting to feel a little one-sided? He couldn't stop thinking about Angie.

Day and night, she was on his mind, and the only time they seemed to truly connect was when he reached for her in the dark. There, without words to mess things up, they were perfect together.

But then he'd come here today and she wasn't wearing the ring he'd given her. What on earth could that mean?

"With each breath out, I want you to release your tensions and worries. Meditation is a time for resetting the mind and— Oh no! Stop!"

Jace sat bolt upright, knowing exactly what had interrupted the yoga session. "Truffle! No!"

Truffle, who'd looked sleepy and adorable not five minutes ago, had mounted one of the toy poodles and was humping away to his heart's content. The poodle, on the other hand, looked entirely bored by the whole thing.

Jace leaped to his feet and dodged the other yoga participants until he got to his mischievous, misbehaving dog. "Dude. Really?"

"My poor Mitzi." The owner of the dog rushed over, glaring at Jace. "You get off her right now!"

"He's fixed," Jace reassured the woman. The whole room had been well and truly broken out of their meditative state now, and most were laughing behind their hands.

"I don't care if he's fixed." The woman snatched the poodle from the ground, and Truffle looked up at Jace as if to say, *What? Dog's gotta do what a dog's gotta do.*

"We're going to talk about this later," he grumbled as he picked Truffle up and tucked him under one arm.

"Well, on that entertaining note, I think we can conclude today's class." Chloe took a bow to some very enthusiastic clapping. "Thank you for joining Angie and me, and we really hope you enjoyed yourselves."

"I enjoyed the peep show!" one of the older gentlemen crowed from the back. "That dog was really going for it."

At the front of the room, Angie dropped her head into her heads. But her shoulders were shaking as though she couldn't contain her laughter.

"You've always got to be the center of attention, don't you?" He looked at Truffle, who craned his small doggy head up. "Yep, and not ashamed of it, either."

"I think he's adorable." Meredith got to her feet and gave Truffle a scratch on the head. "He reminds me so much of my little Andy. He was a Chihuahua mix, feisty as can be. But when he decided he liked you, it was like the whole world was shining."

"He sounds like a great dog."

"He was. Lived until he was fourteen and could barely see a damn thing." Meredith was misty-eyed now, and she gave Truffle another pat. "Bring him along again, okay? It makes us all so happy."

"I certainly will." Jace bid her a good day and went to find Angie.

She stood at the front of the room, chatting with the residents. It took a full fifteen minutes before the room cleared out, but every single person—bar the woman who'd been horrified by Truffle's deviant behavior—left with a smile on their face.

"I would say it was a success...on balance." Chloe winked, and Angie groaned at the pun.

"That was really great, terrible jokes aside." Angie gave Chloe a hug. "Thank you so much for giving up your time. It's incredibly generous."

"We need more people around here to remember why this community is so amazing. So I'm happy to do my part." Chloe turned to Jace. "And thank *you* for bringing that little troublemaker along."

Jace let Truffle down to the ground, now that everyone had cleared out of the room. The staff of the retirement home had come in to start putting all the furniture back into place. The little dog flopped straight down onto the ground.

"Did all that sex wear you out?" Angie folded her arms and gave him a mock-stern expression. "Seriously, you take your eyes off him for two seconds..."

"I'm thinking I might need to get him a chastity belt." Jace chuckled.

"Well, I declare it a cracking success."

Jace smiled at the Aussie-ism. Angie was clearly still working on her Australian vocabulary.

"What's next on the plan?" Chloe asked. "I'm assuming you're shooting for small-town domination. Glen Powell is going to rue the day he said no to you. I give it five years before you're running this place."

Five years.

Angie studiously avoided Jace's gaze. "One step at a time. I've got my meeting with the board on Friday and several businesses lined up to provide classes should we get the go-ahead. The bakery has offered a cake-decorating class, and they seemed really interested, so they'll probably be up next."

"That's a long way from Grannies on Poles," Jace commented.

Angie shrugged. "Maybe it was too ambitious."

"You know," Chloe said, "I have a friend who runs a burlesque studio in Melbourne. It's too far for her to come and volunteer on a regular basis, but I'm sure we could swing some accommodation for her and get her to come overnight for a special onc-off class."

"That would be amazing!" Angie clapped her hands together. "Burlesque. Now, why didn't I think of that? It's sexy and fun. Just what Meredith said they needed."

"Let me put in a call." Chloe pulled out her phone and typed a note to herself. "And now I have to run. I'm teaching another class in forty minutes."

As Chloe packed up her things, Angie and Jace stood around awkwardly. Truffle slapped his little paws up onto her legs, and she bent down to give him some love. "Did you have fun?"

"Actually, I did." He raked a hand through his hair. "I wasn't expecting to, but it was…entertaining."

"Well, we happened to have a certified ham in the class today. Didn't we, Sir Humps-a-lot?"

Truffle made a satisfied little *hmmph*.

"How come you didn't wear your engagement ring today?" He wanted to give her the benefit of the doubt—maybe it was because a ring might interfere with the yoga poses. Or the dogs. But he wanted to know if something was wrong.

He *wouldn't* be blindsided again.

Angie looked like a deer caught in headlights. Okay, so it must not have been something to do with the yoga class. "Let's talk outside."

They took Truffle through the front of the retirement home, and Angie waved to the staff. Outside, the suburban street was even quieter now that school had started up for the year.

"Is something going on?" he asked. "Ever since we got engaged, you've been acting strange, and I'm starting to feel like you don't want this."

"I *do* want this," she said.

"But every time I mention telling people, you shut down." He raked a hand through his hair, trying to shake out the frustrated energy. He *wanted* this to work between them, because the more he got to know Angie, the more he knew losing her would be a mistake.

The memories of that rehearsal dinner—even knowing what he did now—haunted him. He hated feeling like a laughingstock. Or worse, someone people pitied. What if Angie did that to him?

"Are you…ashamed?"

"No! God, not even a little bit." She shook her head. "More like the other way around. I know you think people won't care or pry into my past, but honestly, I've found very few people who mind their own business. People are going to have an opinion about the fact that we went from being friends to being engaged without much in-between."

"So what? We don't need anyone's permission."

"But I want to make this my home." Her eyes welled, and the sight was a sucker punch. He hated seeing her sad, even more so because he knew it upset her to let her emotions out like that. "We'll have to live here, with people gossiping."

"You seem to be more focused on everybody else than on us." Jace sighed. Truffle swung his head back and forth between the two of them, as if watching a ping-pong match. Poor guy could probably sense the tension. Hell, he was pretty sure they could feel it on the other side of the world.

She looked at him incredulously. "One, I've been busy with planning for the board meeting because it's important to me—"

"You know that's not what I'm talking about."

"And two," she continued, her dark eyes blazing with indignation. "I've made breakfast for you almost every morning. I've cleaned that whole house from top to bottom, and I've tried so damn hard to be perky and happy no matter what was going on in my head."

"Exactly!" Jace threw up the hand that wasn't holding Truffle's leash. "I don't want a maid, Angie. I don't expect you to pick up after me and pretend to be happy when you're not. You're not my employee. And frankly, I like my plain porridge every day."

Her cheeks flushed bright pink, and she pursed her lips. "Well excuse me for trying to be helpful."

"Why are you trying to be helpful? You don't need to earn your place in my house." It killed him that she thought that way, like she needed to *do* things for him in order to make up for some imaginary deficit she thought she had.

Or maybe it wasn't that. Maybe it was that Angie was starting to understand what she'd signed up for—marriage to a man who wasn't perfect. Who wasn't always able to be a hero, like men in the movies she watched. Who was flawed and struggled with his thoughts and who sometimes at the end of a long day just needed to be alone.

Maybe she started to think this was all a big mistake.

CHAPTER TWENTY-FOUR

Angie wasn't sure what was happening right now. But it felt like everything was falling apart—just as she feared it would. And Jace's comment had thrown her for a loop. *Did* she think she needed to earn her place?

"The second I proposed to you, it was like you turned into someone different, and I'm struggling to make sense of it," he said.

"Do you know how many guys would *love* a fiancée who did those things for them?" She planted her hands on her hips, but then she felt like a toddler having a tantrum. So she dropped them by her sides, but that didn't feel right, either.

"Most guys would love a fiancée who wasn't covering up how she felt with fake smiles and who actually wanted to tell people she was engaged."

"That's not fair."

"What's not fair is the fact that you're acting like you're on audition. But you don't need to. I know what we've got between us is something special."

"Are you sure about that?" It was the doubt deep under her skin, the thorn that wouldn't stop pricking her. "Are you *really* sure?"

He blinked. "This is because I told you about Julia, isn't it? I thought couples were supposed to share their mistakes without judgment."

"I'm not judging you. I'm afraid you're going

to do the same thing to me that you did to her."

"For a woman who packed her bags and moved to another country knowing nobody and nothing about where she was going, you sure are afraid of a lot of things at the moment." He cringed as soon as the words were out of his mouth.

But they were like a slap across her face.

"That came out harsher than I meant." He held up a hand.

"We *should* be able to be honest with each other. After all, we haven't got much time to figure this all out, and if it fails, then I have to leave." Panic clawed at the back of her throat at the mere mention of it. Dammit. Why did she have to be so emotional? If she could cut her tear ducts out right now, she would.

"Is that what's gotten you so wound up? The thirty-day thing?"

"There's nothing like a ticking time bomb to make a girl feel like she can't mess up," she muttered. It wasn't Jace's fault—she knew that. Hell, it wasn't even really her fault. But it seemed that running away to Australia hadn't vanquished her demons after all—it had simply put them to sleep for a bit. But now they were roaring and hungry and demanding more. More doubt, more insecurity, more of the softest parts of her.

"I don't expect you to be perfect," Jace said. "That would be pretty bloody hypocritical of me."

"But if I'm not, then I'm out of options. If I don't do a good enough job at playing your fiancée, it could mean going back to everything

I've been trying to escape my whole life." It was too much pressure—she could see that now. Even with the opportunity laid out in front of her, the fear of losing it all was strangling her. "It's hanging over me."

"I get that, but a relationship can't be based on two people playing a role instead of being themselves. That's false and insincere."

Angie's cheeks were hot. She'd never felt more embarrassed, more like a failure. She had a great guy in front of her who wanted to give things a shot, and she was too messed up to be happy. What if this was a sign that she'd *never* be able to love someone else? What if everything that had happened—the abandonment of her family, the foster parents who couldn't handle her, the lawyers who took advantage of her—had left her so broken and so untrusting of both herself and others that she was destined to be alone?

"I like you as you are—I like that rom-coms make you smile and that you're always fighting to make things better and that you're talkative and thoughtful. I like that you've become part of this town, that you know everyone's names and what they do and that you're working hard to beat the things that have held you back."

"But every time I think I've gotten better...I haven't." Her breath was coming quicker now, her chest aching. "I'm never good enough."

"Yes, you are." He looked so frustrated with her, it made her heart ache. "I don't know how many times I need to tell you."

"I have given *so* many chances in my life and

every time, people have walked away." Her lip trembled, but she dug as deep as she could to hold on to her emotions and crush them down into a little box. "You have no idea, Jace. You grew up with your perfect family who loved you, who supported you. I...I'm not used to that."

It was like everything could be so good, and the possibility of it terrified her. Because if she screwed up and lost it all, how would she ever recover?

"I know how lucky I am," he said quietly. While control was doing its best to wriggle out of her grip, he was turning in on himself. Shutting down. She could see it—the light in his eyes dimming, his mouth drawing into an even, flat line. The walls were going up. "You could have had my family care about you, too."

Could have. Past tense.

A wave of sickness swelled in her belly, threatening to bring up the smoothie she'd had for breakfast. "I wanted this to work."

"So did I. But you didn't even give it a chance. Can't you see what you're doing? You're cutting yourself off at the knees, so when it fails you can say, *See, I knew that would happen*. Instead of actually trying to make it work, you're doing everything in your power to sabotage it."

"I'm trying to *sabotage* it?" How could he say that when all she'd done her whole damn life was try, try, try? Try to make friends, try to find parents who might love her, try to find a new home, try to fit in. "That is the most hurtful thing you could possibly say to me."

"Don't you see the pattern?" He looked at her like she was truly lost. Like she was blind. "You left it to the last minute to check on your visa application, by which time it was too late to do anything about it. You create this outrageous plan to fall in love so you can stay, but you pick guys you aren't really that interested in. Then you have an opportunity with me to really have a go at it… and what? You start shutting me out, focusing on all the wrong things."

"So it's all my fault?"

A stone settled in her stomach. But at the same time, she felt…angry. Why didn't anything come easy?

"The funny thing is, I've been feeling like *you* aren't being yourself around *me*. You haven't been surfing anywhere near as much as normal. Your sketchbooks are nothing but blank pages." She ticked the items off on her fingers. "You barely touch the breakfast I make for you, and that's when I find a stupid amount of oats in your cupboard. It didn't even click until we went for brunch. That's what you normally eat, but you won't even tell me something basic like that."

"What was I supposed to do? Reject this kind gesture?"

"You threw the food in the trash, Jace. It took a few days to figure that out, but I saw it yesterday. I saw you sneaking into the kitchen to do it." She shook her head. "Why couldn't you just communicate with me?"

He let out a growl of frustration and turned away from her, which hurt more than anything.

It was like he was shutting her out. Pushing her away.

Why wouldn't he? This whole thing is a complete mess because you're aiming for something that clearly you're not destined to have.

But she couldn't stop herself. "Then you get to the end of the day and you're hollowed out. Like your brain is somewhere else, and I've been in so many houses where people's eyes glossed over me, Jace. I don't want that with you. I can't…live like that."

He was quiet, his eyes trained on the distance as though he was counting birds in the sky. *This* was what she was talking about. He shut down sometimes and wouldn't tell her what he needed. The ridiculous thing was, that whatever he needed, she would give it to him.

"All the change has been…tough," he admitted, shoving his hands into his pockets. Truffle sniffed around their feet, the end of his leash hooked around Jace's wrist. "I'm okay messing up my routine for a day here or there, but this has been…a lot."

"I kept telling you to go work if you needed to. Or to go and do…whatever. I kept giving you options because I didn't want you to turn your whole life upside down for me."

But was that exactly what she'd done? Maybe her mere presence was too much. Like it had been for all those families…no matter how hard she tried.

"You were so busy buzzing around my house, doing all these things for me, that I felt like if I wanted time away, that you wouldn't understand. That you'd take it personally."

Hadn't she proven that she *would* understand? Jace's quirks took some getting used to, but that wasn't because of his autism. *Everybody* had quirks. Everybody had needs mismatched from those around them because they were all unique. Wasn't that something every couple dealt with?

"And truthfully," he added, "I wanted you to treat me like you'd treat any person in a relationship. I didn't want you to see me as different."

"But you *are* different, Jace. We all are. Because the only way we're not different from each other is if we're freaking cardboard cutouts!"

"Maybe I'm sick of being different," he said stonily.

"You say that and yet *I'm* the one sabotaging things." That comment had *really* stung.

Did he really believe that all this time *she* was the reason her life sucked? That she was subconsciously ruining any chance at happiness she might have had?

"You have to *believe* you deserve to be happy," Jace said, turning back to her. "And I don't think you do."

"Well, then what's the point in my staying here?" Biting down on the inside of her cheek to help her focus on something other than the giant pain slashing like a scalpel across her heart, Angie hitched the strap holding her yoga mat higher up on her shoulder. "If I'm going to be miserable, I might as well do it in a country where I can stay as long as I like."

She couldn't believe Jace thought that she was self-sabotaging. It was like he didn't even know her.

"Angie, stop." He reached out for her, but she jerked away. "I don't want this to end in a fight."

"I can't talk to you right now," she said, backing away from him. "I need some space to clear my head."

"Don't run away, okay?" His blue eyes bored into hers, but she looked at the ground. "Please."

But what else could she do — running away was the only way to make the pain stop. Maybe she should stop trying to find a place to fit in and simply find somewhere to hide. For good. It was clear she wasn't capable of making anyone happy.

"I'm sorry," she said, swallowing down every little bit of emotion she felt until it was as if her body had turned to stone. Then she jogged in the direction of home.

Please don't follow me. Please don't follow me.

She needed some time to herself, to really think about what she was doing here. About her next steps. Nothing would happen before Friday, because she'd be damned if all her hard work on the proposal went to waste. But then what?

It's over. You failed.

The words came on a loop, following the thump of her heart.

It's over. You failed.

She'd let herself down. She'd let Jace down. What was there left to do except go back to America with her tail between her legs — head down, hoping nobody would notice her return?

Maybe she could find another country to travel to, keep moving until she found another "dream home" location.

In her heart of hearts, she knew that wouldn't happen—Patterson's Bluff was where she wanted to be.

Only Jace wouldn't want to marry her now. Not when it was clear he thought so little of her—self-sabotaging, indeed. That wasn't her. She was a trier. A doer. A give-it-a-goer.

And frankly, if he couldn't even tell her that he wanted to eat plain freaking oats in the morning, then…well, maybe she didn't want to marry him, either.

When she reached Jace's house, she glanced behind her. He hadn't followed—since he'd driven to the retirement home, he would have beaten her there. But he'd obviously decided not to chase after her. Probably for the best—she wasn't sure what to say to him anyway.

Unfortunately, she had her big meeting with the retirement home's board to present her plans for the community business partnership, and she refused to leave before getting it over the line. Only she couldn't stay here now. Not knowing Jace was so close. The meeting was due to take place in three days. She'd call Chloe and ask if she could crash on her couch until then.

She walked down the path alongside his house, letting herself into the backyard via the gate. Her bike was sitting against the fence, where she'd left it—the basket adorned with sunflowers mocking her. It looked so happy, so carefree—designed to have the wind streaming along its colorful body and upright handlebars.

Something wet nudged Angie's hand. Tilly.

"What are you doing outside, girl? It's hot today." There was no fear left when it came to the big black dog. She'd spent her share of time checking in on the old girl after her encounter with the jellyfish. "You're looking good. Got that sparkle back in your eye."

Tilly nudged her hand again. *Scratch me!*

"Yeah, yeah." Angie found the spot she liked, the one that always made her tongue flop out of her mouth. "You needy thing."

Tilly made a little grunting noise as if to say, *Who, me? Never.* Angie crouched down, her heart heavy from all that had transpired. She wrapped her arms around the dog's neck and pressed her face into the fur. Tilly remained still, letting it happen.

"I'm going to miss you," she said, her voice scratchy. "And Truffle and Meredith and Jean and Betty. And the ladies who run the coffee shop. And Chloe."

And Jace.

She couldn't say it aloud, because that one hurt most of all. And Jace. God, she would miss him like nothing else.

"Things got messed up again," she whispered. Tilly turned and licked up the side of her face, the gently textured tongue catching all the tears clinging to her cheek. "Like they always do."

She sat there for a while until the sun made her shoulders roast. And Tilly didn't budge. Funny how in the end, the one resident of Patterson's Bluff who'd scared her the most ended up being the most comforting.

• • •

Jace was still stewing over his fight with Angie the following day. He'd given her time to get home and lock herself away—thinking he was doing the right thing by giving her space. But he'd come home to his worst fears: Angie gone and in her place…a note.

Another fucking note.

He'd unfolded and refolded it so many times, the paper had worn thin along the center crease, tearing at the top.

Dear Jace, I'm sorry things got messed up. I wanted it to work with all my heart. I've gone to stay with a friend until I'm finished up at the retirement home.

You're a great guy, even if you don't see it. Here's the thing—all the stuff you worry about are the things I love about you.

I love that you need routine, because I never had that growing up and it comforts me, too. I love that you don't always know what to say, because I tend to mess up my words as well. I've always had trouble expressing myself because I was worried that if I wasn't smiling and happy, then I wouldn't be welcome. But you made me feel like an equal. And like maybe you could love all my quirks, too.

Ultimately you deserve someone you can be

yourself around. I wish I'd been that person for
you.
    Angie

The note had been waiting for him in an envelope that also contained his great-grandmother's
ring, her key, and her last month's rent. He'd
wanted to scream and throw the lot at the wall.

Hadn't he asked her not to run away? They
could have talked this through, gotten on the right
foot. All he'd needed was some time to compose
his thoughts, maybe write himself some notes
because things spiraled when he had to improvise
and speak from the top of his head.

It was like the rehearsal dinner was happening
all over again...but worse. He *wanted* to be with
Angie. That much was evident from the sleepless
night he'd spent sitting on his deck and staring at
the moon, pretending he was cuddling the dogs
for their benefit and not his.

Now his eyes felt like forty-grit sandpaper, and
his head was more useless than a bowl of custard.
He'd gone over to the flat this morning and found
evidence of her everywhere—her trinkets, the
painting of the ocean she'd been so excited to buy.
All the throw pillows that compensated for his
poor decorating skills.

Everywhere he looked around the flat, Angie's
mark was there. The scent of her perfume—that
soft and sugary-sweet lemon—lingered as though
she'd only just left the room. There was a to-do
list on the fridge held with a magnet from The Big
Pineapple. Probably written from before she'd

started sleeping in the house with him.

This was his fault. Yesterday, instead of thinking about what she needed, he'd gone in with his blunt honesty. Classic Jace—subtle as a sledgehammer. He'd pushed her too hard and she'd run, like he feared she would. For all her smiles and sparkly laughter, Angie had deep wounds. And instead of being a balm, he was salt. Rough, coarse. Painful.

He wanted to kick himself.

In the living room, he found the box of VHS tapes and the old player he'd rescued from under the house. It, too, had a note sitting on top: *Sorry I didn't have time to donate the tapes.*

The memory of watching that movie with Angie washed over him—the sound of her laugh, the way she sighed happily and teared up when the characters kissed for the first time, the look of seriousness on her face when she explained why romantic comedies were important. He hadn't understood it then. But now…

Well, the idea of knowing everything would turn out happily ever after was suddenly appealing.

He pulled the player from the top of the box and plugged it in. Since he had no idea where Angie had gone and she wasn't picking up his calls—only texting to say she was safe—he had to occupy himself somehow. Jace riffled through the box of movies until he found one called *Clueless*.

The title certainly seemed fitting to his situation. He pushed the tape into the player and hit the Play button. An hour and a half later, Jace's mood was a little buoyed. So he reached into the box and looked for something else to watch. *The Wedding Singer*. Was Drew Barrymore in, like, 90 percent of these movies?

Jace found himself grinning stupidly when Adam Sandler walked down the aisle of the plane, singing and strumming his guitar. Maybe Angie was right, and there *was* something to these movies.

He put in *10 Things I Hate About You* and watched that. More singing. Everybody knew the boom-box trope, so maybe there was something to declaring one's feelings with song. Too bad Jace had neither a boom box nor a singing voice that would endear him to anyone.

So he watched *She's All That*. He couldn't remember the last time he'd watched so many movies.

Or neglected work and exercise for a whole day for no reason at all.

Truffle and Tilly were waiting by the back door, probably starving. Poor things. He fed them both and then collapsed on the couch, too tired to even walk the extra couple of feet to his bedroom. Knowing Angie was gone zapped all his energy. Without her, what was the point of any of this?

Before Jace could formulate a plan about what to do next, he found his eyes drooping. In that hazy limbo of sleeping and waking, something sparked in the back of his brain. Like a tiny candle flickering to stay alight, an idea shimmered.

What if Hermit didn't have to be against the world anymore? What if he lived happily ever after?

CHAPTER TWENTY-FIVE

Angie stood outside the Patterson's Bluff retirement home, her bag resting heavily on her shoulder. She'd put on her most formal dress for this occasion—a silvery-lilac shift with a gauzy overlay patterned with tiny purple flowers. It had delicate cap sleeves, a subtle scooped neck, and hit at the perfect spot at the top of her knee.

It was a dress that said, *Take me seriously.*

Because she was going to knock this meeting out of the park. The board of the retirement home would hear all about her plans to make the place better, and they would give their blessing. It would be the legacy she left behind, a positive mark on this town. And on its people.

Because even though things hadn't turned out the way she wanted, she still had a chance to do something good.

"You got this." She sucked in a breath and walked up the driveway toward the retirement home's entrance.

Part of her wished Jace was here, holding her hand and smiling that beautiful, crooked smile. The other part of her still had its head screwed on properly and shut out all thoughts of her *failed before it really began* relationship. She couldn't look at what she'd lost—she could only look forward.

The front doors slid open with a quiet *whoosh*,

and the blast of cool air-conditioning was a relief to her heated skin. It was a scorcher today—hotter than any day she'd experienced so far. So the plan was to kick butt at her presentation, go back to Chloe's, and then head to the beach for one last swim in the pristine Aussie waters. Then she would be packing her bags and getting a good night's sleep before starting her journey to the Melbourne airport first thing in the morning.

"You look lovely." Nadesha came out from behind the front desk, her arms outstretched. "We are so excited for what you're doing."

Nobody knew she was leaving yet. Angie had decided to leave that not-so-little piece of information for the end of her time slot, because she wanted the board members to focus on her plans. Chloe had already put up her hand to help find someone to take over the project, and she had someone great in mind. Angie would leave all the documents and everything that person would need to execute the Learning Enrichment Program.

"Thank you." Angie smiled. Surprisingly, she *did* feel confident today. Not a lot, but a little—and that was better than none. Her hard work and dedication would speak for itself, and the "doga" class had been such a raging success that the home's suggestion box had been flooded with requests for more sessions.

"Mr. Powell is in there now, and you will head in as soon as he's done." Nadesha led Angie to a little waiting area.

"Glen Powell." Angie wrinkled her nose.

"What's he talking about?"

"Funding cuts." Nadesha rolled her eyes. "Trust me, you'll be a breath of fresh air after him."

Nadesha left Angie waiting in the small, blandly decorated area, and she wiped her sweaty palms down the front of her dress. Twenty minutes, that's all she had to convince them to approve the special volunteer contracts and changes to the facility's insurance required to execute her plan. The latter was going to give her the most trouble. Because contracts were one thing, but money was another.

Just as Angie was going over her opening lines, three friendly faces came around the corner. The poker gang.

"We had to come and wish you good luck." Meredith swanned over and enveloped Angie in her Chanel No.5–scented hug. "I know they're going to think you're amazing just like we do."

"And if any of those old men try to talk over you, don't accept it," Betty added, muscling her way in for a hug as well. "Your ideas *will* be heard."

Jean hung back, waiting her turn, and when the other two women were done, she came forward. Without a word, she wrapped her slender arms around Angie's neck and squeezed. They stood there for a minute, without saying a word, and Angie's throat was suddenly tight. She would miss her three awesome grandmas so much.

How on earth was she going to break the news to them?

Meredith and Betty retreated with a wave, as if wanting to give her and Jean a moment together.

The older woman had a coy smile on her face as she sat down next to Angie.

"I have news," she said primly. "I've taken a lover."

Angie clamped her hand over her mouth to stifle a squeak. "What?"

"Marcus and I have decided to court. I like him very much." Her eyes twinkled mischievously. "I wanted to tell you because it was your dog yoga class that helped me see I was being very stubborn about not ever caring for another man."

"Really?" Angie's heart melted.

"Yes." She nodded. "When we held hands, I felt something that I haven't felt for a very long time. I felt young again. I felt…alive. It's wonderful."

"I'm so happy for you. You deserve it."

"For a long time, I didn't think that way. I was a widow, and that was my lot in life after Winston died. I shut myself off to so many possibilities." She shook her head. "I had many chances to move on and find love again. But any time a man got too close, I would purposefully ruin things."

Angie sucked in a breath. "Why would you do that?"

"Because I was scared. I didn't know if I was able to love anyone else, and I thought it easier not to try." She gave a sweet, faraway smile. "And I was frightened of getting hurt. I'd been so lucky the first time around, I couldn't possibly experience that again. But Marcus has helped me see that the past doesn't need to dictate my actions now."

"You were self-sabotaging?" Jace's words rang in her ears.

"I was. But not any more."

Angie wanted to know more; she had a million questions and confessions dancing on the tip of her tongue. But the door to the boardroom swung open, and Glen Powell walked out, his slimy gaze flicking over Angie and Jean. Was it her imagination or did the edge of his lip curl up in a subtle sneer?

"I hope you have better luck this time," he said to Angie, sounding as though he didn't mean a word of it.

Suddenly invigorated and full of burning passion, Angie jumped to her feet and squared her shoulders. She was here not for herself but for the people like Jean and Meredith and Betty who wanted more out of life.

And you? Do you want more out of life?

This wasn't the time to ponder her own situation. But the word "yes" hissed like a snake in her ear, tempting her. Calling to her.

"Miss Donovan." The board's chair held the door for her. "We're ready for you."

Jean reached over and squeezed Angie's hand in support. "Thank you, dear. For everything."

Angie walked into the room, her heart in her mouth. Blood rushed in her ears. Eight people sat around an oval table, staring at her expectantly.

"Thank you so much for having me." Her voice wobbled, just like it had when the judge asked her those awful questions.

I'm not perfect, but I've come a long way. I will keep trying.

"I'm here to present my plans for the Patterson's

Bluff Retirement Home Learning Enrichment Program." Angie forced herself to pause so nerves didn't send her into talking overdrive. "In a National Institute of Health study, people who continue to learn new skills and challenge their brain are less likely to develop Alzheimer's and dementia."

She glanced around the room. No one was nodding along enthusiastically as she'd hoped. One of the people had started to check her phone, and another had opened his laptop. *Not* a good sign.

"I've collected a lot more research that links learning new skills and the slowing or prevention of degenerative brain disease, but I get the impression that a bunch of stats and figures isn't the best way to show you why I think the people who live here need more opportunities to stretch themselves. So I'm going to tell you something personal instead."

That seemed to get people's attention.

"When I came to Patterson's Bluff I wasn't necessarily looking for beautiful beaches and rugged cliff-lined coasts and perfect orange sunsets, although I found all of that and more. I was looking for a chance to become the person I'd always wanted to be." The guy to her left closed his laptop lid and turned his chair to face the front. The woman who'd been on her phone was also now looking at Angie. "Back home, a lot of people knew my name for all the wrong reasons."

There were furrowed brows and cocked heads

all across the room.

"I grew up in the foster care system and the last home I lived in sealed my destiny as a person unable to escape public scrutiny. A lawyer who wanted to make a name for himself decided to use me as his vehicle to legal notoriety—regardless of what was best for me as his client." The memory made her clench her fists. "So I moved to Australia. I fell in love with this country instantly. The person I wanted to become wasn't someone who relearned to trust or overcome her fears. No, I'd decided I needed to be a person with a home. Because a person with a home is a person who belongs. Who won't be rejected."

The story was tumbling out of her now, and she was so off script that she placed her speaking cards down onto the table.

She laced her hands in front of her. "Only in trying to do that, I will still hanging on to my fear that I wasn't worthy. That I wouldn't be able to change and grow and get rid of my past. I let it stifle a relationship that was very important to me."

She could see it clear as day now—Jace sensed when she wasn't behaving authentically. Because he knew her, the *real* her, and that was the person he was attracted to. The Angie who was scared of dogs but wanted to love them, the woman who could easily face fears on behalf of other people but wasn't so good at doing it for herself. And she had sensed in him the same things.

"You might be wondering what the heck this all has to do with the people who live here,"

Angie continued. "Well, it's my belief that you're never too old to want more. To be more. We're conditioned to think that the past defines us, that if we haven't been able to do something before that we won't be able to do it now. Learning is a fundamental human experience. Whether it's something small like taking a pottery class or trying a new yoga pose, learning opens us up to new experiences. To personal growth and fulfillment. And *that* isn't limited by age."

What had she learned since she'd come to Patterson's Bluff? That there *were* good people in the world. She'd learned that not all dogs were scary and that the beach here was the most calming place on earth. Most importantly, she'd learned that a home wasn't worth anything if she pushed people away when they tried to help, when they were honest with her.

It certainly wasn't worth anything without love.

The thought was like a wet fish slapping her across the face. Love. The one thing she'd been most afraid of her whole life, because her childhood taught her it could be taken away in an instant. Only nobody had ever loved her before, and she had never tried to love anyone in return.

Until Jace.

She loved Jace.

She loved him because he didn't accept her excuses. She loved him because he was thoughtful and kind and loyal and always willing to lend a helping hand. She loved him because he was creative and good with dogs and because when he wrapped her up in his arms, she felt like a piece of broken pottery that had been lovingly put back together.

She loved Jace.

"The people who live here don't always have the option to leave and seek out the enrichment they deserve in their lives. Perhaps their best version of themselves is someone who works with their hands every day, who ticks off one more shoot-for-the-moon dream on their bucket list. Maybe they simply want to try a bunch of things to find out what they're passionate about in life. If we bring these opportunities here, even the people who think it's okay to do the same thing day in and day out might be tempted to change. To grow into the person they've always wanted to become. They just need a helping hand."

Like she had needed a helping hand—and Jace had been there, willing to give things a shot. Willing to help her even when it meant facing his own demons.

Home wasn't Patterson's Bluff...home was wherever love was. And that meant wherever Jace was. Wherever the poker ladies were. Wherever Chloe was.

Home wasn't the place. It was the people.

"So how can we help the residents of this home become the people they've always wanted to be?" Angie picked up her speaking cards again. "That's where my plan to harness the expertise and generosity of local businesses comes in..."

CHAPTER TWENTY-SIX

Jace stared at his inbox. Usually after a new strip was released, he'd get emails…but nothing like this. After the first hundred, he turned off the alert sound because it was upsetting the dogs. But the emails continued to roll in, one after another after another.

He almost couldn't believe he'd done it.

Last night, the idea of Hermit finding his happily ever after must have burrowed into his brain. Because he'd dreamed about it—the final *Hermit vs. World* strip. The bridge to the mainland was complete, and it seemed as though the mayor had won. But Hermit had woken early so he could be the first one there. He vowed to stand at the end of the bridge every day, with his new canine companion by his side, and he would stop people from coming over to the island.

So Hermit went to the end of the bridge with a sign that said no entry and a determined look on his face. But when he got there, a woman came to him. Her smile made Hermit stop in his tracks— when she smiled, it was like the whole world turned to color. And when she reached out her hand, Hermit put down his sign and slipped his hand into hers. The final vision was of the two of them walking back across the bridge toward the island, the dog at their feet. It was in full color.

Only in Jace's dream, the woman wasn't a

cartoon figure. It was Angie—smiling, beautiful, determined. The woman who'd brought light and hope into his world.

The second he'd woken up that morning, he'd raced into his studio—skipping his morning surf and breakfast—and the drawing flew out of him as if his hands were possessed. This was it, the way *Hermit vs. World* had to end. Angie had been right all along: What story was he telling if his character never changed or grew?

That's why he'd had so much trouble these last few weeks—because he knew what needed to happen to Hermit, but it was at odds with what he thought he wanted. Stopping the comic now would kill the syndication deal. It would kill his chance to be the next Calvin and Hobbes, the next Peanuts. It would mean having to start from scratch.

But instead of terrifying him, Jace felt totally and utterly free.

Hermit had been stifling him for a while, because he was no longer in sync with his misanthropic protagonist. *Jace* had changed; his desires had changed. Instead of holing himself up in his studio, working quietly and alone, he wanted a life filled with other people—with Angie. And his family. And maybe a dog…or three. Hell, why not four dogs?

For a moment, he was giddy, and the emails kept coming. Question marks adorned the subject lines…and exclamation points. Some people were furious. Others were sad but saw it as a natural conclusion.

TRENT: wtf man?? You ended Hermit vs. World??

Jace laughed. He hadn't even known that his brother read the comic.

JACE: It had to be done.

TRENT: What happens next?

That was the big question mark hanging over his head. He'd contact the people at the American comic syndication company and politely withdraw from their consideration, but beyond that…

There was only one thing he cared about.

Jace pulled the comic up and stared at it. The single colored panel at the end packed a punch. It wasn't perfect. Jace was not an advanced colorist by any means—since almost all his work was in black and white—but the contrast had exactly the impact he was looking for. The two characters were facing away, so the reader could see the backs of their heads and bodies, and they were holding hands. The little dog had his tail in the air, wagging.

On the last panel, Jace had used the clouds in the sky to spell out a message: *For Angie.*

Because without her, he might have continued down the same path for years—believing he was incapable of change, being stuck and lonely and missing out on all life had to offer.

He still hadn't spoken to Angie since she left the flat out back, and each moment had made him more and more miserable. The dogs seemed to sense it, too, because they were hanging around him even more than usual. Tilly had kept vigil by his bedroom door, and he'd found her asleep in that same spot in the morning. He couldn't imagine what his life would be like when they returned home to Eugenie.

But even worse, he couldn't imagine what his life would be like when Angie returned home. The very thought was like a knife to his gut. And he hadn't known how to reach her, how to tell her that he'd fallen madly and irreparably in love with her. That he wanted to marry her, not only so she could stay in the country but so she could stay with him forever.

JACE: I don't know, man. I'm free-falling.

TRENT: If I was the emotional type, I might shed a tear. Good for you, bro.

He pocketed his phone and leaned back in his chair, staring up at the ceiling. He *was* free-falling, but it felt...good. Like having everything out in the open was a relief. Only, he *shouldn't* be feeling relieved because he'd lost Angie in the process.

Go to her. Tell her you love her and that you want to do whatever it takes to make it work, but both as the real versions of yourselves.

Would she give him a chance? He couldn't worry about that now. All that mattered was getting to Angie and telling her how he felt. How much she meant to him.

He shoved his chair back so hard it almost

toppled over, and just as he was about to go to the front door, a noise shattered the quiet of the house. *Bang, bang, bang!*

"Jace Walters, you'd better open up this door right freaking now!" The angry knocks continued. "I saw Truffle in the window and your car is out front, so don't try to hide from me."

At the sound of his name, Truffle slapped his paws up against the window. "Yip, yip, yip!"

At one point, all the commotion might have sent him ducking for cover, but now it filled his heart with joy. He jogged over to the front door and yanked it open. Angie stood there, eyes wide and hair wild as if she'd raced over on her bike at full speed. Wayward tendrils surrounded her face, and he wasn't sure he'd ever seen her look more beautiful.

"You didn't have to kill him," she said, poking him in the chest and marching into his house without an invitation.

"Kill who?"

"Hermit." She looked up at him, eyes shimmering.

"I didn't kill him." He frowned. "In fact, I think I did quite the opposite of that."

"But you killed the comic, Jace. You shouldn't have done that." She folded her arms over her chest.

Oh no. His momentary joy that she'd kept reading *Hermit vs. World* was squashed by the fear that maybe this was her way of saying that she didn't love him. That this really was the end.

"I was coming straight over from my meeting

with the retirement home board to tell you that I'd been wrong about everything. And you were right—I *haven't* been myself, and maybe I wasn't intentionally self-sabotaging, but there was a part of me that never believed I could be accepted. So perhaps subconsciously I'd shut myself off from it."

She swallowed. Jace wasn't sure exactly where this conversation was going, and it was a little tough doing it with an audience. Truffle and Tilly watched on, the older dog staring unwaveringly at him as if to say, *Don't you dare screw this up.*

"And then I saw that beautiful last panel." She dropped her hands by her sides, then knotted them, then dropped them again. "I'd thought that maybe we're actually perfect for each other. Maybe everything that's caused us pain is *exactly* the reason we'll work. But then you had to go and put Hermit's death on my shoulders. I can't handle that kind of responsibility!"

"Not his death, Angie. His life. I set him free."

She sucked in a breath. "But what about the syndication deal? You had so much riding on that. And all the fans, won't they be mad?"

Some of his fans *were* mad. But many understood Jace's decision and loved the way he'd ended the comic. But ultimately, it didn't matter what any of them thought.

"It was time. Hermit was a phase of my life and…I guess I don't connect with him so much anymore." The misanthropic character represented who Jace had been in the past—someone frightened of judgment from the outside world.

Someone who feared he'd never be accepted because of his autism. "And yes, I'll be a cliché broke artist for a while, but I have more than one idea in me. Besides, you never know. A book publisher might want to bring *Hermit vs. World* to a new audience. Or maybe my next idea will be even more successful than this one."

"So you didn't ruin your career?"

"No, Angie." He clasped his hands around the tops of her arms to steady her—he knew what it was like to spiral. He knew how important it was to have someone to ground you. "I took a risk, but I couldn't keep writing about a person who wanted to be alone when…when I don't want that anymore for myself."

Part of him wished he'd had the forethought to write some of this down before now, because that would have made everything a lot simpler. But this was life—there *wasn't* always time to prepare. And if he wanted to show Angie how much he loved her, then he would just need to come out with it.

"Angie, I—"

"I love you!" she blurted out, and Jace laughed. Okay, so maybe he wasn't the only one in this relationship without a filter.

"Did you steal my thunder?" he asked, shaking his head. "You *totally* did. I was about to say it, and then you bust in here and steal the spotlight."

She gave him a watery laugh. "I'm sorry. I couldn't hold it in anymore."

"Welcome to my world," he quipped.

A hopeful smile passed over her lips, and she

placed her palms against his chest. "You could always say it back, you know."

"I guess I could…" He laughed when she tried to punch him in the arm. "Angie, you're perfect for me. I don't know if I can be perfect for you—"

"You can."

"Could you please stop interrupting me, Miss Motormouth? I know you're used to getting more words out every day, but I've got something to say right now." He brushed a strand of hair behind her ear, and Angie made a motion of zipping her lips shut. Her eyes were glittery and her cheeks pink, and he knew that he never wanted to go a day without this incredible woman ever again. "But maybe perfect shouldn't be our goal. Maybe our goal should be *real*. I want us to be ourselves, to be able to say what we want and to support each other. Because… I love you, too. And the thought of being without you is the most terrifying thing that's ever entered my head."

"Does that mean you're going to tell me when you want a plain breakfast?" she asked. "Or when you need some alone time, because I promise that I *do* understand."

"I will. And I don't want you wearing a fake smile all the time because you think if you're having a bad day or feeling sad that I won't love you anymore. Because I want a wife, not a… robot."

"What if I was a sex robot?" She smile through her tears.

"As much as I *thoroughly* enjoy that part of our relationship, it's not the most important thing.

Waking up next to you every day—that's what I want. Knowing that if you need to lean on me, I can be there for you."

"Oh, Jace." She blinked back tears that had started to gather in her eyes. "I know that now—you're absolutely the man for me."

• • •

Angie's stomach twisted and turned—the day had been full of emotion. Full of a roller coaster–like feeling that had left her head spinning. But being here with Jace, being honest…God, she'd never felt better.

But there was still one big thing that she needed to address. Because if they were going to make things work between them, then it could never be on unequal footing. Never with anything hanging over them.

"Why do I feel like there's a 'but' coming?" He looked so worried, it was like a stab to her gut.

"I can't marry you here." Even though the words sucked the life out of the room and it was like she was dancing along the edge of a cliff face, it was the right way forward. The *only* way forward for her to show Jace what he meant to her. "I won't marry you with any shadow of doubt about my intentions. Because I don't ever want you to wake up and wonder if I cared more about staying than I cared about you."

"So you're still leaving?"

"Yes." She nodded. "Will you come with me?"

He blinked. Devastation morphing to shock

and then shifting into surprise...and wonder. Today, he was letting her see everything he felt. Every emotion like paint splashed across a canvas.

He trusted her.

"I can't be afraid of my past anymore," she said. "But I want to marry you, and I want it to be for all the right reasons, because home is where love is. I need you to know that I married you for love and not for anything else."

"You're serious?"

"I've already thought about places we can go that have amazing beaches for you to get in your morning surf. At the very least, we'll stay in places that have a pool, because I know how much you love being in the water." She smiled, hope filling her heart until she wasn't sure how much goodness she could fit in there. "I will keep our cabinets stocked with plain oatmeal, and you can bring your work with you. I promise to give you as much alone time as you need. Because I really hope that you keep drawing and creating and being you."

"You thought about my routine that much?"

"I know how vital it is for you." She nodded. "So will you say yes? To travel and marriage and love and making a home no matter where we are. I want to build a life with you here, but we can see the world in the meantime."

"Angie Donavon, I will follow you anywhere." He dipped his head to hers and captured her mouth in a long, searching kiss that was filled with the fizzing excitement of all that lay before them.

"Does that mean you're going to bring Hermit back?"

"No, Hermit told the story he needed to tell. But you know I've had this idea in my head for a while about two dogs who love order and routine but who also love going on big adventures." They both swung their heads to Tilly and Truffle, and they both cocked their heads at the same time as if to say, *Who, us?*

"So we're doing this?" she asked, her hands curled into his shirt and her perfect body lining up with his. "You and me and the world."

"And then we'll come back, make this our home together. Maybe make a family, too."

She pressed into him, coaxing his mouth open with hers and infusing him with all her love. "I couldn't think of anything better."

EPILOGUE

One and a half years later…

Angie crept across the floorboards on tiptoes, dodging the one that always squeaked. It was Jace's birthday, and they'd officially been back in Patterson's Bluff for two months. Therefore, it was a special day on several levels.

And, being a special day, Angie had planned the surprise of all surprises. She bit down on her lip to keep an excited squeal from popping out. They'd talked about this day ever since they got married in a sunlit Tuscan villa after leaving Australia for their grand adventure. It had been a perfect afternoon, with their closest friends and Jace's family.

And now, that family was going to be expanded by one.

She pushed open the door to the bedroom where her husband slept peacefully, unaware that he was about to be surprised again. Angie had a habit of doing that to him. First there was the watch she'd bought him in Paris with the words "I'll always cross the bridge with you" engraved on the back. Then the fact that she'd secretly arranged for his family to meet them in Tuscany for a real wedding, instead of a simple ceremony with the two of them. Then there was the private tour of Universal Studios when they made it to

America. There, on home soil, she'd started to conquer her fears.

And now…this.

"Good morning, sleepyhead." Angie crawled onto the bed and planted a chaste kiss on his cheek. But Jace wasn't having it. He crushed her down to him with strong arms and coaxed her mouth open.

"Mm, you taste like coffee."

"And you taste like morning breath," she teased. He didn't really—somehow Jace managed to avoid most gross guy-related things like bad morning breath and stinky boxers. Which didn't do much to dissuade Angie from thinking her husband was actually a god and not a man. "Happy birthday, husband of mine."

"Does this mean I get a present?" He waggled his brows in a way that told her he wanted to unwrap something…and it wasn't a gift.

"Yes." She grabbed his hand and tugged him into a sitting position. "Come on. I have something to show you."

He looked at her for a long moment. "Oh my God, I thought we were waiting."

"I think we've waited long enough."

Since Angie had recently been promoted to day manager at the retirement home, overseeing the learning program, event planning, and making sure the residents were happy and engaged, she'd been busy. And since Jace's new comic, *Big Adventures, Little Dogs*, about a small Chihuahua and a black dog that looked a heck of a lot like a miniature version of Tilly had taken the internet by storm, he'd also been kept busy.

Angie grinned. "Out of bed. Now."

She took Jace into the living room. Sure, she wanted to give him the birthday present he desired, but that would happen later. For now, she had an introduction to make.

Nestled in a small wicker basket padded with the softest of blankets was a tiny puppy. She yawned, and her long pink tongue curled out and over her nose. Then she blinked sleepily, and Angie was pretty sure she turned into a puddle on the spot.

"Oh my God." Jace's eyes lit up, and she'd never seen him so excited.

"I picked her up this morning. The litter came from an older woman who couldn't care for all the puppies—and don't even get me started on the fact that she didn't spay her dog. So, Mira was trying to find homes for them."

"How many more?" He looked up at her.

"There are six total. Three left when I went this morning."

Jace's eyes gleamed.

"No." Angie shook her head, but Jace scooped the puppy up and cradled it to his chest so lovingly she knew there was no way she'd ever be able to deny him. "Seriously?"

"You want to break her up from her family?"

Angie laughed and shook her head. "You want four dogs? This from the guy who was determined to live alone."

Jace leaned over and kissed her cheek. "Pretty please."

"How are we going to take care of four dogs with us both working full-time?" She shot him a look. "*And* you practically begged Eugenie to let you go to her place once a week to see Tilly and Truffle."

Tilly wasn't able to leave the house too much these days, but her tail never failed to wag when Jace walked through the door. And Truffle…well, he was still humping anything he could throw his paws over.

"When we're together, we can do anything. Isn't that what you told me?" There was that crooked grin again—it got her every damn time. "Besides, I work from home. It's the perfect situation."

"And your routine?"

"I'll schedule in dog time." He stroked the puppy's head gently. "What should we call her? How about Drew, after your favorite rom-com heroine?"

Angie leaned over. "Hello, Drew, welcome to our family."

The puppy was fast asleep, so Jace set her back down into the basket, handling her as though he might a glass made of the finest crystal. "You make me so happy."

"You make *me* so happy."

Jace scooped Angie up and she stifled a squeak, not wanting to wake the slumbering puppy. He carried her back toward the bedroom, his light eyes burning into hers and his mouth shaped into a wicked smile.

"What are you doing?" she asked in a mock-stern tone. "What happened to surfing at seven and breakfast at eight and scheduling out every second of your day?"

"What can I say? I know how to take a break from my routine every once in a while. You must be a good influence on me."

"I think I am."

"But I still want porridge for breakfast." He tossed her down onto the bed and crawled over her, his gaze burning a path from her thighs to her belly, to her breasts and then to her face. "Does that make me predictable?"

"It's makes you...you." Angie pulled her husband down on top of her, hanging on tightly because she never wanted to let him go. "And that's makes you perfect for me."

ACKNOWLEDGMENTS

A huge thank-you to Liz Pelletier for all the opportunities you've given me in my career, including the chance to tell this story and share more of the country I love so much with readers. Thank you for pushing me hard to make each story the best it can be and for helping me to bring these amazing characters to life.

Huge thanks to the rest of the Entangled Publishing team, including Heather Howland and Stacy Abrams for your insightful edits, Lydia Sharp for all the comments pointing out which bits made you laugh, to Jessica Turner for your assistance with all things marketing and promotion, Heather Riccio for always answering my questions, and Katie Clapsadl for making RAGT a blast! Thank you to everyone else whose hands touch my books. I appreciate you all.

Thank you to my agent, Jill Marsal, for going to bat for me and for always helping me wrangle my schedule, no matter how out of control it gets.

As always, huge thanks to my husband, Justin, who keeps me going, making sure I'm fed and plied with coffee during long revision sessions. For listening to me moan about how the book will never be finished and cheering me on when I'm writing a section that brings me joy. You're my everything.

Thank you to my grandparents, who all immigrated to Australia, giving me a beautiful place to grow up. And thank you to my parents for not protesting too hard when I wanted to leave. I know the joy and turmoil of making a new country your home, of leaving things behind and embarking on new adventures. In all of that, thank you to the technology industry for allowing me to stay connected with my family, so it doesn't feel like they're quite so far away.

nothing but trouble

by Amy Andrews

For five years, Cecilia Morgan's entire existence has revolved around playing personal assistant to self-centered former NFL quarterback Wade Carter. But just when she finally gives her notice, his father's health fails, and Wade whisks her back to his hometown. CC will stay for his dad—for now—even if that means ignoring how sexy her boss is starting to look in his Wranglers.

To say CC's notice is a bombshell is an insult to bombs. Wade can't imagine his life without his "left tackle." She's the only person who can tell him "no" and strangely, it's his favorite quality. He'll do anything to keep her from leaving, even if it means playing dirty and dragging her back to Credence, Colorado, with him.

But now they're living under the same roof, getting involved in small-town politics, and bickering like an old married couple. Suddenly, five years of fighting is starting to feel a whole lot like foreplay. What's a quarterback to do when he realizes he might be falling for his "left tackle"? Throw a Hail Mary she'll never see coming, of course.

She's just one of the guys...until she's not in USA Today *bestselling author Cindi Madsen's unique take on weddings, small towns, and friends falling in love.*

Just One of the Groomsmen

by Cindi Madsen

Addison Murphy is the funny friend, the girl you grab a beer with, and the girl voted most likely to start her own sweatshirt line. She's perfectly fine answering to the nickname "Murph," given to her by the tight-knit circle of guy friends she's grown up with. Time has pulled them all in different directions, like Tucker Crawford, who left their small town to become some big-city lawyer, and Reid, who's now getting hitched.

Naturally the guys are all going to be groomsmen, and it wouldn't be the same without "Murph" in the mix. The fact that ever since Tucker's return to town, she can't stop looking at him and wondering when he got so hot is proof that she needs to mix things up. She'd never want to ruin a friendship she's barely gotten back, but the more Addie comes out of her tomboy shell, the more both she and Tucker wonder if there's something more there...

The Truth About Cowboys

by Lisa Renee Jones

I had my life figured out.

Engaged to a successful man.

About to make partner at my firm.

Bought a high-rise apartment in downtown Denver.

And then, poof, it's all gone. Now, like in some cheesy romantic comedy, my car has broken down in the pouring rain on my way to "find myself" in The Middle of Nowhere, Texas. Cue hot guy coming to my rescue and changing my tire. This is the part where we flirt and have a meet-cute, right? That's how it works in romance novels, and I should know — after all, I'm coming to Texas to write my own cowboy romance. But nope. This sexy cowboy lights into me about not being prepared for the country roads and how inappropriate my high-heeled boots are.

Little did I know, Jason Jenks would tilt my world into a new dimension with his sinful smirk and his bad attitude. Every time I turn around, he's there to reluctantly save the day. And every time, I think there may be something to that spark we ignite. But there's a reason the majority of country songs are about broken hearts. The closer I get to this man, the closer I get to learning the truth about cowboys. .

AMARA

an imprint of Entangled Publishing LLC